WHITE OAKS

JILL HAND

Black Rose Writing | Texas

This is a work of fiction. Names, characters, businesses, places, events, and incidents are either the products of the author's imagination or used in a fictitious manner. Any resemblance to actual persons, living or dead, or actual events is purely coincidental.

ISBN: 978-1-68433-283-0
PUBLISHED BY BLACK ROSE WRITING
www.blackrosewriting.com

Printed in the United States of America
Suggested Retail Price (SRP) $18.95

White Oaks is printed in Calluna

To my mother, Vivian Crawford Campbell, who took me to get my first library card and who made me laugh harder than anyone I ever met.

WHITE OAKS

CHAPTER 1: THE ROAD ROCKET

Three days before the murder a lemon yellow Lamborghini Aventador LP 750-4 SuperVeloce swung into the parking lot of Buzzy's General Store in Cobbs, Georgia. It was moving at fifty miles per hour, trailed by an extravagant plume of blood-red dust. Crows perched in the loblolly pines cawed and took wing, startled by the throaty shriek from the exhaust and intake at 4,000 rpms.

The car slewed sideways as its driver fought for control. For a moment it appeared it would keep sliding until it smashed into the black and white police cruiser parked in front. Sun glare on the windscreen made it impossible to see who was behind the wheel. Whoever it was drove like a madman. What sort of emergency could have occasioned such haste?

The Lamborghini lurched to a stop two feet shy of T-boning the cruiser. Gravel kicked up by the big Gallardo tires clattered against the side with a sound like shrapnel hitting a tin roof.

The store's screen door flew open and smacked against the ice machine, which was situated too close to the front door when it was installed, back in 1983. Gordon Buzzy had considered moving it, but he died before he could get around to it. His son, Gordon Jr., inheritor of his father's kingdom, which amounted to the decrepit general store and the living quarters behind it, likewise thought of moving it a little farther to the right.

It goes without saying, Gordon Buzzy, Jr., not exactly being a coiled spring of industriousness, that he too would die without moving the ice machine, as would his son and *his* son, and so on, until either Buzzy's went out of business or the world came to an end, whichever came first.

Boyce County Sheriff's Deputy Ewell Haskins emerged onto the wooden porch, primed for action. In his left hand was a partially consumed moon pie. With his right, he unsnapped the leather guard over the Smith & Wesson M&P semi-automatic pistol in his service holster. The screen door thwacked shut behind him. Above it a hand-lettered sign warned anyone having the effrontery to take the Lord's name in vain not to expect a warm welcome at Buzzy's, where bait, tackle, beer, and sundries could be purchased between the hours of 7 A.M. and 6 P.M. every day except Sundays and major holidays.

Haskins stood open-mouthed, staring at the yellow roadster.

It looked like something from a future century, at once sleek and angular. "Hot damn," he whispered, spying the orange and black New York license plate. A Yankee! Driving recklessly! Perhaps the Yankee speed demon was under the influence of drugs. From what Haskins understood, a large percentage of the Yankee population customarily went around hopped up to the eyeballs. If such was the case, he would soon be a very sorry Yankee indeed.

Haskins licked his lips like a dog smelling steak. The deputy still felt the sting of the conflict that a certain type of white Southerner refers to as the War of Northern Aggression. Arresting a rich Yankee who was endangering the citizens of Cobbs by ramming the roads in what amounted to a deluxe hot rod would soothe that sting considerably. It might also put Haskins in line to become the next sheriff when the current sheriff either retired or dropped dead of the heart attack that must surely be coming to a man who weighed close to four hundred pounds. Haskins rolled his eyes heavenward and offered a silent prayer to the Almighty to please bring about a vacancy for the position of sheriff as swiftly as was convenient. Thank you and Amen.

Haskins squinted at the mysterious vehicle through a shimmer of heat. It was such a bright yellow it made his eyeballs throb. Who'd want a car that gaudy color? Cars should be black, white, gray, or blue, in that order. It was permissible for pickup trucks to be red; that signified a certain self-confident, assertive masculinity, but red sports cars were looking for trouble, their drivers just begging to be given a speeding ticket. A yellow road rocket like this one was utterly and flagrantly wrong, to Haskins' way of thinking.

An idea crossed his mind, one which amazed and delighted him with its breathtaking implications. Could the driver be one of those rappers, all gold chains and surly attitude? Haskins hated rap music, considering it to be nothing but a string of filthy words interspersed with boasts about engaging in criminal activity.

The Lamborghini sat motionless in the baking heat, sun-dazzle bouncing off the windscreen, making its driver invisible. Haskins wondered how large the rapper might be, and whether he had an open container of alcohol in there or anything else that would qualify him for a trip to join the bad boys in the county lockup. If the rapper was riding dirty and he put up a fuss, mouthing off about his rights or illegal search and seizure, the usual crap, then the deputy would deliver a beat down, courtesy of his steel baton.

Haskin's mind was not the most agile. The moon pie began to melt in the heat, its chocolate icing oozing between his fingers as he considered how things might play out. Might the rapper, once subdued, be discovered to have a wallet stuffed full of hundred-dollar bills? Might some of those bills make their way into Haskins' pocket with no one being the wiser, except for the rapper? And who cared what sort of accusations such a person might make against an officer of the law? Haskins offered up another silent prayer to the Almighty to make it so.

The driver's door opened vertically, gullwing-style. In one smooth movement, a woman got out. Her legs seemed to go on for miles in a short white linen dress imprinted in red and cobalt blue with the pictogram that was the international chemical weapons warning symbol. In the merciless south Georgia heat, with the mercury in the rusted Beech-Nut chewing tobacco thermometer nailed to the front of the general store standing at a hair over one hundred and three degrees, she looked as cool as a Rocky Mountain breeze, like a supermodel stepping out of the cover of *Vogue* to grace the humble town of Cobbs.

Haskins gaped, transfixed, as she raised a nearly empty bottle of Southern Comfort to her perfect red lips and took a long drink. Then she headed toward him, her gold high-heeled sandals crunching in the gravel of the parking lot. With three swift strides, she climbed the sagging porch steps.

"Dispose of this, would you," she said, handing him the empty bottle.

This close, he could smell the liquor on her breath as well as her perfume, which reminded him of rich, moist soil in which night-blooming flowers grew. They would be the kind of flowers that had an intoxicating scent but would prove toxic if eaten. Beneath the dangerous flower smell was something else, something he couldn't identify. Whatever it was, it put him in mind of petrochemicals, or maybe plain old road tar.

Wherever her perfume came from Haskins was sure it wasn't Walmart or even Dillard's, where they sold fancy perfume like the Youth-Dew favored by his mother. Haskins' mother devoted herself to running the local chapter of the Eastern Star with the single-minded aim of rewarding her friends and punishing her enemies, in much the same way that Sam Giancana used to run the Chicago mafia. No, perfume like that had to come from one place: Paris, France.

He was correct. The scent the woman wore was made in small batches at a fragrance house occupying the ground floor of a building on the Rue du Mont Thabor, a narrow three-block side street between the Place Vendome and the Tuileries. The perfume had no name and was made expressly for one client: the razor-thin woman with chin-length, glossy chestnut hair who stood before him wearing wrap-around Chopard sunglasses.

"Sure thing, Miz Aimee," Haskins replied, accepting the bottle. He would have tipped his broad-brimmed hat, but his hands were occupied with the dripping moon pie and the empty bottle of Southern Comfort. Instead, he bobbed his head respectfully, the way he did in church when the pastor made a particularly telling point.

Aimee von Helgern was married to a man who lived in a castle in Germany and who held the heredity title of margrave. Such things might matter in Europe, but they cut no mustard in Cobbs. What cut a considerable amount of mustard was who her father was: Blanton Trapnell, the richest and most powerful individual in the state, if not the entire South.

Aimee didn't visit Cobbs often, but when she did, she was treated to bowing and scraping from everyone from the state senator, who lived in a 14,000-square-foot house overlooking the golf course, on down to the semi-literate occupants of the miserable shacks out by the fertilizer factory. Blanton Trapnell owned those shacks, along with the fertilizer factory. He also owned the golf course.

"That's a nice car you got there," Haskins ventured.

She regarded the Lamborghini as if she'd never seen it before.

"It's not the most comfortable car to take on a long drive, but I was tired of flying and thought perhaps driving would make an amusing change." She frowned, causing Haskins to frown in sympathy. Apparently driving had failed to amuse her. "There's no place in it to put my purse." She raised a slim wrist to display a plastic purse with big-eyed Japanese anime characters on it. It was barely large enough to hold a lipstick and a tin of breath mints, plus the black American Express Centurion card that enabled her to buy anything from a cup of coffee to an ocean-going yacht. The purse cost more than Haskins made in four months.

"That's too bad," he said.

"It's not easy finding places to garage my cars near the Dakota." She removed her sunglasses to reveal eyes the same witchy pale green as absinthe. While much of Aimee had been surgically improved and artificially enhanced, her eye color was entirely natural.

"Are you living out West now?" Haskins asked. It was hard for him to follow what she was saying, what with her accent, which sounded part-Yankee and part from someplace overseas. Aimee and her siblings were rumored to own homes all over the world. She might conceivably own one in North or South Dakota.

"*The* Dakota. It's an apartment building on the Upper West Side of Manhattan. I own two apartments there, one for me and one for my snakes. I have a large collection of snakes, including the only known example of a white Darevsky's viper outside of the Ljubljana Zoo."

"Well, ain't that nice!" Haskins said heartily. Snakes gave him the creeps. They had ever since he stumbled onto a nest of baby cottonmouths on the farm where he lived when he was a boy. He'd never forgotten the way they writhed, all balled up together. Snakes not only looked repulsive, they stank to high heaven, as he'd learned to his dismay during a raid on a meth lab. The wild-eyed amateur chemist who produced his wares from a trailer deep in the woods kept cages full of snakes. Their sour-milk stench stayed with Haskins for days, despite his showering repeatedly, scrubbing until his skin was red and raw.

He couldn't imagine what an apartment filled with snakes smelled like.

He tried not to think about it. Instead, he held the screen door open for her. "I got to get back on the road. Y'all have a good day," he said.

He thought about telling her to drive safely but abandoned that idea. The Trapnells could drive any way they pleased.

Aimee gave him a negligent salute. "Goodbye, deputy."

CHAPTER 2 – GONG-GONG'S BIRD BOOK

Thirty minutes later the yellow Lamborghini came barreling down the mile-long crushed oyster shell drive that led to White Oaks, the Trapnell family's Greek Revival plantation. The grass on either side was the deep, vibrant green of the felt on billiard tables. It was sumptuously thick and weed-free, kept that way by six full-time groundskeepers, who also tended to the formal gardens with their central water cascade, as well as the rare orchids and other plants in the greenhouses. High privet hedges screened the property from the curious gaze of anyone passing by on the road.

Aimee parked between her father's 1959 white Rolls-Royce Silver Wraith and a red Ford pickup truck belonging to her brother Trainor. A sticker on the truck's rust-eaten rear bumper said GAS, GRASS OR ASS. NOBODY RIDES FOR FREE. That charming sentiment perfectly summed up Trainor's attitude toward life.

Aimee glanced at the disreputable vehicle as she walked through the muggy heat and up the front steps. She passed through the white-columned portico and into the cool confines of the house, kept at an even seventy degrees year-round by a heating and air conditioning system that was a marvel of engineering.

Old houses tend to have a specific scent, resulting from a long accumulation of years of being lived in. It is a scent made up of dust and fireplace ashes and gently rotting fabric, as well as decades of breakfasts, lunches, and dinners. White Oaks smelled of nothing at all.

In the entry hall, Aimee slammed the item she'd gone to Buzzy's for down on a round ebony and ivory inlaid French Second Empire table. Its gilded, curved columns were shaped like bare-breasted women wearing Egyptian-looking headdresses. Her heels clicked on the black and white marble floor tiles as she veered diagonally, like a bishop moving across the squares of a chess board. She passed through an archway into a room the house's architect had designated as the gentlemen's parlor. There she found her brother Trainor lounging on a Le Corbusier sofa upholstered in black leather with a tubular steel frame.

The room's walls, ceiling, and floor were stark white, like a research laboratory. The sterile theme continued with the furnishings, which were mid-twentieth-century modern, a style better suited to a spaceship than a plantation house. The stark white setting formed a backdrop for the blazing colors of a dozen original works by Roy Lichtenstein, Jackson Pollock, and David Hockney. It was a tiny sampling of Blanton Trapnell's art collection, most of which was on loan to museums.

"I got his darn old Brunswick stew," Aimee informed her brother. She unbuckled her sandals and kicked them off with a sigh of relief. She sank into a powder blue Arne Jacobsen egg chair across from the sofa where Trainor sat and placed her stockinged feet in his lap.

"Rub my feet," she commanded.

He did so, with considerable skill. His first wife had been a reflexologist, and she'd taught him how to give a good massage.

Aimee sighed contentedly as Trainor dug his thumbs into her arches.

"You got it down to Buzzy's?' Trainor asked, meaning the stew.

Aimee wiggled her toes. "Yes. They don't sell the kind he likes at Publix anymore. Rub harder." She eyed her feet unhappily. "I think I might be getting bunions. If I get bunions, I'll be so ashamed. Waitresses get bunions."

"Nurses, too," Trainor said. "Anybody that's on their feet a lot is pretty much condemned to gettin' bunions. Stay off your feet. That's my advice."

Massage over, he pushed her feet roughly off his lap. He took a drink from a glass that was about half full of dark red liquid then set it down on the kidney-shaped Noguchi coffee table in front of him. Aimee immediately picked it up and drained the rest.

"This isn't bad. What is it?"

Trainor reached over the back of the sofa and retrieved a bottle, holding it out for her inspection. "Château Latour 1961. It goes for about fifteen thousand bucks a bottle. I checked online. I swiped this one from the wine cellar when Hillman wasn't looking. There's plenty more; he'll never miss it. Gong-Gong's got enough wine down there to float a battleship."

Hillman Parks was their father's ancient African-American butler. He was also rumored to be his first cousin. Gong-Gong was their father, Blanton Toombs Trapnell.

"I wish you wouldn't call him Gong-Gong. Call him Daddy like we always did. Gong-Gong sounds stupid," Aimee said.

"He likes to be called Gong-Gong; it's what his favorite grandchild calls him, Trainor said smugly, referring to his own six-year-old daughter, Jubilee.

Trainor was in the process of getting divorced from Jubilee's mother, a dog groomer from Milledgeville. She was his third wife and by far the most cunning. She'd managed to maneuver him into giving her the house in Atlanta's upscale Buckhead neighborhood, and the condominium in Longboat Key, Florida, as well as an allowance of twenty thousand dollars a month. Trainor had a team of lawyers battling her demands for more money. Upon advice of counsel, he was feigning poverty, hence the beat-up truck out front, which had rolled off the assembly line in 2002 and been hard-used ever since.

In the meantime, he had Jubilee for a month while Palmer, his soon-to-be-ex, was in Thailand, prowling the beaches and floating markets with three of her girlfriends. Trainor devoutly hoped that while she was there, she would die of food poisoning or be swept away by a tidal wave. In the meantime, he was making the most of it by using Jubilee's adoration of the flinty-eyed old man she called Gong-Gong to insinuate himself into the position of favorite child.

Aimee thought of her own son, Benjamin, whom Jubilee had supplanted as favorite grandchild. Benjamin had grown from a wide-eyed toddler into a sullen teenager who was currently in a drug rehab in Switzerland. One might assume upon first meeting the steely, self-possessed Aimee that she would be the same kind of mother as her beloved snakes, which laid their eggs and slithered off, abandoning their young to get along as best they could. Such was not the case. Aimee doted on Benjamin. His troubles left her feeling panicky and ill, not that she let it show.

"Daddy better not find out what Jubilee did to his bird book," she told her brother.

She was referring to one of the volumes in a four-part folio of hand-colored engravings made by naturalist John James Audubon. Only one hundred and twenty copies of Audubon's *The Birds of America* were known to exist. A complete first edition like the one Blanton owned was worth about ten million dollars. Little Jubilee had scribbled in it in crayon.

"Aw, she just wanted to make a surprise for her Gong-Gong. She didn't mean no harm," Trainor said indulgently.

"He certainly will be surprised," Aimee said, thinking about how best to respond when he found out. *Quiet sympathy,* she thought. *Don't let him see you're glad the brat did something that made him angry.*

Trainor poured himself more wine. "Kids color on things. Remember the time Marsh drew all over that painting Lucian Freud did of Mama? In permanent marker! Mama just about tore him up."

He laughed, remembering their younger brother's screams as he got a whipping from their deceased mother, one of many that short-tempered lady dished out to her offspring. Then his brow wrinkled as he tried to puzzle something out. "I wonder how Jubilee got that big old book out of the display case. It's gotta weigh fifty pounds."

"I don't know. Somebody must have left it out, maybe that guy from England Daddy hired to catalogue the books, Chortney or Hortney or whatever his name is," Aimee said. Let the blame fall on the horse-faced Chortney or Hortney, who bore a close resemblance to the Mad Hatter as drawn by John Tenniel. He'd come to White Oaks with favorable references from having worked in the cataloguing departments of the Bodleian and the British libraries.

Blanton owned many valuable books and manuscripts, which he'd purchased as investments. *The Birds of America* was the prized jewel of his collection.

Aimee was well aware of how heavy the volume was. She'd personally hoisted it onto the long Beaux Arts table in the library that was an exact copy of the ones in the New York Public Library's Rose Main Reading Room. After looking around to make sure she was unobserved, she opened it to a picture of a pink flamingo. Each bird in the portfolio was drawn life-size. The flamingo was bent almost double in order to make it fit on the page. It looked uncomfortable as it morosely studied something in the water at its webbed feet.

Aimee chose that particular page knowing pink was Jubilee's favorite color. She placed an open box of crayons temptingly next to the volume before exiting the room. The trap was set. Jubilee liked to go into the library to look at the children's books that had belonged to her father and his siblings. With any luck, she'd discover the crayons and scribble in the Audubon folio instead of *Green Eggs and Ham.*

At that moment a man entered the room, talking on a cheap cell phone. Looking at the lean and elegant Aimee, with her peridot eyes and knife-blade cheekbones, and the indolent Trainor, who had a scruffy beard and wore frayed denim shorts and rubber flip-flops and who seemed like a perfect example of a dopey, good-natured redneck, one would find it hard to believe that the two of them were siblings. The newcomer was no bigger than a jockey and had a clever, wicked face. He was impeccably dressed, like a miniature James Bond. He resembled neither Aimee nor Trainor, but he was their younger brother, Marsh.

"Sounds good. We'll set up delivery when we meet with the buyers in Majorca in two weeks," he said and ended the call.

"Nice phone, Marsh," said Trainor, who never passed up a chance to needle his brother.

"It's one of those disposable ones, like drug dealers use," Aimee said, joining in the fun.

Marsh was unperturbed. "You should know. From what I hear Benjamin knows lots of drug dealers." He smirked as he leaned against the doorframe, his hands in the pockets of his olive-colored English cotton twill Massimo Cerrato bespoke trousers.

Annoyed, Aimee asked, "How do you like this dress? It's part of my summer collection."

"It's hideous. Don't tell me people actually buy the awful clothes you design." Marsh seated himself in an Eames lounge chair, fussily hiking up the knees of his trousers to preserve the crease. He put his feet in dark brown burnished calf loafers handmade by John Lobb of St. James Street, London, on the matching ottoman. Then he picked up a remote and pressed a button, causing an enormous flat-screen television to descend from the ceiling with a smooth *whirr.*

"This dress is very popular," Aimee told him. Her clothing line was doing well, in part because of the provocative images she used on her garments. The chemical weapons symbol was one of the tamer ones. She'd chosen it largely to irritate Marsh, who was an arms dealer.

He was watching a golf tournament and made a noncommittal noise.

"Chemical weapons are terrible. It's a good thing they're banned," Aimee said, hoping to get a response out of him.

"Just because they're banned doesn't mean there's not a market for them, not that I have anything to do with it," Marsh said placidly, thinking of his upcoming meeting in Spain.

Trainor leaned forward, his belly pressing against his chest as he dug his hand into a bowl of boiled peanuts on the table in front of him. He picked one open, letting the shell fall to the antique silk Kashan carpet. On the TV, a golfer attempted to sink a putt. "Where they playin'?" he asked Marsh. The ball hesitated on the edge of the cup then went in, to polite applause from the gallery.

"Hawaii," Marsh said shortly. He was irritated with Trainor for having moved back into White Oaks and cozying up to the old man. The Trapnell children were as suspicious and watchful of each other as Medicis. If one of them appeared to be pulling ahead in the race to win the ultimate prize of the bulk of Blanton Trapnell's fortune when he finally went to his reward, it made the others furiously resentful.

Trainor scratched his bare chest. "That reminds me. Anybody heard from Karen? She's got a place out by Waimea Canyon, right?"

Karen was one of Blanton Trapnell's four surviving children. (Two others had died, a son from a heart attack and a daughter by drowning, the result of jumping from a yacht into the harbor at Cannes.) Karen was sixty-two, half-sibling to the much younger Aimee, Trainor, and Marsh. She was the old man's daughter by his first wife, a busty Hollywood starlet named Sandra Ames. She had supporting roles in *Wild Bikini Weekend* and *Invasion of the Vixens from Mars,* both of which were considered cult classics. Sandra, too, was dead, the victim of overambitious plastic surgery performed at a clinic in Mexico. Having a facelift, a tummy-tuck, and a butt lift all in one day had proved too much for her.

"Karen's in Nepal, at her school," Aimee said. She poured the last of the wine into the glass and drank it. She didn't offer Marsh any. While he enjoyed fine wine, she knew he'd balk at sharing a glass. He was fastidious that way, while she and Trainor didn't mind drinking from the same glass or eating off of one another's plates.

Karen had won several humanitarian awards for having established a school for girls in Nepal, including an Albert Schweitzer Prize. While the girls, ages eight to fifteen, were taught some basic reading, writing, and mathematics, most of their time was spent making beaded jewelry and painted wooden handicrafts. The results of their labor was sold to stores throughout North America, Europe, and Asia through a shell company called Himalayan Village Treasures. In reality, the Dhaulagiri School for Girls was more of a sweatshop than a school.

Trainor ate another peanut. "Is she gonna be here for Gong-Gong's party?"

The old man's ninetieth birthday was in one week. Feverish activity was underway to make it a memorable occasion. A haughty event planner named Garrison Wickwire was on site, having been flown in from Los Angeles. He was occupying one of the guest suites, annoying the servants by ordering them around. At the moment he was out by the swimming pool, wearing lime green swim trunks with pink whales on them. A red calfskin notebook from Smythson of Bond Street was balanced on one knee as he culled through the guest list of five hundred. He tapped his chin thoughtfully with a gold mechanical pencil engraved with his initials as he decided who merited favored seating in the largest of the greenhouses and who would be relegated to tents outside.

Cordwainer McTavish, the distinguished Scottish actor who'd been snotty to him when he'd tried to strike up a conversation at the BAFTAs? He'd go in one of the tents, the one closest to the port-a-johns. Wickwire smiled. *Take that, you stuck-up old bastard,* he thought, making a note with the mechanical pencil.

Wickwire had confided to Trainor that he expected the party to be bigger than almost any social event, except for a royal wedding. "It will be talked about for years, like Truman Capote's Black and White Ball," he said happily. Wickwire sometimes liked to imagine which famous gatherings of the past he'd attend if he had access to a time machine. The Black and White

Ball, a masquerade held at the Plaza Hotel in New York City on November 28, 1966, was always near the top of his list.

"Was that for his inauguration?" Trainor asked. He and Wickwire were standing beneath the white Corinthian columns of the front portico, smoking cigarettes and watching one of the groundskeepers run a rider mover over the lawn. The muggy air smelled of freshly cut grass, tobacco smoke and the promise of rain from the purplish-gray thunderheads that were stacked up in the distance.

"Whose inauguration?" Wickwire asked, tearing his eyes away from the groundskeeper. If he wasn't wearing a baseball cap, he would have been a dead ringer for Michelangelo's David. *These backwoods Southern boys*, he thought. *They're young gods at eighteen, but by forty they're wizened old men.*

"President Truman's. You said he had a black and white ball. Was it some kind of integration thing?"

Wickwire inwardly smiled. Could Trainor really be such a philistine that he'd never heard of Truman Capote? "The writer, not the president," he said.

Trainor ran a thumbnail in the gap between his front teeth. He removed a particle of food and examined it carefully before flicking it away. "Oh, a writer. You know what writer I like? Jeff Foxworthy. He's comical, the way he makes fun of rednecks and is always askin' if folks is smarter than a fifth grader. Daddy likes him too. Why not invite him?"

"Why not indeed?" Wickwire said, trying to picture the folksy comedian chatting with the three Nobel Laureates and two former vice-presidents who had RSVP'd, expressing their willingness to attend. He tried to imagine how Dick Cheney would react to being quizzed on whether he was, in fact, smarter than a fifth grader.

Answering Trainor's question, Aimee said she didn't think Karen would make it to the party. "The last time I talked to her she said she wasn't feeling well. Her gallbladder's bothering her."

Marsh and Trainor exchanged speculative glances. They weren't fond of Karen, who in addition to gallbladder trouble suffered from high blood pressure. She had already experienced two small strokes. Maybe the next one would permanently remove her from the playing field, leaving more of their father's money for them.

"That's a shame," Marsh said. "Maybe she could FaceTime with him or something."

At that moment labored breathing could be heard coming from the direction of the entrance hall, heralding the approach not of Darth Vader, but of Hillman Parks. Trainor looked around frantically for a hiding place for the now-empty bottle of Château Latour before thrusting it inside a four-foot-high terracotta glazed vase signed by architect and designer Ettore Sottsass.

"Hey, Hillman. What's up?" he asked as the butler dragged himself, wheezing, into the room.

Hillman was nearly as old as his employer. He resembled a Galápagos tortoise, with his heavy-lidded eyes and shriveled little head atop a long, wrinkled neck the color and texture of a walnut. He regarded the three Trapnell siblings with puzzlement, as if unsure of who they were. Then something seemed to click inside his ancient brain.

"Mr. Blanton wants y'all in his study," he said, slowly nodding his head in confirmation. "Right now," he added, more forcefully. "He says he wants to see y'all right now, so I come to get y'all and tell y'all he wants to see y'all *right now!*" The last two words were barked out in an eerily accurate imitation of Blanton's voice. Then he launched into a fit of deep, bronchial coughing.

Marsh turned off the television. Aimee stood up and smoothed the front of her dress. Trainor rose from the sofa and finger-combed his hair, which was in need of cutting.

When Hillman stopped coughing, he asked, "Why's there a can of stew on the table by the stairs?"

Aimee explained that she'd purchased it for her father.

"Why he likes that nasty old stew from a can I don't know," Hillman said, his wrinkled lips pursed in distaste. "I tole him anytime he wants some Brunswick stew Bestie'll make it for him, but he said, oh no, Hill, don't you bother Bestie none. I said it's no bother. She can still make chicken and dumplings and biscuits and gravy and banana puddin' and anything else you want, you jes gotta watch her around the stove, so she don't go startin' a fire."

Bestie was Hillman's wife. She'd cooked for the Trapnells for sixty years before being put out to pasture, having fallen victim to dementia. The revelation that something was wrong came at a formal dinner party when the guests lifted the metal salvers from their plates to discover catfish staring up at them, whole and uncooked, their bulging eyes goggling, rubbery mouths agape.

Bestie was retired with due ceremony, given a dinner in her honor at the country club at which she was presented with a Hérmes crocodile-skin Birkin bag costing ninety-five thousand dollars. She now spent her days carrying on a one-sided conversation with the television, in the snug little house Blanton had bought for her and Hillman on Jackson Avenue, under the care of her twin granddaughters, Kortney and Kortnessa.

Message delivered, Hillman made his way back to the kitchen, where two of the maids were watching a televised courtroom proceeding in which actual litigants aired their grievances before a judge.

"That's the one's gonna win, that girl right there," said one of the maids, pointing to a young woman who wore enormous hoop earrings. "She didn't swear or disrespect the judge or nothin'. Not like that smart-mouth white boy who keep droppin' the f-word. Judge Jessica gonna tear him a new booty hole, you watch and see."

They watched, engrossed.

Chapter 3 – A Fine Old Southern Family

Marsh, Trainor, and Aimee trooped into their father's study, wondering what on earth he wanted. The thought crossed their minds that he was going to announce he was getting married. He wasn't currently seeing anyone. The lady whom he'd been squiring around, the widow of a former lieutenant governor, had broken her hip and been consigned to an assisted living facility, but that didn't necessarily mean anything. Despite his age Blanton was tech-savvy. He spent hours online every day, tracking his investments, and generally poking around. He wouldn't be foolish enough to be ensnared by some gold digger who'd professed her love for him through an online dating site, would he?

Blanton Trapnell's study resembled the office of a used car dealer rather than the inner sanctum of a billionaire. The floor was covered in the type of cheap indoor-outdoor carpeting found in mobile homes. The battered metal desk the pinkish-tan color of Band-Aids had originally come from a used car dealership, one which Blanton purchased using a loan from his father when he was fresh out of the University of Georgia. The desk had witnessed a number of business deals that launched him on the road to riches, and he was sentimentally fond of it.

On the walls were shelves heavy with gold statuettes and loving cups and plaques and framed certificates awarded to Blanton by a variety of civic and philanthropic organizations, as well as photographs of him with five former U.S. presidents. The one of him with Ronald Reagan had pride of place immediately behind where Blanton sat, his knobby-knuckled, liver-spotted hands clasped on the desk blotter.

Like Reagan, Blanton had been handsome in his youth. There was still something of the Gipper in his appearance at ninety, especially the broad shoulders, jet-black hair, and confident smile.

His granddaughter, Jubilee, was perched on a three-legged wooden stool next to Blanton's Hans Wegner swivel chair, which was worth about five times as much as everything else in the office, except perhaps for the clutch of Montblanc Meisterstuk pens in a pewter mug on the desk. The mug bore the image of Uga, the bulldog mascot of the University of Georgia. Aimee felt a pang of envy at seeing her niece seated in the place of favor, on the same stool where she used to sit when she was small.

Jubilee was a chubby child with knock-knees and a potbelly. She had returned from swimming at the home of a little girl her age named Ainsley and wore a yellow-and-black-striped swimsuit that made her look like a bumblebee. She was telling her grandfather about her play date. Ainsley's father was a lawyer and her mother was a dermatologist. They lived in a spacious house on Fortson Avenue, the best residential street in Cobbs, but to hear Jubilee tell it, it might as well have been a sharecropper's shack.

"Their pool wasn't near as big as yours, Gong-Gong, and their little bitty pool house had just a shower and a toilet. No bidet and no soaking tub like you got in your pool house, and no heated towel racks either," she said. Her piping, childish voice expressed horror at this evidence of abject poverty.

Blanton shook his head in amazement. "Mercy! Imagine that!" His teeth, when he smiled, were yellow as old elephant ivory, but they were still his own. Then he grew serious. "Now listen, honey," he told the child, "Just because their house ain't as big as White Oaks, and they got no bidet in their pool house, it don't mean they ain't fine people. Ainsley's mama's people go way back, as do her daddy's. His great-great granddaddy had his horse shot out from under him at Chickamauga."

Jubilee mulled that over. "What was the horse's name?"

Blanton said he didn't know; maybe Ainsley's daddy would know. She should ask the next time she saw him.

"I've got a horse. His name is Hold My Beer," Aimee told her niece.

It was true. She'd purchased the thoroughbred colt sight unseen. Her accountant had recommended investing in a racehorse, and so far the young chestnut showed promise.

"Where is he? Can I ride him?" Jubilee asked excitedly.

"He's in California. That's where his trainer lives," Aimee explained.

"Oh," Jubilee said, crestfallen. She turned to her father. "Mommy said to ask you if I can have a pony.

She would, thought Trainor sourly.

"I wish I could get you a pony, Jubilee. I'd get you the nicest, prettiest pony you ever saw," he said, his voice dripping with sincerity. "But I can't. I have to give all my money to your mama, so she can go off to Thailand and have fun with her friends while she leaves you here." He let that sink in before deciding to go ahead and really twist the knife. "I know for a fact that *my* mama would never have gone away to a fun place like Thailand without takin' me along. Thailand's the funnest place in the whole world, even funner than Disney World," he said, naming Jubilee's favorite theme park. He sighed heavily. "My mama loved me. She wouldn't think of goin' off and having a good time without me."

That was a blatant lie. Their mother had often gone off without them when they were children, sometimes for weeks at a time. Trainor, Aimee, and Marsh were always relieved when she did.

Aimee rolled her eyes. She put the can of Brunswick stew on the desk.

"Here's the stew you wanted, Daddy. I went down to Buzzy's for it, special," she told him. Her voice, as it always did when she addressed her father, morphed from its usual transatlantic crispness into honeyed tones redolent of magnolia blossoms and molasses, like the speech of Scarlett O'Hara.

"Bless you, honey. To think you went out on a hot day like this to fetch supper for your old daddy! That's so thoughtful I don't know what to say. I'm overcome." He beamed at her, having made it sound as if she'd trudged to the store and back barefoot, instead of driving there in a four-hundred-thousand-dollar automobile.

Blanton was pleased to note the dismayed expressions on his sons' faces. One of the best things about having children, in his opinion, was making them vie for his approval. He let Marsh and Trainor seethe for a moment, allowing Aimee to savor her victory. Then he prepared to introduce a new item of business.

"Jubilee, honey, I need to have some grown-up talk with your daddy and your aunt and uncle. Go on and change out of your swimsuit."

"But there's nothing to do. I'm bored," the child whined.

"Why don't you find Garrison and help him get ready for Gong-Gong's party?" Trainor suggested. Garrison Wickwire loathed children, but he pretended to find Jubilee enchanting.

Jubilee slid down from the stool. "Okay." She scurried off, her sandals slapping across the varnished cypress boards of the hall, as she headed in the direction of the stairway that led to the upstairs gallery. It was a rare example of a double-reverse spiral staircase, dating to 1831, the year White Oaks rose out of swampland teeming with mosquitos, alligators, and venomous snakes.

Eight of the slaves involved in the house's construction died of cholera and were buried on the grounds, in a patch of land surrounded by a rickety white picket fence not far from the Trapnell family mausoleum. Their ghosts were reportedly seen sometimes on moonlit nights, pacing restlessly back and forth inside the fence, as if waiting for the overseer to summon them back to work.

The white granite Trapnell mausoleum resembled an old-fashioned bank building. It had stained glass windows depicting some of the lesser-known scenes from Greek mythology. (The one of Laocoön and his sons being attacked by snakes was Aimee's favorite.) It stood on a rise overlooking another small cemetery, one where the slaves who'd survived the cholera outbreak and their descendants, among them free blacks who worked for the family, were buried. Even in death, the Trapnells liked keeping an eye on their former property, and the offspring of their former property.

"Shut the door. I don't want anybody hearing this," Blanton told Marsh, who was standing closest. Marsh did so, with a sense of foreboding. *He's getting married, I knew it,* he thought. *Some skinny twenty-three-year-old from Kazakhstan or some other stan has her hooks in him. He'll bring her here, and she'll get pregnant, and then we're all screwed.*

Blanton looked off into the middle distance, biding his time and letting the tension build. Then he swept his glacial gray gaze over his children. "Y'all asked me what I wanted for my birthday. I told y'all I'd think on it and get back to y'all."

Aimee, Trainor, and Marsh nodded their heads. It didn't sound like he was getting married, which was good, but they didn't like the expression in his eyes. Something about it hinted that he wasn't about to request they make a donation to a charity in his name, or bake him a cake.

"That's right, Daddy," Aimee said.

The three of them wondered what the old man was going to ask for. He was obviously hesitant to name it, so it might not be legal, but whatever it was, they'd get it for him. There was too much riding on it to refuse. He couldn't live forever, and he was currently worth around forty billion dollars, by best reckoning.

It's something weird, Aimee thought, noting the old man's reticence. *It's probably a prostitute, or several prostitutes, or maybe even several dwarf prostitutes.*

It's gotta be drugs, Trainor thought. *The old guy wants to try some cocaine or who knows? Maybe even meth, and that's totally fine because I can help him out in that department.*

Oh, God, thought Marsh, noting his father's solemn expression. *Whatever it is, it's bad.*

Marsh was correct. It was bad. A bevy of the most degenerate prostitutes imaginable bearing a kilo of the purest cocaine would seem like a Sunday School picnic compared to what Blanton wanted for his ninetieth birthday.

"I want to kill a man," he said.

There was a shocked silence. Finally, Trainor spoke. "Anybody in particular?"

Blanton ran his tongue over his teeth, thinking. "I don't care for the fellow that does the weather on Channel 8. He's got this prissy little face with the features all smushed up in the middle that makes you want to beat the tarnation out of him, but no, I can't say I want to kill him."

His children relaxed a little at that. They didn't want to be party to the murder of a television weatherman, but if not him, then who was Blanton's intended victim?

"I wouldn't mind killing my brother Shindell. He used to hold me down and rub my face in the dirt when we were boys and laugh when I cried, but the Germans got him, back in forty-three." He sounded regretful at being deprived of the opportunity to murder his brother. The rest of his siblings were dead, as were both his wives, two of his children, and all his old business rivals, whom he'd enjoyed humiliating before driving them into bankruptcy. At ninety, he'd outlived just about everyone.

Blanton removed one of the Montblanc pens from the mug on his desk and examined it meditatively. "I dreamed of Shindell the other night. We were right here, in this very room. He was laughin' at me, callin' me a crybaby the way he did. I grabbed him by the neck and throttled him, just choked the life out of him. Squeezed 'til his eyes bugged out! I kept right on squeezin' 'til he was dead. It felt wonderful." He smiled, mentally reliving it, his powerful old hands, corded like tree roots, making flexing motions on the desk blotter.

"That's good," said Aimee. She could relate. She'd once dreamed she throttled one of her neighbors at the Dakota while holding her underwater in the Sophie Loeb memorial fountain in Central Park. The woman struggled fiercely as car horns honked on 60th Street. Dog-walkers and joggers went past and children played in the nearby playground, unconcerned by the life-and-death drama taking place before them. Aimee held on, squeezing her victim's neck as hard as she could, until she lay limp and lifeless at the bottom of the fountain, the jacket of her Chanel wool bouclé suit soaked. The lady was a member of the board of trustees of the Whitney Museum, and Aimee found her insufferable. It had been a pleasant dream.

Blanton replaced the pen in the pewter mug. He leaned back in his chair, folding his arms across his broad chest. "It don't matter who it is; I'll leave it up to you to take the initiative in that department. I just want to kill *somebody*. I'll be turning ninety in a few days. If I'm ever gonna do it, now's the time."

"But Daddy, killing people is against the law. You'd go to prison, and you wouldn't like it there," Aimee told him in her syrupy Scarlett O'Hara voice. "You know how you complained about how crowded it was on that cruise you took, and how the food wasn't very good? Prison would be like that, but worse." She sounded as if she were speaking to a small child, one who didn't understand there were consequences for committing murder.

Blanton regarded her expressionlessly from beneath tangled eyebrows that were as black as his uncannily dark hair. With a stab of alarm, Aimee realized she'd made a misstep. She tried again.

"What I mean is, of course, we'll help you, Daddy. We have to figure out a way to do it so you won't get caught." She turned to her brothers for support. "Right Trainor? Right Marsh?"

Marsh had been considering the problem. Now he stepped up to the plate. "How about this? We find a vagrant, bring him here, and you can shoot him as a trespasser. How's that sound?"

Trainor, not to be outdone, eagerly elaborated on the plan. "What we do is we go to Atlanta or Tallahassee, someplace where they got homeless people. We find one, tell him we're gonna pay him to do some yard work or somethin'. Then we bring him here, and you can pretend to discover him breakin' in and shoot him. You're allowed to shoot somebody who's breakin' into your house. Even if you weren't, ain't nobody gonna put up a fuss over a dead homeless guy."

He smiled, pleased with himself.

Blanton pounded his fist on the desk, making the pens in the cup jump and his children flinch. "No, damn it! Y'all ain't listening! I don't want to shoot somebody! Hell, if I wanted to do that, I'd go out to the gun club and shoot Ash Gaynor or Hoss Delacroix or any them fellows that hang around out there and call it an accident. Shooting ain't how I want to do it. I want to strangle a man with my bare hands! I need to do it. I won't feel right until I do. I'm your father. If y'all weren't such piss-poor excuses for children you'd help me."

Glowering savagely, he held out his hands, blue veins bulging, fingers spread like claws. He was breathing hard. A vein thick as an earthworm throbbed in his forehead.

His children wondered if he was about to have a stroke. As one, their gazes slid to the heavy antique steel floor safe in one corner of the room. It was made by the Herring-Hall Marvin Company of Ohio and was painted black, with red and yellow roses twining up the front. It contained a copy of his will, among other things. Forty billion dollars split four ways was ten billion for each of them, counting Karen. There would be other bequests, and some taken out for taxes, but ten billion dollars, give or take, was a nice, solid sum. Of course, if Blanton dropped dead, they'd have to cancel the birthday party, but perhaps it could be turned into a funeral.

The waited to see what would happen but he didn't die and the moment passed. "Don't worry, Daddy," Trainor assured him. "You can count on us. We'll find you somebody to strangle."

CHAPTER 4 – THE PRINCESS'S COLLECTION

Three nights later the Trapnell siblings were in Trainor's disreputable truck, rattling down a narrow country road that wound beneath live oaks, their limbs draped with nets of gray Spanish moss. Frogs croaked in the muddy ditches beside the road, and crickets kept up a constant trilling. They were headed south, toward Waycross, on their way to pick up a man for their father to strangle.

It was horribly hot and humid, and the truck's air conditioning was broken. Aimee fanned herself with a copy of *Southern Living* magazine. She wore khaki shorts and a sleeveless cotton top. She was sweating and her thighs stuck to the vinyl upholstery patched here and there with silver duct tape. She was in a foul mood.

Marsh was seated next to her, drinking from a bottle of sweet tea. Aimee held out her hand and waggled her fingers. "Gimme some," she said.

"I'd rather you didn't," he said.

"Marsh, I'm getting dehydrated. I mean it, give me some," she ordered.

He relented, knowing she'd pester him until he gave in. "Okay, I guess I was done with it anyway," he said, handing it over. "Be careful not to spill any on me. These trousers cost..."

Too late. The truck hit a pothole, and a spurt of tea shot out of the bottle and splashed onto Marsh's lap, making it look as if he'd peed himself. He swore and blotted at the stain with a handful of paper napkins from Krystal, a fast-food chain favored by his brother.

"You shoulda known better than to wear nice clothes in this truck," observed Trainor, who was driving and eating a Krystal burger. He was full of himself, having found a way to grant Blanton's birthday wish. *My brother might be an international arms dealer, and my sister's a big-shot clothing designer, but when push came to shove, it was good old Trainor who came through in the clutch,* he thought smugly.

At first, they were leery of the idea of allowing their father to strangle someone. They were aware that they could face the death penalty for arranging a murder, along with their father for actually committing it. They didn't relish the idea of ending up on death row in Atlanta, but they couldn't say no to the old man. He might decide to change his will, leaving everything to Karen, or Hillman, or to his Irish setter, Seamus.

It was with considerable trepidation after leaving their father's study that they gathered for a conference in Aimee's bedroom, the same one she'd occupied as a girl. A poster of her adolescent heart-throb, Don Johnson, in his role as Sonny Crockett from *Miami Vice* grinned down at them from one wall.

"Can you imagine what would happen if the media got ahold of the story?" Marsh spread his hands, simulating a news ticker crawling across the bottom of a TV screen. "I can see it now: Murder was Birthday Gift for Dad."

"Maybe he'll forget about it," Aimee suggested. She was sprawled on the canopy bed, examining her manicure. The bed came from France and had been shipped to Cobbs on a riverboat from New Orleans while the house was being built. Its tall rosewood posts were gorgeously carved with flowers and fruit and trailing vines. The original horsehair mattress was long gone, replaced most recently by a Kluft Palais Royal costing forty-five thousand dollars. It was hand-stitched and stuffed with a springy mixture of cashmere, mohair, silk, and wool. Aimee had an identical mattress on her bed at the Dakota, and another in the room where she slept in the castle in Germany, where her husband lived. Aimee went to Germany a little more frequently than she visited Cobbs, which is to say not terribly often, but she liked to sleep in comfort wherever she was.

"When did you ever know Daddy to forget about anything?" Marsh asked. He was prowling around the room, picking things up and setting them down again. "If we get caught it's premeditated murder. You realize that, don't you? We stalked a victim and delivered him up to get killed. My God, they'll throw the book at us! Daddy would probably get let off for being old and having diminished capacity or whatever they call it. But not us, oh no, not us! No indeed. They'd want to make an example out of us. It'll probably get turned into a made-for-TV movie, with us looking like psychopaths."

He turned savagely to Trainor. In a mocking, sing-song voice, he whined, " 'Don't worry, Daddy, we'll find you somebody to strangle.' Why in the blue blazing fuck would you *say* something like that?"

Aimee leaned on the goose down pillows piled against the headboard and considered the situation. "It's not normal to tell your children you want to strangle someone to death. It could be he's got Alzheimer's, like Bestie. A lot of old people do. I heard that half the people over eighty-five have got it. Maybe we should think about taking him to a neurologist and getting him tested. We could see about getting him declared incompetent."

Trainor gave a short laugh. He was seated at the makeup-cluttered vanity, on a pouf upholstered in pink and green Scalamandre paisley fabric. With his scruffy beard and hairy shirtless chest, he looked like a troll that had crawled out from under a bridge and into a lady's boudoir. "You wanna try haulin' him up in front of a judge for a competency hearing? Go ahead, be my guest. It'll make him mad, and he'll write you outta the will."

"Then what'll we do?" she asked.

"Let me think on it," Trainor replied, scratching his beard.

Just then they heard shouts coming from downstairs, carried up through the double-reverse staircase, which acted as an amplifying device. Blanton's bass bellow was answered by indignant upper-class squawks from Chortney or Hortney, the library cataloger.

"Daddy's hollering at that English guy," Marsh said, listening with interest. Down in the entry hall, something hit the floor with a resounding crash. It sounded like someone had knocked over the Second Empire table with the gilded caryatids. Blanton's shouts became more enraged.

"Daddy sounds mad," said Trainor. "D'you think he's gonna strangle him?"

Aimee had a good idea she knew what was happening. Their father had discovered the damage to his bird book and was fit to be tied. *Maybe he is about to strangle him,* she thought. That would solve the problem of finding him a victim, although the police would get involved and there would be a trial with all the attendant publicity and inconvenience, but maybe not, not if some smart lawyer could prove Blanton was senile or crazy. She smiled, thinking of the money that would come to her and her siblings if the old man were to be declared insane.

"Daddy sounds like he's about to kick his ass. That Englishman don't stand a chance. He's kinda wimpy. A lot of them fellows from over there are. It's from all the inbreeding they do," Trainor said. He didn't sound concerned, and he made no move to intervene.

Marsh went to the door and leaned out into the hallway. "Here he comes now," he said.

Footsteps pounded furiously up the stairs, followed by the appearance of the Englishman. He was red-faced and gasping, breathing through his mouth and exposing rabbit-like front teeth. He looked into the room at the three Trapnells, who looked back at him.

"Hey there, what's going on?" Marsh asked pleasantly.

"I've been terminated, told to pack my bags and get out," the Englishman replied. His voice quivered and his lower lip trembled.

"That's a shame. How come?" Aimee said.

He shut his eyes as if he couldn't bear to think about it. "That horrid grandchild of Mr. Trapnell vandalized an extremely valuable book. He's blaming me for it. I swore to him, on my honor, that the last time I saw the Audubon folio, it was put away correctly. He didn't believe me. He called me a liar. No one has ever spoken to me like that before."

Trainor got up off the pouf and advanced on him. "That's my daughter you're talkin' about. I don't appreciate you callin' her names."

"She called me a name," the cataloger replied.

"What did she call you?" asked Aimee.

"I don't want to repeat it."

"Go on, what did she call you?" Aimee persisted.

"If you insist." He straightened the cuffs of his blue and white striped Oxford shirt and cleared his throat. "She called me a poopy head."

The childish insult was delivered in a stuffy upper-class accent, making him sound like a BBC broadcaster forced to repeat a disgusting obscenity. Trainor laughed. Then he recovered. "That ain't nice. I'll talk to her. She can't go around callin' grown-ups names. How come she called you that, anyway?"

"Because I refused to play with her," the cataloger said with dignity. "I told her I was engaged in important work and was not her nanny, or her babysitter, or whatever you people call someone hired to entertain unruly children. I suspect she retaliated by scribbling in that book." His voice dropped to a horrified whisper. "In crayon. She drew all over plate number four hundred and thirty-one in crayon. I doubt it can be salvaged, although there are ways it might be possible. Mr. Trapnell refused to hear my suggestions. He was absolutely livid." His narrow shoulders sagged. "My career is ruined."

"Not necessarily. Let me see what I can do. Go get your passport," Marsh said.

The cataloger left the room and returned with his passport. Marsh opened the burgundy-colored cover and paged through it. "Wait here, Mr. Chern-Humley. I need to make a couple of calls." He left the room with the passport. The cataloger looked after him hopefully.

"Do you think he's going to intercede with Mr. Trapnell on my behalf?" he asked Trainor.

"I doubt it. Once Daddy gets riled up he don't change his mind," Trainor replied. He had returned to the pouf and was idly lining up bottles of nail polish on the dressing table's glass top, in order of color, from darkest to lightest.

"Oh God, I've been terminated. Things seemed to be going well, too. I can't believe this is happening," Chern-Humley moaned. He sank into an armchair upholstered in a turquoise and white Ikat fabric.

Aimee tried to distract him with small talk. "Whenever I'm in London I like to stay at the Connaught," she said, naming a venerable five-star hotel in Mayfair. "I prefer one of Sutherland Suites, the one with the grand piano. I don't play the piano, but I like looking at it. They put on a good afternoon tea, scones and clotted cream, the works. There's so much to do in London: theater, shopping, museums, fine dining, it's not like Cobbs. There's nothing to do in Cobbs." She gave a light little laugh to show how unlike London Cobbs was. "Who was it that said the man who is tired of London is tired of life?"

"Samuel Johnson. The exact quote is, 'When a man is tired of London, he is tired of life,' Chern-Humley replied. "London's all right. My people are from Devon. Good heavens, what shall I tell my wife? I've never been fired before. She'll be heartbroken." He buried his head in his hands.

"You've got a wife?" Trainor said, sounding surprised.

The cataloger nodded miserably.

"I got a wife, wife *numero tres*, in fact," Trainor told him. He chuckled reminiscently. "Man, oh man, is she ever taking me to the cleaners! My advice is, stay clear of marriage. Become a monk or somethin'. Once a woman's got her hooks in you, she don't let up until there ain't nothin' in your pockets but lint."

"I happen to love my wife," the cataloger said stiffly. "She's going to be upset when she hears I've lost my employment. Goodness knows I'm upset. This will reflect poorly on my CV."

"Aw, don't worry about your old CV," Trainor said with a casual wave of his hand, having no idea what a CV was. "Heck, jobs is easy to get. Lighten up."

It was apparent from the sullen way the cataloger looked at him that he was well aware that Trainor had never worked a day in his life.

"All set," said Marsh briskly, returning to the room. He handed Chern-Humley his passport. "It's been taken care of. Pack your things. I'll drive you into town. You can get a cab from there. It's better if you don't stick around here any longer than necessary, with Daddy on the warpath."

The cataloger regarded him, doubt struggling with rising hope in his mild blue eyes. "A cab to where?"

Marsh entered something in his Blackberry. "Atlanta. I got you a ticket on a flight leaving at 8 P.M., going to Kennedy Airport."

"I'm going to New York?" Chern-Humley's expression brightened. Could Marsh have secured him a position at one of the city's great libraries, something in the manuscripts and ephemera department at the Museum of the City of New York perhaps? Or possibly even at the Morgan Library? Chern-Humley would give his right arm to work with the medieval manuscripts in the Morgan's collection. He looked at Marsh with new respect.

"It's just a stopover. Your flight to Gander leaves at...let's see," Marsh consulted his Blackberry. "Eleven-twenty. Air Canada. The plane'll be mostly empty that time of night. It's about an eleven-hundred-mile trip, up the coast into Canada, past Nova Scotia and Prince Edward Island. I got you a seat in first class so you can stretch out."

"Gander," the cataloger said dazedly. "That's in Newfoundland. I'm going to Newfoundland?"

Marsh shook his head. "You'll just be changing planes there, on the way to Iceland. Did you bring any warm clothes? You'll need a parka."

"No, I packed for warm weather, knowing I'd be going to the southern United States. I didn't bring a parka. Why am I going to Iceland? Will I be staying there or is that a stopover, too?"

The idea crossed his mind that Marsh was planning to keep him perpetually on the move, like the hapless protagonist of The Man Without a Country.

"Iceland's where your new job is," Marsh told him. "The weather's not too bad there right now, about eight degrees Celsius, but the nights get cold. They won't be selling anything warmer than sweatshirts this time of year in the shops at Kennedy. I'll have someone meet you at the airport in Gander with a parka, and a couple of sweaters, and a wool hat." He sized up the cataloger, eyes narrowed, like a tailor eyeballing a prospective customer. "You take a men's medium. Johnny Rolex will meet you by the baggage carousels and give you the clothes."

"Who is Johnny Rolex?" Chern-Humley asked with a suspicious frown. He'd watched enough American television to know that somebody with a name like that was probably up to no good.

"He's a friend of mine. Don't look like that," Marsh laughed. "Gosh! You look like you think I'm sending some kind of criminal to deliver your clothes."

That's exactly what he was doing. Johnny Rolex was part of a gun-running network with which Marsh was loosely affiliated. He happened to be in Newfoundland on business and Marsh had taken advantage of that fact to ask him to do him a favor and go clothes-shopping.

"Don't worry, Johnny's a great guy. He's a Pacific Islander. You'll recognize him because he's huge and brown and he's got these tribal tattoos." Marsh ran his fingers over his face, to demonstrate where Johnny Rolex's tattoos were. Chern-Humley looked unconvinced, so he added, "He calls himself Rolex because his last name is hard to pronounce and he likes Rolex watches. Really, he's fine. Besides, you're only going to see him for, like, ten seconds, just long enough for him to hand you the clothes. Here's some money, by the way, for cab fare and incidentals." From his trouser pocket, Marsh removed a sterling silver money clip inset with a cabochon of white jade and counted off some bills.

"This is too much," said the cataloger, examining the bills. He wasn't too familiar with American currency, but he knew it was a lot more than was necessary for meals and tips and whatever else he'd need between Cobbs and Iceland. What was he going to do in Iceland, anyway?

"Keep it," Marsh said. "It should make up for any inconvenience. What's your email address? I'll send you the contact information for the lady who wants you to look at her pornography."

Chern-Humley wasn't sure if he'd heard correctly. "Pornography?"

Marsh reconsidered. "It's not exactly pornography. A lot of it is valuable first editions. High-class art books with illustrations that are somewhat, how should I put it? Stirring."

Aimee laughed. "Marsh, you mean erotic art, like Beardsley prints, Baudelaire-type stuff."

"Yes, that kind of thing. She's also got some extremely old Japanese woodblock prints that are along the same line, as well as scrimshaw carved on whales' teeth by lonely sailors during long sea voyages. It's all very artistic in its own way. It's quite extensive, this lady's collection. She's thrilled to finally have a qualified person to catalogue it for her."

"Who is this lady?" Chern-Humley asked.

"That's the really interesting part. She's the daughter of the Shah of Ishran."

The shah's bloody regime was overthrown in a coup, back in 1985. Nancy Reagan was friends with the Shah and his wife, the Empress Soraya. She prevailed upon her husband to give them sanctuary in the United States. The Shah and his wife were both dead by now. Their daughter, whose erotic art and manuscript collection she wanted someone to catalogue, was their only surviving child, two sons having been blown up by a bomb while they were living in Crete, where they were attempting to rally their supporters to help them take back the throne from the religious zealots who had assumed control of Ishran.

"Princess Farah is a lovely person. She's very cultured and a great conversationalist. She graduated from the Sorbonne and speaks six languages. You'll enjoy working for her," Marsh told Chern-Humley.

The cataloger thought it over. Having a job was better than not having one, and Marsh had gone out of his way to help him when he was under no obligation to do so. That was kind of him, but something about this seemed fishy.

"Why is the princess living in Iceland?" he asked.

"She likes it there. The scenery's spectacular: natural hot springs and rugged mountains and so on. Her home has every comfort imaginable. It'll be like staying in an English country home, only better. You'll love it." Marsh thought it best to leave out the part that the princess' home, while luxurious, was essentially an armed compound. Attempts on her life had diminished in number in recent years, but they still happened occasionally. Hence her moving to a remote part of Iceland, where the cold climate coupled with the compound's fortifications and inaccessibility would deter any but the most determined assassins.

Chern-Humley thought it over. He knew little about Iceland. There were puffins there, he'd heard, and it was similar to the Hebrides, in that from mid-May to mid-August a sort of a lingering twilight took place at night, instead of complete darkness. *The land of the midnight sun,* he thought, feeling an exciting sense of daring foreign to his timid nature. Why not? It would be an adventure.

"Very well," he said. "I'll go."

"Atta boy," said Trainor.

Trainor wouldn't have lifted a finger to help him, and he wouldn't have cared if Chern-Humley had been reduced to begging in the streets. He was as self-absorbed and simple as a snail, existing mainly to eat, drink, and fornicate. His brother Marsh was a more complex character. While he sold weapons that were responsible for the deaths of hundreds, if not thousands of people, he had a strict moral code. He gave generously to Habitat for Humanity and Médicos sin Fronteras, and a dozen other charities, all anonymously. Persons who set up GoFundMe accounts asking for help paying medical bills, or for a loved one's funeral were astounded to receive large amounts of money from someone who didn't give their name. That was Marsh. He didn't bother to investigate whether the requests were genuine or not; he gave anyway. If he thought about it, which he didn't like to do, he would have considered it a way of making amends by helping to restore order to a chaotic world, knowing that some of the chaos was of his own making.

"Thank you," Chern-Humley said fervently, shaking Marsh's hand. "I'm indebted to you."

Aimee, not wanting Marsh to get all the credit, opened a drawer in the nightstand beside her bed. Like the bed it was a French antique. She took out one of her business cards. "Here, if anyone asks you why you left White Oaks tell them to get in touch with me. I'll explain that you didn't do anything wrong. It was a misunderstanding, that's all. I'll tell them the family in no way holds you responsible for that book getting messed up."

She gave him a card, which he placed in his billfold, along with the money Marsh had given him.

"Thank you," he said again. He had hardly any chin, but what there was of it trembled as he fought back tears. "You've all been so good to me I don't know what to say."

He shook hands with Aimee, and with Trainor, who winked and told him to have fun with the princess' collection.

That was three days ago. Now they were in Trainor's truck, on their way to procure a murder victim for their father.

CHAPTER 5 – SIDESHOW ROYALTY

While pondering how to grant their father's birthday wish, Trainor did what he always did when faced with a difficult problem, one calling for underhandedness and secrecy. He got in touch with one of his old college fraternity brothers, a man named Peach Walker.

Peach was a shady character who owned a moving and storage company in Mobile, Alabama. He was rumored to have ties to organized crime, and for that reason Trainor held him in awed respect. The fact that Trainor had graduated from college at all was surprising, considering how little he studied, and that all the papers he turned in consisted either of poorly spelled ramblings that had only the vaguest connection to the topic under discussion or were blatantly cut and pasted from things he'd stolen off the internet.

If his father hadn't made a large endowment to the school, Trainor would have been kicked out long before he managed to receive a degree in communications. He'd chosen that as his major because he'd heard it was the easiest one to complete without putting in too much effort. In the end, it had taken him six years.

Peach was every bit as lazy and pleasure-loving as Trainor. The two of them hit it off right away. They'd stayed in touch since college and had many merry misadventures. Trainor laid the problem out to his old buddy, explaining that Blanton insisted on strangling someone to death. Peach, as he'd hoped he would, came up with a solution.

"See, you gotta know the right people," Trainor told his siblings as the truck shimmied and bounced its way through the humid dusk. It nearly bottomed out hitting a deep pothole, coil springs groaning beneath its rusty chassis. Hot, soupy air blew in through the open windows. Trainor licked ketchup from his fingertips then wiped them on his orange Hawaiian shirt, an exuberant garment on which there were palm trees, surfers, and hula dancers. The paper bag rustled as he reached inside for another burger.

"Me and Peach go back a long way," he said around a mouthful of cheeseburger. "I called him up, and he said, sure, Trainor, I'll be glad to help, and he told me about this guy…"

Aimee interrupted. "Are you sure we can trust him?"

"Who, Peach? Of course! We were in the same pledge class in Alpha Tau. I'd trust him with my life."

"No, the other guy, the one we're going to get. How do you know we can trust him?" Aimee slapped a mosquito that had landed on her arm, reducing it to a smear of blood and a couple of threadlike legs. Sweat dripped down her back. She hated to sweat, unless she was working out at the gym and could take a shower afterwards. She tipped the bottle of lukewarm tea to her mouth, wishing this dubious errand was over with.

"He's a professional. He used to be on the carnival circuit," Trainor said, as if that were proof of trustworthiness.

According to Peach, the man they were on their way to meet used to perform in carnival sideshows as Novak, The Czech with the Iron Neck. He'd stand on a platform inside a tent, chains wrapped around his neck. Carnival-goers would pay ten dollars each to pick up an end and tug as hard as they could. Novak claimed to be endowed with superhumanly strong neck muscles, enabling him to survive strangulation. He'd done it for years with no ill effects.

"Since he left the carnival he works freelance," Trainor explained. Peach had hired Novak to intimidate someone he described as a knucklehead who owed him money. Peach summoned the knucklehead to his office in the guise of having a friendly chat. He then pretended to fly into a rage and strangle Novak, whom he'd introduced as a business associate.

The carnie thrashed and gurgled, clawing at Peach's hands. After a dramatic struggle, he collapsed to the floor, apparently lifeless.

"The knucklehead paid up, pronto," Trainor told his siblings. "As soon as I told him Gong-Gong wanted to strangle somebody, Peach thought of Novak."

The sun was a flaming red disc setting behind the longleaf pines when they reached Novak's home, a double-wide trailer situated at the end of a dirt road. It was the only structure in sight. It rested on cinderblocks, an enormous satellite dish sprouting from its roof. Several brown and black coonhounds leaped and bayed inside a chain-link dog run set off to one side. A gleaming new Cadillac Escalade was parked on a patch of red clay in front.

"The strangulation business must be good," Marsh said, climbing down from the truck behind Aimee.

"That's only a sideline. Peach says Novak's got various projects he's working on," Trainor said.

Alerted by the barking dogs the trailer's front door opened and a leathery-skinned man with a bandana knotted over his shoulder-length gray hair stepped out. He stood silhouetted in the light from behind him, holding a rifle leveled in their direction.

Trainor hailed him cheerfully. "Novak? How ya doin'? We talked on the phone, remember? I'm Trainor, and this is my brother Marsh and my sister Aimee. That's a nice rifle."

"Thanks," replied the grizzled former carnie. He lowered the gun's barrel, so it was no longer pointing at them. "It's a Pre-64 Winchester Model 70. Bolt action." He eyed Aimee's legs and smiled at her, revealing a gaping hole where his front teeth used to be. "It's light enough for a lady to shoot," he said shyly.

"Nice," Trainor repeated. "You ready to take a ride?"

"If you got the money, I got the time," Novak replied. "Five thousand, in cash. That's what I charge for a private performance."

Trainor nudged Marsh. "Show him the money."

Silently fuming at being relegated to the role of henchman, Marsh reached into the cab of the truck and brought out a briefcase covered in dark brown pebbled calfskin. He opened it to show Novak stacks of greenbacks neatly secured with rubber bands.

Novak nodded briskly. "All righty. Since y'all are friends of Peach I ain't gonna count it. Let me freshen up, and we'll get going."

He emerged from the trailer a few minutes later, hair neatly combed, minus the bandana, and with his bridgework in place. He'd gargled with spearmint-flavored mouthwash and splashed himself liberally with drug store cologne. Before Aimee could prevent it, he climbed in the truck next to her. Leaning close, he breathed spearmint-scented fumes in her face.

"You look familiar, honey. Didn't you use to dance at the Crystal Slipper?"

"No," she said.

"Really? Because I swear I seen you at the Slipper."

"It wasn't me," she told him truthfully. Aimee had done many things in her life, but hustling truck drivers and oil rig workers for tips in a hardscrabble Georgia strip club was not one of them.

Novak did his best to impress her during the ride to White Oaks. He boasted of his exploits in the colorful world of traveling carnivals, where he claimed to have shared top billing with such luminaries as Pepe, the Mexican Dog-Faced Boy, and Fatima, the Five-Hundred-Pound Favorite Concubine of the Sultan of Raz-mul.

"Truth is, there ain't no such place as Raz-mul. Fatima was from Hackensack, New Jersey," Novak confided.

"How interesting," Aimee said, trying to scoot over, so Novak's leg wasn't pressed against hers.

"Quit it. You're jamming me up against the door," complained Marsh, who was seated on her other side. Aimee glared at him.

"After we're done, how about you and me go somewhere and have a drink? Get to know one another? I don't know if your brother mentioned it, but I'm single and lookin' to mingle." Novak gave her a roguish look.

"That's nice of you to ask, but I'm married," Aimee told him.

"To a marmot, from over in Germany," Trainor said. He crumpled the empty Krystal bag and tossed it out the window.

"That so? 'Cause I noticed you ain't wearin' a weddin' ring," Novak said.

"It's too hot to wear rings," Aimee said. She slapped at another mosquito, this one on her neck. "Besides, my husband's a margrave, not a marmot. A marmot is a rodent."

"Well, if you change your mind about that drink, let me know," Novak said, being no more enlightened as to what a margrave was, except that it wasn't a rodent. "Now, like I was sayin' about Pepe and Fatima. They were what you call born freaks, making them sort of carnival royalty. They was born the way they was, see? Next comes made freaks, like the tattooed lady, or Mister Sharp, the Human Pincushion. They had to have stuff done to them so's they could be in a carnival. Then there's gaffed acts, like Og, the caveman entombed alive inside a block of ice. Og never was alive; he was made outta rubber. Gaffs are fake, to fool the rubes."

The truck bounced and shuddered as it rolled toward White Oaks, Novak continuing his lecture on sideshow hierarchy. "Born freaks are those fortunate enough to be born with natural talent. My talent is my neck of iron." He pressed closer to Aimee, unwilling to give up his amorous pursuit. "Wanna feel?"

"No, thanks."

"Aw, come on, feel it."

Marsh came to her rescue by suggesting they rehearse what was going to happen when they reached their destination. "We'll go along to the side of the house, where Daddy's study is," he told Novak. "He'll be in there because he sits up late, thinking about things."

"Plottin'," Trainor put in. "He likes to stay up late, plottin' and schemin'."

"Right, so anyway, we'll tap on the window to get his attention. Then we'll motion him to come around to the back of the house. Once he comes out, we'll tell him we picked up a hitchhiker."

"That'll be me," said Novak, nodding.

"Right. You're the hitchhiker. We tell Daddy you tried to rob us, but we overpowered you and brought you home with us to ask him what we should do with you."

Novak frowned and sucked his teeth. "I dunno. Why would a hitchhiker try and rob three people? That don't seem likely." He brightened. "You could say you caught me gettin' fresh with your sister. We could rehearse that part, too." His eyes took on a lascivious gleam.

"No," said Aimee firmly. "We'll say you had a gun, but we got it away from you. Trainor and Marsh can hold you while Daddy strangles you. He'll think he killed you and go to bed happy. Then we'll pay you and take you home."

The others considered that scenario. "One problem: we don't have a gun," Trainor told her. He turned to Novak. "Unless you brought one?"

He shook his head. "I left the Winchester at home, and both my AR-15s, and my Glock and my Sig Sauer P320, and all my other firearms. You didn't say nothin' about needin' to bring a gun."

"Don't worry about it; I've got a gun in my car. We'll say it was yours," Aimee told him.

"Okay, so long as it ain't one of them pink ones they're makin' for ladies nowadays. It ain't, is it?"

It wasn't. The gun Aimee retrieved from the glove box of the Lamborghini was a Smith & Wesson 9mm compact semi-automatic pistol. It was matte-black and appropriately sinister in appearance. She handed it to Trainor.

Novak gaped at the white antebellum mansion and at the yellow roadster parked in front and at Blanton's white Rolls-Royce and the silver Porsche 911 Turbo belonging to Marsh parked next to it.

"This is quite a spread y'all got. That big ol' house is bigger than the Motel 6 in Valdosta. How many rooms y'all got in there?"

"I don't know; we never counted," Aimee said. She peeled her sweaty shirt away from her back with a grimace of distaste. Night had fallen, but it was still brutally hot. Insects made a droning chorus in the shrubbery. Aimee thought again how much she hated Georgia.

"How come y'all came and got me in an ol' truck when you got vehicles like these here? I ain't never rode in a Rolls before. It's on my bucket list," Novak said, gazing with longing at the Silver Wraith.

Marsh explained that the Rolls-Royce belonged to their father. Asking to borrow it would spoil the surprise. The other cars weren't roomy enough to hold three passengers.

"Whose is that?" Nova asked, pointing to a black Nissan Maxima. Wickwire had rented it at the Atlanta Airport. The Trapnell children had hoped he'd be out somewhere, indulging in what passed for nightlife in rural Georgia, so they wouldn't have to worry about encountering him and having to explain Novak's presence. It appeared he'd chosen to make an early night of it.

"It's the event planner's," Trainor told him.

"What's that?"

"Somebody who throws parties for a living."

"You're kidding! People get paid to do that?"

"Yes. Keep your voice down. Come on, Daddy's study is over this way," Aimee hissed, gesturing toward the wing that jutted out from the building's left side, a twin to the one on the right. The servants had gone home for the day. Aside from Wickwire and little Jubilee, whose bedtime had passed hours ago, there should be no one inside the house. Seeing Trainor fiddling with the gun, she told him, "Don't mess with that; it might go off."

"All right. Quit naggin' me. You're always naggin' me."

Their footsteps crunched in the crushed oyster shells as they crept through the parking area. They walked through the *porte cochère*, the covered porch that was designed to shield passengers disembarking from carriages in bad weather. Marsh led the way, followed by Novak, followed by Trainor, holding the gun. Aimee brought up the rear.

A light was on in a window to their right, spilling a buttery yellow square of illumination onto the neatly clipped turf below. Moths threw themselves against the window screen, attracted by the light, their bodies making twanging sounds as they hit.

From the formal gardens behind the house came the lush scent of vegetation. The water cascade, a series of artificial waterfalls pouring over stone steps, could be heard gurgling and splashing.

"That's Daddy's study," Marsh whispered to Novak, indicating the lighted window. "Remember, act mean, like you're a desperate criminal who robs people at gunpoint, got it?"

Novak nodded. "Got it."

The looked in the window. Blanton was seated at his desk. He was paging through a stack of papers in the glow of a green-shaded banker's lamp. He selected one and examined it, his face taking on the gloating, avaricious expression that his children knew well. It was the expression he wore when he was about to put the screws to somebody.

Novak seemed taken aback by the sight. "Holy cow! He looks tough. I thought you said he was a little old man?"

"He's ninety. Relax, there's nothing to worry about," Trainor told him. He tapped on the screen. Blanton looked up sharply.

They saw his lips move, forming the words, "Who's that?"

He went to the window and raised the sash, demanding, "Who's out there?"

"It's us, Daddy, me and Marsh and Aimee," Trainor told him.

Blanton frowned down at them, his hands on his hips. "What are you doing out there? Who's that with you?"

Aimee stood on her tiptoes and leaned closer to the window. A gnat buzzed in her ear, and she brushed angrily at it. "It's a hitchhiker, Daddy. We were out riding around in Trainor's truck, and we picked him up. He had a gun, and he tried to rob us. Marsh and Trainor got it away from him. We brought him here to ask you what we should do."

"What do you mean, what should you do? When somebody tries to rob you, you call the police. Everybody knows that." Blanton turned as if to pick up the phone on his desk. His children looked at each other in panic. This wasn't going the way they'd planned.

Trainor called out, "Daddy, wait! Wasn't there somethin' you always wanted to do, somethin' you *told us* you always wanted to do?"

Blanton paused, one hand outstretched toward the phone. He rubbed his chin, thinking. "Can't say I recall."

Marsh made strangling motions behind Novak's back. "Remember, Daddy, what you said you wanted to do to Uncle Shindell?"

Understanding dawned in the old man's eyes. "Oh, yes!"

Novak decided he'd better start playing the role of villain. Scowling ferociously he snarled, "I didn't do nothin'. I was just foolin' when I said I was gonna rob y'all. You rich folks can't take a joke."

"Shut up, you," Trainor told him, jabbing him in the ribs with the gun.

"Come on out back, Daddy. We'll meet you by the greenhouses," Aimee said.

"Be right there," Blanton replied. He sounded chipper, pleased at the prospect of strangling an armed robber. He lowered the window and moved toward the study door with surprising swiftness for a man his age.

"Come on," Marsh said. They hurried around the side of the house and into the gardens.

The formal gardens were extensive, covering many acres, with a boxwood maze and carefully tended flower beds. Slate paths led to the greenhouses, lined by solar-powered lights in the form of brass carriage lanterns that gave out a dim but adequate illumination. The air grew cooler as they passed the water cascade, where water from the swamp behind the house was constantly recycled by underground pumps so that it flowed endlessly over the limestone steps.

To their right, the turquoise water in the swimming pool rippled in the moonlight. The lounge chairs around it were empty, the umbrellas beside them closed for the night, giving the pool a ghostly and foreboding appearance, like the set of a horror movie. Bobbing in the water was an inflatable pink sea serpent, one of Jubilee's pool toys. Its face wore a secretive smile, and its long-lashed eyes held an expression of vicious cunning.

The tents were already set up for Blanton's birthday party. Chairs were stacked inside, ready to accommodate the behinds of the rich and famous and their plus-ones. Grow lights inside the greenhouses cast a purple glow on the palm fronds and vines that pressed against the glass.

The three Trapnells and Novak hurried to the shadow of the greenhouse closest to the house and waited for Blanton to arrive.

CHAPTER 6 – INTO THE SWAMP

"You don't suppose he's calling the police, do you?" Aimee asked when several minutes passed with no sign of the old man.

"Naw, he's probably makin' sure all the lights are turned off downstairs. You know how he hates it when he finds a light left on when nobody's in the room. Okay, get ready, here he comes," said Trainor, seeing the top of their father's head appear over the cypress hedge that surrounded the patio outside the kitchen.

"Over here, Daddy," Marsh called.

"Shush, we don't want Garrison to hear," Aimee told him. A light was on behind the curtains in the second-floor window of the bedroom occupied by the event planner. He was evidently in there, reading or doing something on his laptop.

As Blanton approached, Novak launched into his role as a modern-day highwayman. "You people think you're better'n anybody else 'cause y'all got money," he groused. "I ain't afraid of you. Think you can scare me by havin' an old man come out an' holler at me? Ha!"

His show business training on the carnival circuit paid off, for he made a convincingly defiant brigand. Unfortunately, one thing he'd forgotten to mention when he was bragging about his neck of iron was that, like Harry Houdini, he needed to tense his muscles before performing his trick. If you've read about how the great magician met his death, you know it was due to a college student punching him in the abdomen unexpectedly while Houdini was preoccupied with reading his mail.

A muskrat chose that moment to rustle through a clump of pampas grass, on its way to take a dip in one of the ornamental ponds formed by the water cascade. As Novak turned to look, Blanton launched himself at him, giving him no chance to prepare.

"Gotcha!" Blanton shouted, knocking him to the ground. He clamped his hands around Novak's neck and squeezed. Novak struggled and kicked, but the old man hung on like grim death. The carnie's eyes rolled back in his head. He turned the color of a ripe strawberry, then the deep purple of an eggplant. Blanton throttled him, growling, as his children looked on. The struggle seemed to go on forever. The Trapnell siblings were impressed.

"He's good," Aimee murmured. "Very convincing. He looks like he's really being strangled."

Novak really was being strangled. With a rattling gurgle that sounded like a straw sucking the last drops of liquid from the bottom of a glass, he gave a final spasm and lay motionless.

Blanton staggered to his feet, his hair hanging in his face. There were grass stains on the knees of his trousers, and he was breathing hard, as if he'd run a marathon. "You killed him, huh? Good for you! That'll teach him to go around robbin' people," Trainor told him.

Blanton didn't respond. His eyes appeared to be looking through his eldest son and into a fathomless void. Something was wrong with his face. Aimee was the first to realize what was happening.

"Oh my God, I think he's having a stroke!" she cried. "Daddy? Daddy! What's wrong?"

"Ummmpf,"Blanton grunted and collapsed.

Trainor nudged Novak with his foot. "Get up! Somethin's wrong with Daddy."

Novak didn't respond. Trainor nudged harder, rolling him over. The carnie was unresisting. He sprawled, legs spread, one arm flung over his head. His eyes were open and his mouth hung slack. Bloody foam dribbled out.

"Shit, I think he's dead," Trainor said, backing away.

Aimee's hands flew to her mouth. She stared down at the carnie, her eyes huge. "Do either of you know CPR?"

Marsh knelt beside Novak and felt his neck for a pulse. After a moment he shook his head. "CPR won't do any good. He's gone. Looks like his windpipe's crushed. His hyoid bone's probably broken. You don't come back from that."

"You sure? Maybe you could do the Heimlich maneuver," Trainor said. He kept a safe distance, rattled by the sudden proximity of a dead body.

"I'm sure." Marsh got up and went to their father.

"Are you really sure?" Trainor persisted. He wasn't looking forward to delivering this news to Peach Walker.

Marsh didn't answer. He was probing his father's neck, feeling for a pulse.

"How do you know so much about strangling, anyway?" Trainor asked.

"I've seen it done, okay? I don't want to discuss it further. Daddy's alive. We'd better call an ambulance."

Aimee gave a shriek and shoved Trainor. "We can't. What if Daddy wakes up and tells the doctors he strangled somebody? There's a dead carnival worker in the garden. We could go to jail. Damn you, Trainor, I should never have gotten involved in this mess. This was all your idea, you and that damn Peach Walker," she wailed.

"Calm down. We can't let Daddy lie here. He needs medical attention. Let me think," Marsh told her.

A querulous voice called out from the direction of the house. "What's going on out there? Is everything all right?"

Garrison Wickwire stood on the balcony outside his room, his hands on the balcony's railing, looking down in their direction. He'd heard the commotion and decided to investigate. Fortunately for Aimee, Trainor, and Marsh, they were concealed by a deep shadow cast by one of the greenhouses, so he couldn't see them. Wickwire was all too visible. He wore a maroon silk dressing gown over blue and white striped silk pajamas. He'd applied a clay mask as a pore-tightening skin treatment, and his face in the motion-sensor lights that came on when he leaned over the balcony was an eerie shade of neon green.

"Fuck a duck, it's that prancing idiot Wickwire," Marsh muttered. He hissed at Aimee, "Tell him you and Daddy were taking a walk and he got sick. Tell him to call an ambulance and wait out front for them. Trainor and I'll get rid of Novak's body. Come on, Trainor, help me get him into that wheelbarrow over there."

Aimee walked into the light cast by one of the carriage lamps. She called out, "Garrison, Daddy's sick. I think he had a stroke. Call 911 then wait out front for the ambulance so you can show them where he is. Hurry!"

Marsh grabbed Novak's legs as Trainor hoisted him under the arms. He was heavier than they would have thought. *Dead weight* was the term that crossed Trainor's mind, making his stomach lurch. A mix of stomach acid and onions from the Krystal cheeseburgers he'd eaten earlier rose in the back of his throat. He swallowed, forcing it down again.

They lugged the body to a wheelbarrow one of the gardeners had left next to a pile of mulch and dumped it in. Trainor took the wheelbarrow by the handles as they made their way through the gardens. The wheelbarrow's single wheel resisted as Trainor strained to push it over the roots of a stand of white oaks from which the house got its name. He sweated and struggled, trundling it past the mausoleum and the little cemetery surrounded by the white picket fence, toward the swamp at the rear of the property.

It was a large swamp, covering many hundreds of acres. Years before, Blanton had deeded it over to the state for use as a nature preserve. It was home to a variety of wildlife, including birds, fish, frogs, and snakes, some of them venomous. Wild boars lived in there, growing to enormous size. They were highly aggressive and extremely intelligent. Experienced hunters claimed they were more dangerous than bears. There were also plenty of alligators.

It was no place to venture without boots and waders and high-powered rifles. Marsh and Trainor were heading into the swamp wearing a Hawaiian shirt, jeans and sneakers (in Trainor's case) and bespoke trousers, a Turnbull & Asser bespoke shirt, and hand-sewn Italian loafers, in the case of Marsh. Trainor still had Aimee's 9mm pistol, but it wouldn't be much more useful than a BB gun against an alligator.

As they trundled their lifeless burden over the marshy ground dozens of pairs of eyes watched them, some fearfully, some greedily.

"Do you think Daddy's gonna be okay?" Trainor asked Marsh.

"He'll probably be fine. He's a tough old bird," his brother replied.

"I hope he's better in time for the party. It would be a shame to cancel it, what with all the people we got comin'. You know what else is a shame? That we went to all that trouble to get somebody for him to strangle and then he killed him by accident." Trainor panted, the unaccustomed exertion was taking its toll.

Marsh agreed it was a shame.

"Daddy didn't even get to enjoy it for long before he had a fit and passed out," Trainor said sadly. "At least now we don't have to pay Novak. We saved five thousand bucks."

"That's the spirit, keep looking on the bright side," Marsh told him.

The wheelbarrow bumped over the uneven ground as they left the carefully tended confines of the garden and encountered hillocks from which weeds sprouted, and washed-out places. The body nearly fell out at one point. Marsh heaved it back in. It was horribly hot, the air close and sultry. He ran a hand across his sweating forehead. "You said Novak was working on various projects."

"Yeah, that's what Peach said." Trainor lowered the handles of the wheelbarrow and swatted at a cloud of tiny black gnats buzzing around his head. He examined his palms. "I'm getting blisters. Do you want to push for a while?"

"No," Marsh said. "Now getting back to what Peach said about these projects, did they seem like the kind of thing that could lead to him disappearing suddenly? I mean, if something went wrong, did it sound like whoever Novak was doing these projects for might get mad and decide to get rid of him? Permanently?"

"That's the impression I got, from the way Peach was talkin'," Trainor said. He took up the handles of the wheelbarrow and continued trundling it toward the swamp. As they got closer the smell of muddy water and rotting vegetation intensified. The chorus of insects and frogs grew louder and more insistent.

"Peach didn't say exactly what Novak was doin', but yeah, he made it sound like it was the kind of thing where if you screw up somethin' really bad would happen to you," Trainor said. Then he was struck with an idea. "Listen, how about we leave him here?"

Marsh started at him in disbelief. "Just for a few minutes," Trainor said hastily. "I left my phone in the truck. I think I should go get it and call Peach, ask him what to do. That might be better than dumpin' him in the swamp. I mean, what if somebody finds him? It's our swamp; it would look bad. Peach has probably dealt with this kind of thing before. He'll know what to do. Gravel pits, cement mixers, acid to burn off fingertips so there'd be no fingerprints for the cops to trace in case the body gets found, you know:

professional murder victim disposal-type stuff."

"I'd rather not have Peach involved," Marsh said. Peach's friendship with Trainor might prevent him from blackmailing them, but then again it might not. He suspected it was only a matter of time before the feds took an interest in Peach Walker, if they hadn't already. Once in custody, he would start talking, naming names in a desperate bid for leniency. Marsh preferred it if his name wasn't among those mentioned.

"I know Peach is absolutely trustworthy," he said, not believing it for a moment. "Ordinarily I'd say it would be a good idea to ask him for help, but we're kind of pressed for time here. The ambulance is on its way to take Daddy to the hospital. We can't be standing around when they arrive, waiting for Peach and his body-disposal expert to show up and take Novak off our hands. It would look suspicious. The ambulance people would want us to go to the hospital along with Aimee, to fill out forms or whatever. We've got a swamp right here. It's got places where nobody ever goes. Let's take advantage of it. If Peach asks, tell him we dropped Novak off at his trailer, and that was the last we saw of him. Stick to that story and everything will be fine. Peach will think Novak went into hiding, or that somebody he was doing business with killed him."

"It's stuck," said Trainor, when the wheelbarrow sank into the mud and couldn't be dislodged.

Marsh grabbed the handles and shook it violently from side to side, tipping the body out. Grunting with the effort, he proceeded to drag it by the ankles toward a flat-bottom boat moored at the end of a rotting wooden dock. The dock looked out over of a body of stagnant water full of pungent-smelling skunk cabbage and water hyacinths, a pretty but highly invasive species from the Amazon basin that was rapidly taking over waterways in the southern United States.

The heat was intense, close and insistent. It was like being in a sauna.

"Man, it's hotter than blazes. Don't tell me we're takin' the boat out. I don't feel like rowing. I've already got blisters," Trainor complained.

"You're not having a good time? That's too bad. I'm enjoying myself immensely, out here in a swamp with a dead body," Marsh snapped.

The bottom of the boat had about five inches of brown water in it. There was nothing to bail it out with except for a rusty coffee can. With a muttered expletive Marsh started bailing. "To think that only a few days ago I was worried I'd be bored at White Oaks. I should have known my big brother could be counted on to liven things up. Brilliant idea, by the way, hiring a carnie for Daddy to strangle. That turned out well, didn't it?" he told Trainor. "Now stop whining and help me get him into the boat."

They got Novak's body into the boat, taking care not to tip it over. Marsh wrestled with the wheelbarrow, finally managing to pull it free from the mud. He was sweating profusely in the hot, stagnant air as he shoved it off the dock and into the water. It fell in with a splash, and dark brown water closed over it.

Trainor extended a hand and Marsh took it and climbed into the boat. He sat on one of the splintered wooden thwarts and sadly regarded his loafers. "They're ruined. I got them the last time I was in Rome, in an exquisite little jewel box of a shop on the Via Condotti. I knew I should have bought an extra pair." He examined his mud-flecked shirtsleeves and let out a cry of dismay. "Oh no! I've lost a cufflink. They were antique scarab ones, from Cartier. The scarabs were carved out of lapis lazuli. Beautiful workmanship."

"Never mind your shoes and your stupid old cufflinks. What about Daddy? What if he's dead?" Trainor took up a long pole lying on the dock and proceeded to pole the boat through the water, avoiding the jagged cypress stumps that stuck up here and there.

They decided to leave the body on a grass-covered hummock that rose out of the water about a mile away. They used to play there when they were boys, naming it Skull Island and pretending they were pirates. They figured animals should make short work of the corpse. Marsh had already taken the precaution of removing Novak's wallet, so he wouldn't be identified by the contents on the off-chance someone stumbled on the body and went to the trouble of informing the police.

From Novak's driver's license, Marsh found that the dead man's first name was Mitchell, and that he had expressed a desire to be an organ donor. His fatal visit to White Oaks had cancelled out that option. Novak's corneas wouldn't be giving anyone the gift of sight, and no lucky dialysis patients would be getting his kidneys, but at least he'd provide a meal for hungry animals.

After a brief internal debate, Marsh stuffed the money – ninety-three dollars – in his pocket. He'd round it up to an even one-hundred and give it to Sean, one of the attendants at the parking garage where he kept his Porsche. The garage was near his condominium on fashionable Abercorn Street in Savannah. Sean looked out for the Porsche as diligently as if it were his own. He was a young man with a baby and another one on the way. Marsh knew he could use the money.

The narrow channel leading to Skull Island would be nearly impassable to anyone who didn't know their way around. The foliage was so dense it was hard to see more than a few feet in front of them. The bird watchers and nature lovers who visited the swamp didn't venture that far back. Hunting and fishing weren't permitted in the nature preserve, not that poachers didn't sometimes sneak in, but poachers would be unlikely to report finding a body, so that should be all right.

Marsh gave a short laugh and ducked his head as the boat passed beneath a tangle of kudzu vines dangling from a low-hanging tree limb. "Daddy's the least of my worries. He'll probably be fine. Remember, he beat prostate cancer and skin cancer, and God knows what else. I'm beginning to suspect he's immortal. Don't you worry about him. Worry about how we're..."

At that moment a water moccasin dropped from the kudzu onto Trainor's shoulders, causing him to instinctively grab it by the tail. He flung it away with a cry of disgust. The snake sailed through the air, convulsing like a length of angry brown rope. It hit the water with a slap, rousing an alligator which was floating half-submerged. It rose with a bellowing roar.

The two men scrambled to one side of the boat as the alligator glided toward them. The boat rocked crazily then tipped over, spilling them and Novak's corpse into murky, chest-deep water. Marsh grabbed the push pole that Trainor had been using to propel the boat and swung it at the alligator. It was enormous, a real monster, easily the largest they'd seen. It batted the pole aside with an angry swipe of its head. Marsh swung again. The pole grazed the beast's armored back. It hissed and fixed them with a malevolent glare, swimming closer.

"Hit it again," Trainor shouted. Marsh thrust the pole, aiming for the alligator's nose. He missed.

"Shoot it," he said to Trainor.

"Huh?"

"You've still got the gun? Shoot it."

In all the excitement Trainor forgot he had Aimee's gun. He fumbled for it in the back pocket of his jeans. He managed to get it out, but before he could aim and pull the trigger, it slipped through his fingers and fell into the water.

He and Marsh shielded their heads and screamed as the alligator surged toward them, its jaws open, exposing razor-sharp teeth.

CHAPTER 7 – A HOUSE IN MOURNING

One month later, Ewell Haskins drove his patrol car out to White Oaks. The plantation house drowsed in the noonday sun, white and serene, a vision of opulence. Arcs of water shot up from the underground sprinkler system, creating miniature rainbows as they nourished the velvety green lawn. Two gardeners on aluminum ladders were trimming the hedges with electric clippers. It was brutally hot.

Haskins parked in front of the house, where the crushed oyster shell drive made a circle. He surveyed Trainor's beat-up pickup truck, and Marsh's Porsche, and Blanton's Rolls-Royce. He shook his head. Their owners wouldn't be driving them anymore. Somebody would want the Porsche and the Rolls, but the truck would be destined for the junkyard. It was a darned shame what had happened to the Trapnell men.

It took several minutes for someone to answer the old-fashioned doorbell, operated not by pushing a button but by twisting a knob set into an ornate bronze faceplate. Haskins rocked back and forth on his heels, whistling tunelessly as he waited in the shade of the portico. Finally, the door swung open beneath the decorative fanlight and Hillman Parks looked out at him.

"Afternoon, Hillman. How you holdin' up?" Haskins asked the butler. He stepped into the entranceway and removed his hat.

"There are sad times at White Oaks," the old man wheezed. "I'll be eighty-six years old come November, and I can't recall a time when Mr. Blanton wasn't around. Now the young gentlemen are gone. It's tragic, that's what it is."

Hillman led the way through the hushed coolness of the house outside to the swimming pool, where Aimee was sunning herself in a tiny red bikini. The tents for Blanton's birthday celebration had been taken down and removed by the rental company, leaving trampled areas behind in the grass.

Garrison Wickwire had gone back to Los Angeles, bemoaning the party that had to be canceled because the guest of honor had suffered a stroke. Such a shame. It would have been a glittering occasion.

Aimee was the only member of the Trapnell family remaining in residence at White Oaks. Palmer, Jubilee's mother, had been forced to cut short her vacation after Trainor and Marsh went missing. They'd gone for a walk in the swamp on the same night that Blanton had his stroke. Nobody had seen them since. The consensus was that they'd become trapped in quicksand, with one brother blundering in and the other one getting stuck while trying to rescue him. Another possibility was that they'd fallen victim to snake bites, or been attacked by alligators, or possibly they'd drowned. There were a dozen ways to die out there. Searchers had gone in looking for them, but the swamp was so extensive, so dense with vegetation, so filled with sinkholes and knotted cypress roots that the brothers' bodies might never be found.

Palmer did her best to hide the fact that she was furious with Trainor for escaping her attempts to get more money out of him. She arrived at White Oaks wearing a black dress and a black pillbox hat with a black net veil covering her face. She pretended to be grief-stricken, but inside she was fuming. News of Trainor's disappearance had forced her to leave the oceanfront villa in Bophut where obliging beach boys waited on her hand and foot, bringing her cold bottles of Singha beer and offering to clean her sunglasses.

Now she was stuck with the dreary day-in and day-out of single parenthood. There'd be no divorce now, and no fat settlement. She was a widow instead of an ex-wife and all she had to show for it was the house in Buckhead and the condominium in Florida. Both were mortgaged to the hilt and would have to be sold. Jubilee was the beneficiary of Trainor's five-hundred-thousand-dollar life insurance policy, but that money wouldn't be forthcoming until he was officially declared dead, a process that could take years. There would be no more trips to exotic destinations for Palmer Trapnell, not in the foreseeable future. She might even have to get a job. If Trainor wasn't already dead, she would have happily murdered him.

Haskins took in the sight of Aimee stretched out on a lounge chair and looked away. There was a lot of her on display. A hot blush rose to his cheeks. He removed his uniform hat and fanned himself with it, pretending to be overcome by the heat.

"Afternoon, Miz Aimee. Sure is warm today," he said.

Hillman stood by silently, waiting to see if Aimee wanted to offer the deputy some refreshment.

Aimee pushed her sunglasses on top of her head. "Good afternoon, deputy. Would you care for some sweet tea or lemonade? Perhaps a sandwich?"

"That's mighty kind of you, but no, thanks," he told her.

"Thank you, Hillman. We're fine for now. Go on back inside; it's too hot for you to be out here," she told the ancient butler. Despite the heat, Hillman insisted on wearing a black suit of worsted wool with a strip of black cloth sewn around the upper left sleeve. There had been deaths in the family, and he was of a generation that believed in observing the proprieties of mourning.

The old man walked slowly back to the house. In all of his nearly eighty-six years, he'd never seen such goings-on. First, his employer had a massive stroke, and then his two sons disappeared, all on the same night. It was almost as if the Trapnells were cursed, like the Kennedys, now *there* was a family with bad luck.

"Have a seat," Aimee told Haskins.

"How is Mister Blanton?" he asked.

Aimee's pale green eyes were unreadable. "The same. He's paralyzed, and he can't talk. He's going to be released to a nursing home, maybe as soon as next week."

Haskins seated himself on the edge of a wicker chair next to the lounge on which she reclined. Aimee's normally pale skin had acquired a golden glow from exposure to the sun. The sunscreen she was wearing smelled like coconut, reminding the deputy of the tropical drinks with paper umbrellas in them that his wife liked to order when they went on vacation to Tybee Island.

He looked away, not wanting to stare at that taut expanse of golden skin. Instead, he watched the azure water ripple in the swimming pool, trying to think how best to broach the news he was about to deliver.

Aimee's cool, amused voice broke into his thoughts. "Would you like to go for a swim, deputy?"

"No thank you, Miz Aimee. The water sure looks nice, but I'm on duty."

"Are you not permitted to swim while on duty?"

He wasn't sure if swimming was off-limits or not. He wasn't supposed to accept free meals while on duty, although sometimes he did if a restaurant proprietor was insistent. In this case, he thought it best to refuse. He had grim news to deliver. It would be unprofessional to deliver it while splashing around in his Jockey shorts.

"No ma'am, but thank you for offering." He cleared his throat. "I got some news."

She turned to him, her eyes wide. "Is it Trainor and Marsh?"

"Seems some fellows from the state wildlife resources division killed an alligator out in the swamp," he said, motioning with his chin in the direction of the swamp.

Aimee regarded him steadily with those piercing green eyes, saying nothing. Haskins went on quickly, wanting to get it over with. "They said it was almost eighteen feet long. Said they found it near an overturned boat. When they opened it up, there were human remains in its stomach."

He explained what they'd found, trying not to be too graphic. He'd seen the body parts laid out on the metal table where one of the veterinarians under contract with the state had performed a necropsy. He hadn't wanted supper that night, even though his wife made chicken salad, the kind with raisins and walnuts, his favorite.

Aimee listened silently, giving no indication of what she might be feeling.

CHAPTER 8 – HUCKLE BUCKLE BEANSTALK

When Haskins left, relieved to have delivered his unpleasant news, Aimee went upstairs to her room. She went to her dressing table and picked up her tortoiseshell-backed hairbrush with natural boar bristles.

A voice came from behind her. "Hello, Aimee."

She whirled around, dropping the brush. It fell to the antique gold and white Aubusson carpet with a thump.

Her brother Marsh stood there. He was as neatly put together as always in a lightweight gray wool suit the color of storm clouds. He wore one of his Turnbull & Asser custom-made shirts with a silvery gray Roberto Cavalli silk tie.

"Did I frighten you?" he asked.

"You're alive," she said.

"Indeed I am. Are you glad?"

"Of course."

"You don't seem glad."

"Don't be silly. I'm surprised, is all. Everyone thought you and Trainor were dead. Where's Trainor? Is he here?" Aimee bent to pick up the hairbrush. She began running it through her hair.

Marsh seated himself in the armchair upholstered in turquoise and white Ikat fabric. He crossed his legs and smiled. It was not a friendly smile.

"I let myself in downstairs," he said, not answering her question. "Nobody was around but Seamus. He's a terrible watchdog. He didn't even bark; he just lifted up his head and looked at me then went back to sleep. You might want to think about getting a security system put in. Somebody could walk in here and murder you."

"Where's Trainor?" Aimee asked again.

"That's a good question. Where, oh where, could Trainor be?" Marsh went to the armoire and opened it, pushing aside the hanging clothing.

"He's not in there." He got down on his knees and looked under the bad. "He's not under here either."

He got up and seated himself in the armchair again. "He's not in your room. Want to check the bathroom, see if he's hiding behind the shower curtain?"

Aimee didn't answer.

"No? If you want, we could play huckle buckle beanstalk. You could hunt for him around the house, and I could tell you when you're getting warm. Remember how we used to play that when we were kids?"

"Quit screwing around," Aimee said flatly. "I've been through a lot. Daddy's in the hospital, and the two of you were missing. I thought I'd go out of my mind."

"You poor thing," Marsh said, without a trace of sympathy. "Okay, I won't make you play huckle buckle beanstalk. Our big brother isn't here."

"Then where is he?" Aimee asked. She put down the brush and reached for a tube of lipstick. Grooming helped calm her nerves. She was like a cat in that way.

"He could be in Cancun, tending bar at a beachfront resort, or possibly he's in Kalamazoo, Michigan, teaching ballroom dancing. He could be almost anywhere. That's the beauty of faking your death and assuming a new identity, especially if you've got enough money." Marsh said.

Aimee applied lipstick in a shade of red called Countess Báthory's Secret. Her hand was steady as she ran the vermilion cylinder over her lips. "What happened? Did you get rid of Novak's body?"

Marsh uncrossed his legs and straightened the crease in his trousers. "Body? What body? I don't know what you're talking about. Who's Novak?"

Their gazes locked, Aimee staring stonily into the triple mirror on the dressing table and Marsh reflected from where he sat in the armchair, watching her with a teasing smile. Twenty seconds passed before he broke the stalemate.

"I don't know what you mean about a body, but assuming there was one, and assuming it belonged to someone named Novak, it's possible that an alligator ate it, one that came at me and Trainor when our boat tipped over. It's possible that the alligator would have gone after the easy prey of a corpse, rather than bother with two men who were alive, one of whom was armed with a boat pole. But that's just speculation you understand."

Aimee took a tissue from the box on the dressing table and removed a smudge of lipstick from the corner of her mouth.

"Why didn't you come back here, then? How come you disappeared for a month and made everybody think you were dead?"

"Like I said, Trainor *wanted* to disappear. Palmer kept badgering him for money. She had a pack of lawyers after him. It suited him to pretend to be dead. We were in a hell of a state, no boat, soaked to the skin, terrified another alligator would come after us. We got up on some semi-dry land and wandered around, looking for a way out, getting eaten alive by mosquitoes. Trainor's the one who got us out, believe it or not. He's not the sharpest tool in the shed, but when it comes to finding his way out a swamp, he's a sort of idiot savant. We were out of there and onto the two-lane road that cuts through Gaithersburg in under an hour. Some good old boys came along in a pickup truck and gave us a lift into Pontahatcha. We told them we'd been gigging for frogs and our boat sank."

"And when you got to Pontahatcha?" Aimee prompted. "Where'd you go then?"

"Walmart. There's one right in town. They tore down Greenberg's department store and the Criterion Movie Theater and built a colossal Walmart. I'd never been in one before. It was fascinating. They sell an astonishing variety of merchandise, all of it cheap and not particularly well made and yet people were filling their shopping carts with it. It was like being on an anthropological expedition among one of those primitive tribes who've developed a cargo culture and make simulacrums of airplanes, worshiping them in hopes of cases of Spam falling from the sky. Remarkable, really."

"You're a snob," Aimee told him.

"So are you. I just don't pretend that I'm not, the way you do," he replied. "Anyway, we both purchased a change of clothes: socks, underwear, shoes, the lot. I wore tube socks for the first time in my life. I don't understand what people like about them; they're unfashionable." He looked down complacently at his ankles elegantly encased in pewter gray hose woven in Italy from a mixture of silk and Egyptian two-ply cotton.

Resuming his tale of their adventures he said, "We ran into a retired couple in the dining area they have there, a food court I believe it's called. Trainor, of course, was hungry, and he chowed down on hamburgers from McDonald's. It was the first time I had one. It wasn't bad. Not in the same league as Kobe beef, you understand. I tried that in Tokyo, and it was marvelous. The meat comes from cattle of pure Tajima-gyu lineage that were born in Hyogo prefecture and raised on the local grasses and water. Did you know there are only three thousand certified Kobe beef cattle in the world? None of them are permitted to be sold outside Japan. There are all sorts of rules about the way they're raised and how they're slaughtered. They're very strict about it. If you're ever in Japan, you should order Kobe beef. But getting back to what I was saying, those burgers we had at the food court were quite passable, under the circumstances."

"I'll keep that in mind," Aimee said. "Did the retired couple give you a lift to wherever you've been hiding?"

"No, they took us to Savannah. But first, we had to spend the night in their Winnebago because Frank doesn't like driving after dark. That was the man's name, Frank Orlasky. He and his wife, Myra, are from Hatboro, Pennsylvania. They're touring the country. They've been to the Grand Canyon and Yellowstone National Park and all over. They stay at campgrounds, or in Walmart parking lots. A lot of people stay overnight in the parking lot at Walmart, from what Frank told me."

Aimee tried to imagine Marsh spending the night in an RV. "It sounds like you had some interesting new experiences," she said.

"I certainly did. I slept in a bunk bed with Wonder Woman sheets on it. The Orlaskys got them at Walmart. The Orlaskys love Walmart. The next morning they drove us to Savannah. Myra wanted to see the cemetery with the Bird Girl statue from *Midnight in the Garden of Good and Evil*. She was disappointed when I told her it was moved out of Bonaventure Cemetery to the Jepson Center. They wanted to see Bonaventure anyway so we parted company there. Myra couldn't get over the live oaks with Spanish moss on them, and all the blossoming azaleas and camellia bushes. She kept saying it was the prettiest cemetery she ever saw and expressed a desire to be buried there. I told her that as far as I know, there are currently three plots available for sale to the public. If she was interested, she should reserve one right away. Then I gave them directions to the Jepson and told them to be sure and get the museum's senior citizen discount.

After we saw them off, I called one of my business associates to come get Trainor and set him up with a new identity. That done, I went home and took a shower. Then I packed for my trip to Majorca. Thus ends my epic saga." He took a bow.

"Do you know where Trainor is now?" Aimee asked.

"I do, not that I'm going to tell you. Loose lips sink ships." Marsh grinned at her. "How's Daddy?"

"He's paralyzed. He had a bad stroke. He's in Clark General. They moved him out of intensive care about a week ago and into a private room. I go every day. I'm not sure if he recognizes me or not. He tries to talk but it doesn't make any sense; it's just groans and nonsense syllables. It's awful to see him like that," Aimee said.

The doctors hadn't held out much hope that Blanton would regain the power of speech. Aimee counted on them being right, although if he started talking about strangling someone, they'd probably put it down to a hallucination.

"I've been talking to Beau Tetley, getting Daddy's affairs in order. I'm setting it up so we can get him moved to a nursing home in Valdosta. It's called Palmetto Gardens."

Beau Tetley was Blanton's lawyer. He was a courtly white-haired gentleman who resembled Colonel Harlan Sanders, the fried chicken king. Aimee had also begun the process of becoming Blanton's legal guardian and conservator of his finances. She thought it best not to mention that to Marsh.

"Palmetto Gardens is like a hotel. It's got a dining room with linen tablecloths on the tables, not that Daddy will be eating in there unless he gets better," she said, seeing her brother's raised eyebrows at the mention of the lawyer's name. She thought he'd pursue it and ask what they'd talked about, but he didn't. Instead, he asked a different question.

"What did the deputy want? I passed him leaving when the Uber driver was bringing me here. He didn't notice me. I'll go by the sheriff's office later and tell them I'm not missing anymore."

"He said they found human remains inside an alligator from the wildlife preserve."

"Do they know who it is?"

"No. Just that it was a woman. They're checking the missing person databases, but so far no luck."

Marsh straightened the knot in his necktie. "I wonder if it might be Karen," he said.

Aimee put the top back on the tube of lipstick. "That's ridiculous. She's in Nepal."

"Is she?"

"Of course," Aimee said.

"That's interesting because I called her school and they said she wasn't there. They said they hadn't seen her in a while. I thought she would have contacted us by now."

Marsh's questions were starting to make Aimee uncomfortable. Marsh was smart. Once he honed in on something, he wouldn't let go.

"Karen travels a lot. She would have told us if she was coming here. If she's not at her school, she's probably at her place in Hawaii, or somewhere else. You know how she is. Sometimes we don't hear from her for months. She'll turn up eventually," she said.

Chapter 9 – Petulia Puddlehopper

Karen had already turned up. She'd wanted to surprise their father by arriving unannounced for his birthday party. At Aimee's suggestion, she flew into Miami International Airport. It was one of the nation's busiest, where a pudgy gray-haired woman in her sixties traveling alone would be unlikely to be noticed. Once there she took a cab to a Waffle House – again on Aimee's suggestion. Aimee drove there in Hillman's Toyota Corolla instead of the Lamborghini. People tended to remember seeing a Lamborghini while Corollas blend into the background.

Aimee dressed for the occasion in orange gym shorts, black high-topped sneakers, a long blonde wig, and an oversized orange and blue t-shirt from the University of Florida emblazoned with GO GATORS! No one in a million years would have recognized her as the chic Aimee Trapnell Sciotticini von Helgern who was seated in the front row at all the best shows during Fashion Week in Paris, London, and Milan.

She parked far enough away from the restaurant so the Toyota's license plate wouldn't be picked up by any security cameras. Then she went in and stood beside the booth where Karen was drinking coffee, having polished off a plate of raisin toast and scrambled eggs. Karen glanced at her, looked away, then did a double-take.

"Surprise!" Aimee said.

"Aimee? Good grief, I didn't recognize you," Karen said.

Aimee slid into the white plastic booth across from her stepsister. "I had the idea of disguising myself for Daddy's party. I thought I'd put on this wig and dress up in a uniform like the caterers are wearing and mess with him a little bit, just for fun, you know?"

Karen nodded eagerly. "You could spill something on him and see what he does. That would be funny."

"It sure would. Are you about ready? Let's get your stuff, and we'll be on our way," Aimee said.

"Don't you want to order something? They make good cheese eggs."

Aimee shook her head. "I'm not hungry."

"Not even coffee? Or a glass of juice?"

"That's all right." Aimee beckoned to the waitress to bring the check.

Karen reached for her wallet. "You should eat more. You fashion people are all too thin, if you ask me. It's not healthy to be so thin."

Aimee thought it wasn't healthy to be fifty pounds overweight and to be stuffing one's face with buttered toast and scrambled eggs loaded with processed cheese, but she kept that opinion to herself.

"Let me take care of this," she said, placing a twenty-dollar bill on the table.

Karen had a purse, a carry-on bag, and a rolling suitcase. It all went into the trunk of the Corolla. Aimee later threw it in a clothing collection bin, after removing the luggage tags and any other forms of identification. The SIM card from Karen's phone went into the swamp, as did Karen herself.

The orange and blue GO GATORS! t-shirt had been ironic, Aimee thought, since a gator had eaten her stepsister, according to what Deputy Haskins said (not that they knew it was Karen's body inside the alligator the state wildlife guys shot. They thought it was some poor, unidentified woman.) No one had seen Aimee lead a giggling, jet-lagged Karen into the swamp on the pretense of having what she called a "girls' adventure."

"Tricolored herons are nesting in the nature preserve. The bird watchers are excited about it. Apparently, they're rare. Do you want to go see?" she'd asked Karen.

Karen had wanted to go see. She'd been looking up into a tree where Aimee said there was a heron's nest when Aimee crept up behind her clutching a heavy beanbag shaped like a frog. It was made of flowered chintz filled with ball bearings. Aimee had purchased it at a gift shop near the airport, where it was being sold for use as a doorstop. She paid cash for it. She wasn't taking any chances.

"Her name's Petulia Puddlehopper. She's my good-luck charm. She wants to go see the herons' nests with us," she'd said earlier, showing the beanbag frog to Karen.

"Hi, Petulia," Karen said to the frog with the bulging, long-lashed eyes and the red-lipped smile.

Aimee raised one of its webbed front feet and made it wave. "Hello, Karen," she croaked.

Aimee had never liked her stepsister. The difference in their ages meant they didn't have much to do with each other when Aimee was growing up. What interaction there was between them wasn't the kind that made for fond memories. Karen had teased her when she was six and struggling to learn to tie her shoes, speculating whether Aimee might be "special," as she put it. When Aimee was a gawky adolescent with braces on her teeth, she'd called her "metal mouth," and pretended to be blinded by her silvery orthodontics.

It wasn't the old grudges that prompted her to kill Karen. The ugly duckling that turned into a swan had no need to murder the ducks that formerly mocked him. The mere fact that Aimee was slim and beautiful, a major player in the world of fashion, should have been payback enough, but there was their father's fortune to consider. She wouldn't put it past Karen to get him to change his will in her favor. She'd already convinced him to make a large donation to her school, the Dhaulagiri School for Girls. She might try to get an even larger donation out of him by offering to change the name to the Blanton T. Trapnell School for Girls.

Aimee wasn't about to let that happen.

Leading the way to the swamp, she thought of Karen's showy conversion to Buddhism, and how she'd failed to appreciate the birthday gift of a tunic from Aimee's summer collection. It was a one-of-a-kind piece, sized extra-large. The clothing Aimee designed only went up to an American size 10.

In response, Karen sent her a curt thank-you email, followed by a half-dozen wooden bangle bracelets for Aimee's birthday. The bangles were amateurishly painted with dragons and tigers, meant to invoke the mysterious East, undoubtedly by children from Karen's sweatshop-school.

Having lured her to the swamp, Aimee gripped the beanbag by its dangling back legs and swung it at her stepsister's head. The blow sent Karen staggering across a muddy patch of ground. She fell with a splash into the murky water where dragonflies skated and hovered. Aimee waited for her to come up again, but she didn't. If she had, she would have gotten another whack from Petulia Puddlehopper.

Aimee had never killed anyone before. It was easier than she thought. If she'd known how easy it was, she would have gotten rid of Karen sooner.

"Namaste, bitch," she muttered.

An obliging alligator had evidently done the rest. No one had seen Karen at White Oaks, Aimee made sure of that. Petulia having served her purpose, Aimee gave her to Jubilee.

The child had spotted the frog on Aimee's dressing table while waiting for her mother to come and take her home.

"What's that?" she asked, going over for a closer look.

"Her name's Petulia Puddlehopper," Aimee told her.

"She's heavy," Jubilee said, hefting the beanbag in her small hands.

"That's because she's filled with little metal balls," Aimee said.

"What for?" Jubilee asked.

"To make her heavy, so she can be a doorstop, or a paperweight, or whatever you want her to be," Aimee said. *A murder weapon, for instance.*

"Do you want her?" she asked Jubilee.

"Yes. She's funny," the child said. She poked at the frog's bulging eyes. "Boop! Boop!"

"What do you say?" Aimee prompted.

"Thank you, Aunt Aimee."

"You're welcome."

"My daddy got lost," Jubilee told her.

"I know. That's really sad," Aimee said.

With Karen out of the picture, Blanton's forty billion dollars would now be split three ways instead of four. Aimee had been counting on getting it all, until Marsh reappeared. That was disappointing.

"Karen will turn up eventually. She always does," she told him. No way was she going to tell her brother what she'd done. Marsh was an arms dealer. He wasn't unfamiliar with people getting killed, but he might object to one of his close relatives murdering another one.

"If she doesn't turn up we'll have two missing people in the family. That's two more than most families have. It's embarrassing. I won't be able to hold my head up at the country club. It makes it look as if we can't be relied upon to keep each other from disappearing," Marsh said.

He smiled. It was a slightly warmer smile than before, but not by much. In his gray suit, with his cold gray eyes, he resembled a shark, a small one, but a deadly one nonetheless.

"At least Hillman will be glad to see me. It'll be like the return of the prodigal son. We can probably talk him into opening a bottle of that fifteen-thousand-dollar Château Latour '61."

Aimee rose and prepared to follow him downstairs. "What are you going to tell him happened to you and Trainor?"

"I'll say we got split up in the swamp. I'll say I wandered around, calling out for Trainor and getting no reply. I kept going deeper and deeper into the wilderness, plunging through thick vegetation, unable to recognize a single landmark. I must have blacked out because the next thing I knew I was back home in Savannah, staring up at the ceiling in my bedroom, covered in mud, beard down to here, looking like Robinson Caruso. Hillman will believe it, bless his heart. He's a trusting soul."

Aimee thought Hillman would believe it. So would the police, when Marsh went to the sheriff's department to announce his miraculous return. Deputy Haskins wasn't exactly Sherlock Holmes, and the sheriff was even slower on the uptake. His greatest concern was whether to have hush puppies or cornbread with his fried catfish at the dining establishment in Cobbs' former railroad depot called Goober's Grits 'N Griddle. He usually gave in and had both.

"Where were you, really?" Aimee asked as they walked along the upstairs hallway leading to the gallery overlooking the staircase.

"Majorca. I had a business appointment there. The seafood is good in Majorca, particularly the squid, although they tend to go a little heavy on the garlic."

"I see," said Aimee, thinking there'd be more to the conversation. She was right.

"If your talks with lawyer Tetley involved you applying to be Daddy's legal guardian and conservator of his money, I'm fine with you becoming his guardian, but I think we'd better be co-conservators, don't you? That way we can keep each other honest," Marsh courteously motioned to Aimee to precede him downstairs.

"Whatever you say," she told him.

Marsh smiled. This time his smile was sunny as a fine day in Puerto Portals, where he'd recently closed a lucrative business deal aboard a luxury yacht. "Let's go find Hillman. I can't wait to see his expression when he sees I'm alive."

CHAPTER 10 - AIMEE'S HAPPY PLACE

Aimee wasn't the kind of person who thought of herself as having a happy place. She would have scoffed at the term, just as she'd mentally scoffed at Novak's mention of a ride in a Rolls-Royce as being on his bucket list. People like Aimee didn't have bucket lists. She had the resources to do whatever she wanted to do whenever they wanted to do it.

Nevertheless, she had a happy place, although she didn't call it that. She called it her Snake House, although *herpetarium* was the scientific term for the use she'd put to the nine-room apartment across the hall from the one she occupied. Both were in the Dakota, the venerable, exclusive building on Central Park West. It was where John Lennon used to live (he'd been shot outside) and where some of the wealthiest people in Manhattan hung their hats.

When Aimee bought the second apartment, paying ten million dollars for it, some of her neighbors weren't pleased to learn they might be living under the same roof as dozens of reptiles.

"What if they escape?" one of them asked at the meeting of the co-op board when it was revealed that the premises formerly occupied by an investment banker were about to be overtaken by snakes. The person voicing her objection was a pinch-faced septuagenarian of grand old Knickerbocker ancestry, the same woman Aimee had dreamed of strangling while simultaneously drowning her in the Loeb fountain in Central Park.

"They won't escape," Aimee said. "The plans for their containment not only meet but exceed those currently in place at the Philadelphia Zoo, the National Zoo, and the Bronx Zoo."

"But it's not the Bronx Zoo or any of those other places; it's the Dakota," the woman protested. The reverent way in which she pronounced "the Dakota," was reminiscent of the way devout Catholics say "the Vatican."

"Cher was turned down for an apartment, and Madonna, and Billy Joel.

Why would you let snakes live here if they can't?" the woman demanded. "It's not fair."

"It's not a question of fair or unfair," the head of the co-op board said, thinking life wasn't always fair and it was high time Ms. high and mighty de Bruijn-Vanderhuysen realized it. "We review each application individually. We'll consider Ms. von Helgern's application and make a decision after we've gone over the schematics submitted by her engineers. We want to make certain that everything is done according to city and state regulations, and that any animals living in this building are treated with the utmost consideration as to their happiness and well-being."

"But they're snakes. They're not like Muffykins, my bichon frise! They're horrible, slimy snakes. They have no business being allowed in here," Ms. de Bruijn-Vanderhuysen complained.

"They're God's creatures, the same as Muffykins," Aimee said. The members of the co-op board nodded their heads solemnly at the mention of God's array of furred, feathered, scaled, and finned creations. No matter what they privately thought of God himself, like all rich Manhattanites they paid lip service to the idea of preserving the environment and protecting members of the animal kingdom. At least snakes wouldn't have fans loitering outside, bothering the residents while waiting for the snakes to emerge from the building or to pull up in a limousine. Snakes stayed inside, unlike Muffykins, whose cigar-shaped feces littered the central courtyard.

"Snakes aren't slimy. That's a misconception. They're dry. Their bodies have a very pleasant texture. Do you mean to say you've never touched one?" Aimee asked Ms. de Bruijn-Vanderhuysen.

"No, and I wouldn't want to," she replied.

Aimee eventually prevailed. The end result pleased her. The Snake House was smaller than the World of Reptiles at the Bronx Zoo, but what it lacked in size it made up for in the rarity of its inhabitants and the high quality of its equipment. Aimee owned more than one hundred snakes, some of them extremely rare, like the white Darevsky's viper, the prize of her collection.

She owned a Brazilian rainbow boa, and a king cobra, and a speckled forest pit viper. She owned a Boelen's python, a weighty, nonvenomous snake native to the mountains of New Guinea. It had a large head and a thick body with a white underside. The black scales on its back shone iridescently, like an oil slick, appearing opalescent purple one moment and the next emerald green. It was exceptionally rare and difficult to keep in captivity. Aimee loved it, as she did all her snakes, doting on them in much the same way her detested neighbor doted on Muffykins.

She owned a two-headed bull snake that was four feet long. An opaque plastic partition had to be placed between the two heads when it was fed, so they didn't fight each other for the food. It was three years old, an advanced age for a two-headed snake. Every year Aimee threw it a birthday party with Champagne and a cake from Le Vert Poule on E. 60th Street. Last year, thirty guests had gathered to sing Happy Birthday to the two-headed snake, including the mayor of New York.

The snakes were housed in large cases with glass fronts, each with its own artificially created climate, mimicking mountainous, temperate, tropical or desert habitats. There were waterfalls, pools, savannas, and deserts, all meticulously recreated in miniature, down to the exact type of leaves found on the ground in the rainforest of northwestern Brazil.

The stars of Aimee's Snake House – aside from the snakes themselves – were the backdrops. There were ten of them, costing as much as her Lamborghini. The elderly artist who created them was a master of a dying craft. His father had painted the dioramas in Philadelphia's Academy of Natural Sciences in the 1920s and 1930s. He'd passed along to his son the notebooks that gave specifications on how to trick perspective in order to create feats of illusion, making a space the size of a closet look like it stretched to a distant horizon. The snakes wouldn't have known, as they wound around a tree trunk or moved across the sand, that they occupied a small-scale reproduction of a mangrove forest in Sierra Leone, or the sunbaked dunes of the Mojave Desert, but Aimee did. It was the details that counted, in her opinion.

The floor of the Snake House was made of clay tiles in shades of brown and gray, sculpted to resemble flat stones. The original inlaid mahogany floorboards that were installed when the Dakota was completed in 1884 were pried up and recycled. Standing on the stone-shaped tiles, looking into the snakes' habitats, one would swear they'd been transported to some exotic location far from Manhattan, and that the Second Avenue Subway didn't rumble beneath the street a few floors below them.

The Snake House was presided over by a herpetologist named Joaquim Brazos. He had a doctorate in zoology and lived there full-time, occupying a suite of rooms in the rear of the apartment. Aimee had hired him away from the Bronx Zoo, where he'd been part of the research staff, tripling his salary and encouraging him to devote time to his writing.

Brazos was fanatically devoted to Aimee, as was Mildred Pickering, Aimee's housekeeper. Both of them considered her to be the closest thing to a living saint they were ever likely to meet.

At the moment Aimee was in her Snake House, dangling a gerbil by its tail over a ball python's hide box. The python cautiously poked its head out. It flicked its forked tongue, sensing the rodent's presence with the vomeronasal organs on the roof of its mouth.

Aimee held her breath. The python was a new addition to her collection. It was wild-caught, and Brazos feared it would reject the white mice eaten by some of Aimee's snakes that had been bred in captivity. Would it eat the gerbil?

The python had recently shed its skin and was hungry. It began to slide out of the hide box, its shiny new skin catching the overhead lights as if it had been oiled. It moved its head upward, its black eyes intently watching the squirming rodent.

With a lightning-fast movement, it seized the gerbil. The hapless rodent didn't even squeak. Perhaps it was too terrified.

"*Bon appétit*, my darling," Aimee told the snake. She shut the cover on the tank and stepped back. She would have liked to watch it eat, but pythons are notoriously shy. She didn't want to make it uneasy and cause it to reject its meal. Later, perhaps, it would come to trust her, and she could watch it consume gerbils and hamsters. If she was lucky, it might even accept the advances of a male ball python, and there would be hatchlings. Hatch days were exciting times in the Snake Room. Aimee loved watching baby snakes poke their tiny heads out of their eggs.

The phone in her pocket pinged. It was a text from her housekeeper. One of the best things about Mildred Pickering, in Aimee's opinion, besides her devotion, was the fact that she was deaf. Aimee would have liked it if she were also blind, to better ensure her privacy, but deaf and blind housekeepers were difficult to come by. Mildred could speak, but she preferred not to. The text said U HAVE A VISITOR.

Aimee typed back. WHO IS IT?

HE SAYS HE'S UR HUSBAND.

Franz-Albert. What was he doing in New York? Aimee had a feeling that whatever the reason, it wasn't good news. Franz-Albert hated leaving his *schloss* in the mountains of Bavaria.

She looked in on Brazos in his study where he was writing an article for the *New Zealand Herpetological Journal* and reported her success in feeding the python. Then she went across the hall to find out what Franz-Albert wanted.

CHAPTER 11 – AN OLD ACQUAINTANCE

Aimee found her husband in the living room, his hands clasped behind his back, looking down at the leafy green treetops of Central Park.

"Darling, what a surprise," she said, kissing him.

Franz-Albert was in his early fifties, tall and implacable, resembling a column of thick gray smoke. His grandfather had owned chemical manufacturing plants and was rumored to have done business with the people who ran Germany during World War II. Those rumors never resulted in criminal charges, and Franz-Albert's grandfather died in his bed at age seventy-four, evading the fate of many of his less fortunate friends from the days of the Third Reich.

Whatever Grandfather Hermann may have been, there was a distinct echo of Nazi in his grandson's chilly countenance and iceberg-blue eyes. Franz-Albert was the polar opposite of Giovanni, the Italian count who was Aimee's first husband. Franz-Albert was a pale blond while Giovanni was dark-haired and flashing-eyed, effusive and prone to flights of rapturous enthusiasm that turned suddenly to moodiness and dark, furious silences. Aimee suspected he was bipolar. He denied it, saying all Italians were like that.

Giovanni was a knitwear designer. He helped Aimee get started in her fashion career. She appreciated him for that, and they remained cordial after their divorce. Putting up with Giovanni's mood swings had been exhausting. It was a relief when she met Franz-Albert who had only one mood: polite indifference.

"How are the snakes?" he asked, turning away from the window.

"They're fine," she said.

"Good. That is good."

He took her by the shoulders and held her at arm's length. "You are looking well. You have gotten some sun, I see."

"There's not a whole lot to do in Georgia besides lying by the pool," she replied.

"You must be sure to use the sunscreen. When I go outside I always use the sunscreen," he told her.

Franz-Albert seated himself on a curved white leather sofa that appeared to hover in the air on two t-shaped steel feet. Mildred came in carrying a silver tray that held a plate of digestive biscuits, a teapot, and two cups. At a nod from Aimee, she placed the tray on the glass-topped table in front of the sofa and left the room. Aimee sat in one of the matching white leather club chairs and folded her hands in her lap, waiting for Franz-Albert to tell her the reason for his visit.

One thing was certain: he hadn't dropped in because he missed her. Franz-Albert was perfectly content with not seeing her for months on end. Aimee felt the same way about him. Theirs was a very European marriage.

"I see you have a new housekeeper. What happened to the last one?"

"Tomoko retired. She was almost eighty. She went back to Japan."

"I don't know why she came here in the first place if she was only going to go back to where she came from. Servants should work until they die. It is better for them and for their employers, particularly if they die in the night after they have completed their assigned tasks. That way no one is inconvenienced."

Aimee greeted this pronouncement with silence. It was somewhat harsh, but on the whole, she didn't disagree. She thought that when Hillman died, he would contrive to do so in such a way that the Trapnell family experienced the least possible amount of inconvenience.

"The doorman remembered me from the last time," Franz-Albert said as Aimee poured him a cup of dark brown oolong tea. That was five years previously, shortly after he and Aimee were married. He hadn't been back since. He didn't like Manhattan, or the rest of America, for that matter. It was too new, too vulgar, too full of noisy, badly dressed Americans. He sipped the tea and gave a chilly, approving smile.

"Very good. What kind of tea is this?"

"Da Hong Pao, it means the Red Robe. It's grown in the Wuyi Mountains of China's Fujian Province. Some of the original bushes are still alive. They date to the Song dynasty. It's very rare and very expensive."

Franz-Albert's thin lips compressed in distaste. He had an aristocrat's dislike of the mention of money. "Interesting." Taking another sip, he said, "Chinese tea is the best tea, just as German culture is the best culture. Tell me, how is your father? Has there been any improvement?"

Aimee had phoned to tell him about Blanton's stroke.

"No, he still can't move or talk. He just lies there. Daddy was such a vital man. It's heartbreaking to see him like that."

Aimee drank some tea and ate a biscuit. Palmetto Gardens, the nursing facility where Blanton was currently housed, cost ten thousand dollars a month. He'd already been there six weeks. There was no danger of running out of money. It was his in-between state that Aimee found disagreeable. If he were restored to his usual blustering health things would go back to normal. If he died, there would be a funeral to plan and the pleasant business of spending her inheritance. Not knowing whether he'd live another six months or six years was wearing her down.

"And the rest of your family? How are they?" Franz-Albert asked.

That was a tricky question. What could she say? *Karen's dead. I killed her? Trainor's pretending to be dead, according to Marsh? Marsh is busy selling heavy artillery to dictators and terrorists?*

"They're fine," she said.

Franz-Albert uncrossed his legs. "Then I will get to the point of why I have come. I have bad news. It concerns Benjamin."

Aimee's heart lurched. She felt lightheaded as if she was going to pass out.

"Is he dead?"

Benjamin was her son by her first husband, the bipolar Italian count. He was eighteen. Ever since he'd fallen in with bad companions and gotten involved with drugs, she was afraid of him dying. Now here it was. *No, no, oh no,* she thought.

She put her hands over her eyes and sobbed, feeling as if her heart would break. Franz-Albert sipped his tea and watched her impassively. A full minute passed before he spoke.

"Compose yourself. Benjamin is not dead. He has run away from the Institute and has stolen an item that was given into my keeping. It is a serious matter."

"Oh! I was sure you were going to say he overdosed," Aimee said. Franz-Albert passed her his linen handkerchief. She blotted her eyes and blew her nose. Then she balled up the handkerchief and stuffed it in the pocket of her tapered polished cotton slacks. She'd have Mildred wash and iron it.

The Institute's full name was the Institute for Health and Human Potential. It was a high-priced drug rehab located in the Swiss Alps. Benjamin was supposed to be there for at least another six months. Apparently, he'd had enough of being woken up at 6 A.M. to go on hikes, and of lectures given by earnest recovering addicts, and of the Institute's bland diet, lacking even the mild stimulants of refined sugar and caffeine and had decamped for greener pastures.

"He telephoned me, sounding in good spirits. He asked what I was doing. I told him I was about to leave for Munich to take care of some business. While I was gone he turned up with a man whom he claimed was a staff member at the Institute. He told Klaus they were going *wandern* in the mountains and Klaus, suspecting nothing, made them welcome. In the morning they were gone. When I returned I discovered the theft," Franz-Albert said.

Klaus was Franz-Albert's general factotum. He was even more stolid and stony-faced than his employer. Aimee had once seen him doing squat thrusts in the garden wearing lederhosen with knee socks and sandals. It was a disturbing sight.

"I'm sorry he stole something from you. I thought he was getting better." She sighed. Benjamin was likely to steal the copper plumbing right out of the walls if he was on a drug binge. Whatever he took it was probably long gone by now, pawned most likely.

She was so preoccupied with worrying about Benjamin that she didn't notice Franz-Albert get up until he was standing directly in front of her. Fists clenched, he leaned down until his face was inches from hers. His pale blue eyes blazed as he snapped, "Benjamin did not steal some foolish bibelot. What is it called? Some trinket. He took an extremely important item that was given into my family's keeping. I must get it back. You must help me."

Aimee was taken aback, shocked by his vehemence. "Of course I'll help you. Goodness, you're carrying on like he took a Rembrandt or something."

Franz-Albert owned several of what were called "important" works of art. None of them were by Rembrandt, although there was a Vermeer and a muddy brown painting by Albrecht Dürer of a man looking out of a window while a lion drowsed at his feet.

Franz-Albert crossed his arms and glared at her. "It is more valuable than a Rembrandt. You do not understand the seriousness of this matter. Otherwise, I would not leave my home and fly across the Atlantic on an airplane full of revolting people, one of whom took my copy of *Der Spiegel* when I was in the water closet and was reading it when I returned. He called me buddy when I asked for it back."

He sounded as affronted as Count Dracula would be if he were accosted by a peasant asking him to hold his horse while he ducked into a tavern for a quick drink.

"He not only took my reading material he had the gall to address me familiarly when I made it clear I did not wish to speak with him when he made an earlier attempt at conversation. His exact words were, 'Here you go, buddy.' " Franz-Albert's face assumed an expression of utter loathing at the recollection. "He was fat, grinning American, no doubt thinking himself someone of importance because he was seated in first class."

"I'm sorry you had to put up with that," Aimee told him. "Do you want me to call the Institute and find out which of their employees was with Benjamin? He might know where he is now and be able to get him to tell what he did with whatever it was he stole."

Franz-Albert snorted. "It was not anyone from the Institute. That was a ruse. I sent them a photograph from the security camera at the front gate of the *schloss,* taken from a video recorded when they arrived. They said they had never seen the man before. Klaus said he spoke with an American accent. He said it sounded like the accent of someone from the American South."

He turned his accusing blue gaze on Aimee, making her feel like she was pinned in the glare of a spotlight. "You are from the American South. Here is a copy of a photograph taken from the video. Perhaps you will recognize him."

He handed her a folded sheet of paper.

Unfolding it, Aimee said, "The South is a big place. Millions of people live there. It's not as if we all know one another. I'm sure I don't know who it...oh!"

The man in the picture was turned partly away from the camera, but Aimee recognized him. It was Trainor's old college chum, Peach Walker.

"I see you know him," Franz-Albert said, watching her carefully. "I thought you would. That is why I came here in person, to see your reaction, face to face, as they say. It was too much of a coincidence of your son turning up with an American from the South while I was away. Upon making inquiries in the village I was told this man and your son had been seen with another American, one with a beard and shaggy brown hair. The villagers said the other man addressed him as his trainer. I thought they might be in error. I thought he might have been calling him by the name Trainor. You have a brother with that name."

The village he spoke of was located not far from his ancestral home, *Schloss Wilgonhöfferen,* a massive, brooding stone edifice dating to the fifteenth century. It was where Franz-Albert got most of his servants from. There was a post office and an inn and a cluster of trim little chalets with brightly painted wooden shutters, their window boxes filled with carefully tended flowers. The village reminded Aimee of a cuckoo clock, one of the big ones with many moving parts. There was something a little too perfect about it, as if it were a movie set and at any moment the villagers would come pouring out into the streets and burst into song, the women in dirndls and the men wearing Tyrolean hats.

Aimee was aware that Peach was said to be embroiled with mobsters, getting up to all kinds of shady dealings under the cover of running a trucking company, but she hadn't thought his criminal ventures would take him as far afield as Germany. To have him turn up in the company of Trainor and Benjamin was bad news. Aimee didn't like the way Franz-Albert was looking at her. Normally so refined and polite, his expression was one of barely contained rage. For the first time, she felt afraid of him.

"What now?" she asked.

"What now?" He smiled, revealing perfect white teeth. "Now you will summon your housekeeper who is deaf and who would not hear you scream if you were injured."

Aimee felt herself go cold. Franz-Albert went on, smiling placidly, "Tell her to press the formal suit in my luggage. We are going to the opera."

CHAPTER 12 – IT'S NOT HITLER

Of course, Franz-Albert travels with a tuxedo, Aimee thought, as she sat in a box beside him that evening at the Metropolitan Opera, looking out over the auditorium through opera glasses. And of course he didn't call it a tuxedo; that would be too American. He called it a formal suit. Black tie would be another way of describing it. On the jacket's left lapel was a small circular gold insignia. It signaled his membership in an ancient organization, one with a sinister agenda, as Aimee had recently learned.

What little he'd said about her son's theft of an item from a room deep within the foundation of his ancestral castle was enough to terrify her. *Oh Benjamin,* she thought despairingly, *what have you done?*

Fortunately, the opera being presented that night was *Siegfried,* part three of Richard Wagner's four-part ring cycle. Wagner was Franz-Albert's favorite composer. He'd taken her to the festival at Bayreuth shortly after they'd met. Aimee hadn't cared for all the bellowing and carrying on that went with Wagner's operas. Brünnhilde had been enormous, with thick blonde braids, wearing a formidable metal corset and a horned helmet. She'd towered over Siegfried, but Franz-Albert hadn't seemed to mind.

"He is a true heldentenor. Notice how he holds that note? Magnificent," he'd breathed, as the man portraying Siegfried let out a long, anguished wail that went on and on, as if he'd stepped on a board with a nail sticking out of it.

The prospect of seeing *Siegfried* put Franz-Albert in a better mood, making Aimee feel easier. There had been a bad moment when their hired car pulled up in front of Lincoln Center, and he saw that some of the opera-goers were not properly dressed.

"Look there! That fellow is wearing tennis shoes!" he cried, pointing in horror.

"At least he's going to the opera. Young people don't usually like opera,"

Aimee said.

"He's not all that young. He is at least twenty-five. He should be horsewhipped for wearing tennis shoes to the opera. And look! Over there! That woman has on short trousers! *Mein Gott!* Don't tell me they will allow her to go in like that!" Franz-Albert said excitedly.

People were starting to notice his consternation. There was laughter, and some of them held up their phones and began filming him, causing him to retreat into angry silence. Head held high, he took Aimee by the elbow and moved through the crowd, a martyred expression on his face.

"Disgusting Americans, how I loathe them! They don't deserve to attend a great German opera, the nasty tennis-shoe wearing, hotdog-eating creatures," he fumed.

While Franz-Albert's outburst made him the object of amusement, Aimee attracted admiring gazes. She wore a sleeveless teal blue satin gown with a tight bodice and a plunging neckline. It had an organza overskirt and a bolero jacket trimmed with silver trumpet beads in a Greek key pattern, each bead individually sewn on by hand. Her beaded clutch purse contained her opera glasses, a lace handkerchief, and the credit card that allowed her to purchase anything from a cup of coffee to an ocean-going yacht. There was an excited buzz of speculation as onlookers tried to determine whether she was a celebrity.

Around her neck was a diamond necklace, part of a matched set given to her by Franz-Albert on the occasion of their wedding. The von Helgern diamonds were legendary: a parure made up of a necklace, brooch, and bracelet that once belonged to Empress Maria Theresa of Austria, mother of Marie Antoinette. The brooch and bracelet were dazzling and costly, but it was the necklace that was the real show-stopper. It consisted of three rows of ninety pear-shaped colorless diamonds set in a delicate filigree of white gold, with a pendant stone of a flawless green diamond weighing 408 carats, giving it a combined weight of just over one thousand carats.

Breathtaking as the necklace was, it was the pendant stone that set it apart from other large, showy diamond necklaces. It came from the famed Golconda diamond mines of India. Naturally occurring green diamonds are rare, their green color caused by the presence of radiation from nearby rocks that trap electrons. Green diamonds that change color are even rarer.

The stone that hung from the front of the necklace was known as the Imperial Chameleon. It changed color under different lighting and temperature conditions, varying from yellow-green to olive brown. In its vivid green state the Imperial Chameleon exactly matched the color of Aimee's eyes, something Franz-Albert remarked upon the first time they met.

The von Helgern diamonds were priceless, although Lloyds of London reluctantly agreed to insure them for twenty million dollars. The necklace sparkled and flashed brilliantly as Aimee walked beside her husband, the stones catching pinpoints of light from the lights outside Lincoln Center. The Imperial Chameleon nestled in her cleavage. It had been a brooding greenish-brown when she took it from the black velvet case in the wall safe in her apartment. Exposed to the light it was now the vibrant green of a lime ice pop.

Aimee rarely went to the opera, but she considered it good for her clothing business to become a patron. Her status as a benefactor gave her passes to dress rehearsals, an invitation to the Opera Guild's annual luncheon, and access to the Eleanor Belmont members' lounge on the Grand Tier, among other perks. The lounge was named after an actress who'd married a wealthy New Yorker. Truth be told, the Belmont Room wasn't any more impressive than the dining room of the country club in Cobbs. There were the same ficus trees in planters shedding their leaves on the same low-pile carpeting that was chosen because it didn't show dirt. There were the same round tables with chairs upholstered in the same type of easy-to-clean fabric. As for the quality of the food and drink, it was on a par with that served in moderately priced chain hotels. What gave the Belmont Room its cachet was its members-only policy.

Franz-Albert's sour mood was mollified by the sight of the fountain in Lincoln Center Plaza that shot water into the air in concentric rings then briefly receded before shooting back up again. He pronounced it "enchanting." However, he expressed disapproval of the promotional banners that hung over the opera house's long windows, obscuring the view of the pair of thirty-six-foot-high paintings by Marc Chagall and the constellation-shaped Lobmeyr crystal chandeliers blazing with light.

"Tasteless and tawdry," he sniffed. "All these signs in front of what would otherwise be a more or less presentable building, although it is not on a par with the *Festspielhaus* in Bayreuth. Look at that one! Box office now open! Ridiculous. It might as well be the entrance to an amusement park."

Aimee, who thought the *Festspielhaus* looked like a cross between a barn and a police station, agreed that the Met didn't hold a candle to it.

She'd been reassured, while getting dressed for their evening at the opera, to see that Mildred had unpacked Franz-Albert's luggage and put his things in the bedroom room next to hers, although there was a connecting door. Franz-Albert had told her he would be returning to Germany early the next morning, his flight scheduled to leave at 8 A.M. She hoped he wouldn't visit her in the night. If he did, she thought she could manage to feign enthusiasm for his businesslike lovemaking. Still, she was frightened by his unspoken threat that harm would come to her and Benjamin if she was unable to get him to return the item he'd stolen.

"Return it, and all will be well. We will put this unpleasant incident behind us and go on as before," Franz-Albert had told her as he paced the apartment's spacious living room, his hands clasped behind his back.

"But what if he sold it and I can't get it back? What happens then?" she asked.

The temperature in the room seemed to drop twenty degrees. "Oh, Aimee, you really don't want to know what will happen then," he said softly. His expression was not one of anger but of sorrow, which was somehow worse than if he'd struck her.

Franz-Albert's ancestral castle, *Schloss Wilgonhöfferen* was very old. There were dungeons deep beneath its massive stone foundations where rats scurried and where rusted iron manacles and leg irons were bolted to the walls. He'd given Aimee a tour on her first visit. They'd passed through a low oaken door banded with iron straps, descending a seemingly endless flight of stone steps carved into the rock, worn down over the centuries by the passage of feet.

Franz-Albert pointed out rusted sconces on the stone walls where the stubs of tallow candles could still be seen, and the room filled with pikes and ancient muskets, with rotting benches where the guards used to sit when they weren't tormenting the prisoners.

"In my youth, there were skeletons hanging in chains, the bones brown with age," he said, his voice echoing off the dripping stone walls. "My father had them removed."

"That was nice of him to give them a decent burial," Aimee said. She rubbed her arms. It was cold down there. She thought about what it must have been like to be shut up in this cold, damp darkness, never to see the sun again, and shivered.

Franz-Albert was incredulous. "Why would he do that? They were the enemies of our ancestors. They didn't deserve a decent burial. Papa had them thrown into the pit where we disposed of our garbage."

Benjamin had gotten a similar tour of the dungeons, with an extra highlight. Franz-Albert had responded to the boy's questions about his family's history by letting him in on a secret. The secret was hidden in one of the rooms, behind lock and key. The keen-eyed Benjamin had taken note of where the key was kept and later made use of it.

"You keep saying he stole something important, but you haven't said what it was. You're being awfully mysterious. What was it, the Holy Grail? The Ark of the Covenant? The secret recipe for the eleven herbs and spices in Kentucky Fried Chicken?" Aimee asked, hoping to break the tension by injecting a little humor.

"None of those," said Franz-Albert.

"What was it? Don't tell me you had Hitler down there, living in your dungeon."

He made an exasperated face. "Do not be ridiculous. Hitler would be over one hundred and twenty years old by now."

"Then what was it?"

Franz-Albert stopped pacing. From where he stood in front of the living room windows he was lit from behind by the late afternoon sun, throwing his face in shadow. "It is more dangerous than Hitler," he told her. "Far more dangerous. It is the sigil of Jörmungandr."

The story as Franz-Albert told it sounded incredible at first, so much so that Aimee wondered if he'd become unhinged. It concerned a monster, a sea serpent called Jörmungandr, one of three children of the Norse god Loki and the giantess Angrboða. Loki's father, Odin, took the serpent and flung it into the ocean. It flourished there, growing so large that it eventually was able to wrap itself around the entire earth and grasp its own tail. The legend says that when it releases its tail, Ragnarök will begin.

"What's so bad about that?" Aimee asked. Franz-Albert stopped pacing and turned to her in disbelief.

"What do you mean what's so bad about it? Ragnarök is dreadful! Calamities and natural disasters! Three years of endless winter! Earthquakes! Unspeakable suffering! Then a terrible battle among the gods followed by the entire planet being engulfed in flames and then flooded. Everyone will die, except for one man and one woman."

"I know. Benjamin had a video game about it. Anyway, it's made up; Ragnarök's not real. It's a myth. Afterward the water goes away, the world is nice and new again, the man and the woman have babies, and they all live happily ever after. It's a nice story if you look at it the right way, but it's just a story. Don't tell me you actually believe it."

Franz-Albert lowered himself onto the white leather couch and regarded her with narrowed eyes. "If you are asking me whether I believe there is a giant snake wrapped around the earth, no, I do not. That is a legend handed down from ancient times. However, I believe there is often a grain of truth to be found in legends. The object known as the sigul of Jörmungandr is very powerful. In the wrong hands it can do untold damage, perhaps even bringing about something closely resembling Ragnarök, or Armageddon, or whatever you choose to call the end of the world."

Aimee thought about that as the house lights dimmed and the crystal chandeliers slowly rose toward the ceiling covered in 23-karat gold leaf, signaling the curtain was about to go up. There were murmurs of anticipation from the audience and the sound of program pages turning. People shifted in their seats, settling themselves in more comfortably. Aimee counted the hours before Franz-Albert would leave for the airport to catch his flight back to Germany. As soon as he was gone, she had some traveling of her own to do.

CHAPTER 13 - BRING ME MY GUN

White Oaks drowsed in the summer sun, the baking heat pressing down over its broad green lawns like a suffocating blanket.

Aimee and Marsh were in the gentlemen's parlor. They were drinking tall glasses of iced tea with sprigs of mint in them, brought to them by Hillman. The ancient butler had put off his black wool mourning suit and was dressed in his usual navy blue blazer, neatly pressed trousers, and starched white button-down shirt with a plaid bow tie. There was a spring in his step and renewed brightness in his eyes. Blanton Trapnell, his employer, and lifelong companion, was on the mend.

"I wouldn't have thought it possible, but he really seems to be bouncing back. A stroke that bad should have killed an ox," Marsh said. He was nattily attired as usual in an ocean blue silk suit by Tom Ford. With it he wore a coral and lime green striped shirt from Huntsman of Saville Row, and bespoke black leather Oxfords made by George Cleverley of Old Bond Street, London. He put his feet up on the ottoman of the Eames lounge chair and took a long, appreciative draught of iced tea.

"I believe there is whiskey in this," he said.

"I told Hillman to put some in. My nerves are absolutely frazzled," Aimee replied. She sat opposite her brother in a Ludwig Mies van der Rohe Barcelona chair with tufted ivory pigskin leather cushions and X-shaped polished stainless steel legs. She wore black cotton Capri trousers, low-heeled black sandals and a t-shirt from her fashion line. The front of the shirt was entirely taken up with a picture of a dead pelican drenched in oil.

"What the hell is that on your shirt?" Marsh had asked her when he picked her up at the airport in Savannah. She'd flown from New York to Atlanta that morning and from there to Savannah, leaving her apartment in the Dakota minutes after the mahogany double front doors closed behind the departing Franz-Albert. Placing his sister's Louis Vuitton carry-on bag in the trunk of his Porsche, Marsh asked her, "Is that all your luggage? You didn't bring much."

"I packed in a hurry. I've got more at the house," she said. She gestured to the oil-soaked pelican on the front of her shirt. "This is from my clothing line. It expresses outrage over oil spills that kill wildlife."

Marsh got in and started the engine. "Daddy's certainly going to be outraged if he sees it. He's on the board of two major oil companies, one of which was responsible for a bad oil spill a couple of years back."

"Daddy wouldn't realize what I've got on. He's pretty much a vegetable," Aimee replied. She got into the passenger seat and fastened her seat belt. They had yet to hear the news that Blanton was, against all odds, starting to recover. She put on her sunglasses. "I need you to tell me where Trainor is. He and Peach Walker sprung Benjamin out of rehab. They stole something from Franz-Albert, and he's hopping mad. He came to see me yesterday, talking all crazy about the end of the world."

"All right," Marsh sighed. "I should have known Trainor would get in touch with Peach. He always does when he gets in a jam, and sooner or later he always manages to get into some kind of jam."

He braked to allow an SUV filled with young people to pull out in front of him. "They're probably on their way to Hilton Head," he said, meaning the occupants of the SUV. "It's full of beer-guzzling oafs this time of year. Let's get to White Oaks, and we'll deal with it. The traffic's a nightmare this time of day on I-95. It might be better to take Route 221."

As they drove Aimee related what Franz-Albert had told her about the stolen relic.

"The seagull of door-minder? What the fuck is that supposed to mean? Has Franz-Albert been inhaling paint fumes?" Marsh asked.

"Not seagull, sigul, like signal. And it's Jörmungandr. It's a giant sea serpent, from Norse mythology," she told him.

"Oh, well then, that's totally normal. Benjamin stole the signal of a giant sea serpent from your husband's dungeon. Nothing weird about that," Marsh said.

Up ahead a rusted pickup truck was pulled over to the shoulder of the road. A crudely painted piece of plywood leaned against the tailgate advertising 'Watermellons, peeches & cantillopes 4 Sale.' Two gaunt, leathery-skinned white men loitered next to the truck. Broad smiles lit their faces when they saw the Porsche.

"Rednecks," Marsh said happily. He pulled over behind the truck and turned on his flashing caution lights. "Let's get a watermelon and some peaches. We can have peaches and vanilla ice cream for dessert. Maybe Louetta can make peach cobbler." Louetta was the cook at White Oaks, having replaced Hillman's wife, Bestie. She was almost as good a cook as Bestie, although she didn't have her predecessor's light touch with pie crusts.

When they arrived at White Oaks, Hillman met them at the front door. He was practically bubbling over with excitement. "Praise God! There's been a miracle," he said. "Mr. Blanton can speak."

Aimee put the brown paper bag filled with peaches they'd bought from the roadside fruit vendors on the ebony and ivory inlaid table in the entryway. It was the same table where nearly two months previously she'd put the can of Brunswick stew that had so pleased her father. One of the table's legs had been cracked when Blanton kicked it over in a fit of rage upon finding his Audubon folio damaged. The crack had since been expertly mended, leaving a nearly invisible line to show where the damage had been. Marsh placed the watermelon on the polished black and white marble floor tiles.

"What did he say? When was this?" he asked the butler.

"He said my name, as clear as could be. He looked right at me and said Hill."

"When?" Marsh asked, stunned.

"Yestiddy. I go ever' day to visit with him. I tell him how things are at White Oaks, and how me and Bestie is doin' and all the news from Cobbs. The nurses said to keep talkin' to him, even if it seemed like he weren't listenin', so I did. I read from the Good Book, too, prayin' for the Lord to work a miracle upon Mr. Blanton, and yestiddy he spoke, clear as could be."

The old man's eyes filled with tears. He smiled tremulously. "His eye is on the sparrow! Alls you need is faith the size a mustard seed and shazam! A miracle!"

Marsh and Aimee looked at each other. Aimee said, "Are you sure he said your name? Maybe he was just making noises."

Hillman shook his head, triumph shining from his rheumy eyes. "No, Miz Aimee. He looked right at me and called me by my name. No mistakin' it. He knew me. Then when I said, Hey, Mr. Blanton! You're back! Praise the Lord! What you need? What can I get you? You know what he said?" He waited to see if Aimee and Marsh wanted to hazard a guess as to what their father said then. When they didn't reply, he grinned broadly. "He said Seamus. Bless his soul, he wanted his dog."

Seamus, Blanton's Irish setter, was sleeping in his basket in the entranceway close to where they stood, his feathery russet tail fanned out on the cool marble tiles. He lifted his head at the sound of his name and thumped his tail twice.

Hillman went on, delighted to share his good news, "I tol' him I'd bring Seamus to see him. Then I asked if he wanted anythin' else, besides Seamus, and guess what he said! Go on, guess."

"I can't imagine," Marsh said.

"He went, 'Bring me my gun.' Said it clear as could be! He wanted his dog and his gun! He wanted to rise on up out of that bed and go huntin'. Don't that beat all?"

"I wouldn't be surprised if he makes a complete recovery," Marsh said to Aimee as they sat in the gentlemen's parlor, drinking iced tea laced with whiskey. They planned to go and visit their father later that evening after Aimee changed her shirt into one that wouldn't be likely to anger him.

"If he brings up strangling Novak I don't know what we're going to do," she said morosely.

Marsh drained his glass and set it down on the glass top of the kidney-shaped Noguchi coffee table. "Deny, deny, deny," he said. His voice took on an innocent, astonished tone. "Daddy, what are you talking about? What hitchhiker? There was no hitchhiker. You must have been dreaming. That's how to do it. Deny everything."

"At least Hillman knows better than to bring him his gun. Can you imagine if Daddy got mad at one of the nurses? He'd be liable to blow their head off."

"I doubt Daddy has the strength to handle his Ithaca Mag 10 semi-automatic shotgun. It weighs almost twelve pounds, and it's got a kick like a mule. A nurse would be able to duck if she saw he was about to shoot her, but you never know. If he keeps on getting better, they might release him and let him come home. Then we'd be right back where we started."

Aimee ran her hands through her hair. "I'm not getting him someone else to strangle if he forgot about strangling Novak and starts in again about wanting to strangle somebody. That's non-negotiable; I'm not doing it."

Blanton was sleeping when they arrived at Palmetto Gardens, where he occupied one of the largest and most expensive rooms. The public spaces and the individual "residences" as the rooms were called, featured mass-produced imitation Chippendale furniture, dark green and red plaid wall-to-wall carpeting, and dark green wallpaper with big orange and blue pineapples on it that matched the fabric of the curtains. The curtains would almost certainly have been referred to as "window treatments" by the decorator who supplied them. They had an abundance of layers, including sheers, fishtail swags, rosettes, and valances. The tie-backs were fastened to the walls with brass knobs the size of tennis balls. The chandeliers, too, were brass.

There were ginger jar lamps and life-sized carved wooden swans with gingham bows tied around their necks and wicker baskets filled with potpourri. The time frame of Palmetto Gardens' interior décor was firmly anchored in the nineteen-eighties, a cluttered, fussy decorating style that was still much admired in the Deep South. Despite its fancy décor Palmetto Gardens had the same urine and disinfectant smell common to all nursing homes.

The heat was cranked up since the elderly inmates liked it warm. It was nearly as hot inside Palmetto Gardens as it was outside, where the thermometer in Marsh's Porsche registered 104 degrees.

A sweat bee landed on Aimee's forehead, its shiny green head and thorax contrasting with the vivid black and yellow stripes on its abdomen. It was attracted by the beads of perspiration that sprang up along her hairline almost as soon as she got out of the air-conditioned car. She irritably flicked it away. There were too many bugs in Georgia, big bugs, little bugs, flying bugs, hopping bugs, crawling bugs, stinging bugs. That's one of the reasons why she hated it there: the bugs and the heat and the languid way people meandered through their days, never in any hurry to get things done.

Blanton's room overlooked a courtyard with a fountain at its center. Arranged around it were white wooden benches and rustic wooden barrels planted with white impatiens and pink and green coleus. Blanton could look out at it if he happened to be sitting up, but at the moment he lay flat on his back in bed, mouth wide open, snoring loudly. Aimee and Marsh perched in a pair of molded plastic chairs, waiting to see if he'd wake up and recognize them.

"Listen to him. I'm surprised he doesn't wake himself up, snoring like that," Aimee said as he let off a particularly noisy exhalation.

"He's got a deviated septum. He may have gotten it when Uncle Shindell smashed his face in the dirt one of those times when they were kids," her brother said.

They gave it almost an hour before giving up and leaving when Blanton failed to wake up. The nurse in charge confirmed that he had begun to speak. She said that while it was unusual for someone who'd had such a severe stroke to regain the power of speech, it wasn't unheard of.

"Your father's a fighter," she said, shaking her head in admiration. "I've seen men forty years younger drop dead from a cerebrovascular accident, but he's hanging in there. There's still considerable paralysis. We're going to get him sitting up in a chair and start a more aggressive course of physical therapy. He might surprise us and be up and around again. You never can tell.

CHAPTER 14 – IT CAME FROM OUTER SPACE

On their way back to White Oaks, Aimee and Marsh stopped at the Publix supermarket in Cobbs to pick up a quart of vanilla ice cream. The Publix would have driven Buzzy's General Store out of business long ago if it wasn't for the fact that Buzzy's sold live bait and Publix didn't. Nightcrawlers and crayfish and minnows were what kept Buzzy's alive, those and the fact that Gordon Buzzy, like his father and grandfather before him, sold moonshine whiskey out of a shack in the woods behind the store. The moonshine was clear, oily, and potent and was called Old Rocking Chair. The citizens of Cobbs were, on the whole, as proud of it as the residents of France's Loire Valley were of their Sancerre and Pouilly-Fumé.

The sheriff and his deputies knew Buzzy sold moonshine, but he did it quietly, without fanfare. They considered it a time-honored local tradition and saw no need to get the state alcohol and tobacco enforcement officers after him.

Aimee and Marsh sat at the long marble-topped kitchen table at White Oaks. The servants had cleared out and gone home for the night. The siblings were eating vanilla ice cream with the ripe clingstone peaches they'd bought earlier that day from the roadside fruit vendors. Before she left Louetta had cut up the peaches and mixed them with syrup made from brown sugar, cinnamon, vanilla extract, and butter. This fruit compote was currently warming in a saucepan on top of the Thermador range.

Marsh licked his spoon. "What I don't understand is why all this fuss over the sigul thingamajig? Why is Franz-Albert so hot to trot over it? Where did it come from and what's it supposed to do?"

"The sigul of Jörmungandr," Aimee said. "He said it came from outer space."

Marsh put down the spoon. "Are you serious?"

"That's what he said. I know it sounds crazy, but you should have seen him. He was all worked up. I've never seen him like that before. He insisted it has the power to destroy the world."

Marsh got up and helped himself to more ice cream from the walk-in freezer. "I'd say Franz-Albert could use a check-up from the neck up. He always was kind of creepy, but this is weird even for him."

"I know," Aimee sighed. She held out her dish, and Marsh scooped ice cream into it. She went to the saucepan on the range and added some warm peaches and syrup.

"So it came from outer space, huh?" Marsh made *Twilight Zone* noises. "What does it look like?"

"Originally it looked like a rock. Franz-Albert said it fell out of the sky, like a meteorite. A farmer in Saxony out searching for a lost cow discovered it. He saw a streak of light in the sky, and when he went to investigate, he found a crater punched into a hillside and these glassy-looking gray rocks scattered around. He thought they might be valuable, so he gathered them up and took them to the home of a man who lived nearby who had a cabinet of curiosities. Those were sort of an early type of natural history museum. The man bought the rocks and then when he died his heirs sold them along with the rest of his collection to a museum in Dresden."

"When was this?" Marsh asked.

"In the sixteenth century."

Marsh whistled. "How did Franz Albert get ahold of it?"

"The Age of Enlightenment came along. Scientists got the idea there couldn't be any rocks in the sky and that people were wrong when they insisted they saw them fall. The museum took the meteorites out of public display. They were going to throw them out when one of Franz-Albert's ancestors happened to be visiting and offered to take them off their hands. He took them back to his castle and started cutting them open."

Marsh almost choked on his ice cream. "What?"

"He wanted to see what was inside. Maybe he thought they were geodes and had sparkly crystals inside. Whatever the reason, he started cutting into them, and in one, there was a flat round disc about this big, made of gold-colored metal." Aimee made a fist to show how big Franz-Albert said the disc was.

"What did he do then?" Marsh asked.

"He tried cutting it open."

"That's not the smartest thing to do with a mysterious object of unknown purpose," Marsh said.

Aimee agreed. "It seems foolish. He tried, but he couldn't even make a scratch on it. He figured it wasn't gold because gold would have scratched. When the saw blade broke off, he got frustrated and went outside to chuck it away. That's when he looked up in the night sky and saw a bright beam of light coming right at him."

"A spaceship?"

"Franz-Albert said his ancestor didn't see what was making the light. He ran inside, scared to death. He slammed the door shut and barred it. Minutes later there was a loud *Boom! Boom! Boom!* on the door. Franz-Albert's ancestor was terrified. His wife and the servants were in an uproar. He yelled at them not to open the door when *wham!* it flew open. The thick wooden bar was shattered into splinters. Franz-Albert's ancestors and their servants stood there gaping as in walked two people."

"Spacemen?"

"Apparently. Franz-Albert's ancestor wasn't specific about what they looked like. In the written account he left Franz-Albert said he described them as 'men and yet not men.' "

Marsh guffawed. "Men who weren't men? Sounds like transvestites from outer space, like Frank N. Furter in *The Rocky Horror Picture Show.*"

Aimee scraped the last of the ice cream from her dish. "Laugh if you want, but that description gives me the shivers. It's as if he was saying they were only vaguely humanoid. I'm just as glad he didn't go into it. Anyway, Franz-Albert's ancestor seemed to be in awe of them. He invited them into his library and told his wife and servants not to disturb them. They had a chat, the visitors communicating 'in a language without words in which they made their thoughts and wishes perfectly understood.' That's a direct quote, exactly how Franz-Albert repeated it to me. Then they left, telling Franz-Albert's ancestor to guard the sigul, that it had the power to destroy the world. He got some of his friends together, and they formed a secret society. They had gold circle pins made up and wore them in their lapels to identify them as belonging to the fellowship of the Jörmungandr. They had meetings. They still do. Franz-Albert is one of them. He was in charge of keeping the sigul safe."

"So far I'm not impressed," Marsh said. "Lots of secret societies started up back then. It was a trend. They made up all sorts of fantastic backstories about angels and other supernatural beings appearing and giving them magical documents and showing them mystic rituals. For example, the Freemasons? They started out in medieval times as a stonemasons' guild. It was later that they became a secret society. They claimed their 'craft,' as they call it, was handed down from Euclid of Alexandria, the father of geometry. It's bullshit. I should know. I am one."

Aimee raised her eyebrows. She had no idea. She couldn't have been more surprised if he'd told her he was a lion tamer. "You're a Mason?"

"Yes. It comes in handy sometimes in my business. Quite a few of the less-Westernized gentlemen with whom I come in contact through my business dealings are fellow craftsmen. They're flabbergasted when they learn I'm a brother Mason. It's quite touching, really. There they are in their regalia, their lambskin aprons, and whatnot, going through the old rituals, and to see their astonishment when I deliver the responses correctly! It gives one faith in humanity when people from such different backgrounds are able to put aside their differences and come together like that."

"That's great, Marsh. You can exchange secret handshakes and make friendship bracelets while you're selling them rocket launchers and fighter jets," Aimee said. "The thing is, the sigul of Jörmungandr may be fake, but even if it is, Franz-Albert and his friends believe it's real. They want it back, or they're going to do something awful to Benjamin, and to me, too. That's why we need to find them and get it back."

She leaned her elbows on the table and put her head in her hands. "I'm worried sick about Benjamin. It's bad enough he escaped from rehab. Nothing good ever happens when he escapes from rehab."

Marsh patted her gingerly on the back. "He's done it before, huh? The little scamp! Don't worry, we'll find him. Please don't cry. I hate it when someone cries. It always makes me cry too."

"You don't understand. You don't have children. I couldn't stand it if anything happened to Benjamin. He's all I have."

"It's not out of the realm of possibility that I might have children somewhere," Marsh told her. He collected their empty ice cream dishes and spoons, rinsed them in the sink, and put them in the dishwasher. "I'm widely traveled. There could be a little Marsh or Marsha in Belarus or Rabat, or in lots of other places. Since I don't know one way or the other, I can't say it bothers me. Look on the bright side: Benjamin isn't all you have. You have your snakes. Your snakes love you."

Aimee blinked back tears. "You're right, and I love them, but not in the same way I love Benjamin."

"We'll find him, don't worry," Marsh said. "I know where to start looking.

CHAPTER 15 – POKER WAS NOT TRAVIS MONTENAY'S GAME

Peach Walker ran a moving and storage company in Mobile called Friendly Neighbors Southland Trucking. That's where Marsh proposed to start looking. It was unlikely Peach and Trainor and Benjamin would be holed up in one of the garages where they kept the fleet of moving trucks, but somebody there would likely know where Peach was.

"Mobile's almost a five-hour drive away. I don't feel like fighting the beach traffic down through Tallahassee and out along I-10. We'll fly and get a cab from the airport," Marsh told Aimee the morning after their visit to Palmetto Gardens.

Aimee had spent a sleepless night, tossing and turning on her cloudlike mattress. She was sick with worry about Benjamin. Trainor and Peach weren't the most reliable traveling companions. They might have ditched him, leaving Benjamin to roam the streets somewhere, broke and hungry. She turned the plump goose down pillow beneath her head over to the cool side and willed herself to go to sleep, but sleep evaded her. She kept picturing her son's face, frightened and hollow-eyed. She was determined to find him, but what if it was already too late?

"Valdosta's the nearest airport. Delta flies out of there, I think. We can check the schedule and see when the next flight to Mobile is," she told Marsh. They were seated beneath a green canvas umbrella at a table on the flagstone patio outside the kitchen at White Oaks. Before them were tall glasses of freshly squeezed orange juice and plates of eggs Benedict.

The sky was a harsh, cloudless blue. It promised to be another scorcher of a day.

They could hear the splashing sound of water flowing over the stone steps of the water cascade. From the swimming pool came the scent of chlorine. The patio where they sat used to be the site of the old summer kitchen. When it was torn down in the nineteen-fifties a little tin box was discovered behind a loose brick in the fireplace. It contained human teeth with chicken bones wrapped around them, arranged in the shape of a cross. Blanton kept the box and its grisly contents in his office, showing it to visitors with the single whispered word: "voodoo!"

The kitchen windows were open to let in fresh air. Aimee and Marsh could hear the clatter of pots and pans. A radio was playing a song in which male voices chanted a chorus that went, "nothin' but hos, hos, hos here in this club!"

Marsh cut into his eggs Benedict and neatly forked some into his mouth. He patted his lips with a linen napkin monogrammed with the initials BTT for Blanton Toombs Trapnell. Looking at it, he remarked, "Daddy's initials look like they spell butt. What were his parents thinking?"

Aimee had heard the story from their late mother. "Blanton was the first name of one of our ancestors who was a blockade runner during the Civil War. He sailed a ship to Bermuda, slipping past the Yankee blockade and bringing back arms supplied by the British. It was all very dashing and romantic, the way Mama told it. The Toombses were bankers and landowners on great-granny Mobley's side. She was a Toombs before she got married. She had a lot of money. Mama said Daddy's parents were hoping she'd fork over a generous christening gift if they gave him the middle name of Toombs."

"And did she?"

"She came to the christening in a chauffeur-driven Packard, wearing a full-length sable coat. Daddy's parents were all excited, thinking she'd give them a big check, but then she handed them an envelope with five crumpled one-dollar bills in it. Daddy's parents were fit to be tied. They were going to give him a different middle name, they were so mad, but they couldn't think of one. There was still the chance she'd leave Daddy something in her will, so they went ahead and had him christened Blanton Toombs Trapnell. Then when she died, she left all her money to the Savannah garden club. Daddy's parents were furious."

Marsh laughed. "That's a good story. You ought to write it down. Benjamin might be interested in reading about it someday. Speaking of Benjamin, it'll take too long to fly out of Valdosta. Delta only has three flights a day leaving from there, and they don't go to Mobile. They go up to Atlanta. Then you have to change planes to fly down to Mobile. That's a waste of time. We'll get Skeeter Thibodeaux to take us."

Aimee poured coffee into her cup from the insulated carafe on the table. "Does Skeeter still have a pilot's license? Isn't he too old to fly?"

Marsh helped himself to some coffee. "He's not that old, maybe seventy-five or so. He used to take Daddy all over in his Cessna. I called him last night after you went to bed. He said he'd be glad to take us to Mobile, said he was looking for a reason to go there and get some fried crab claws."

He looked at his watch, an 18-karat white gold Patek Philippe. "Finish your breakfast and change into something appropriate to wear to a meeting with the leader of a gang of criminals." He smiled at her over the rim of his coffee cup. "I suggest your white piquet sundress with the blue stripes and your red patent leather slingbacks. That's a fetching summer ensemble."

Skeeter Thibodeaux was a farmer who had a dirt airstrip on his property outside the nearby town of Pontahatcha, where the Walmart was that Marsh and Trainor visited after they were lost in the swamp. Pontahatcha had, in addition to a Walmart, an Eddie's Po Boy sandwich shop, a branch of a national chain of workout studios called Prison Fitness, a Ford dealership, and a children's indoor playground featuring trampolines called Funz-a-Bouncin'. Pontahatcha was really only a wide place in the road, but compared to Cobbs it was a booming metropolis.

Marsh turned the silver Porsche in at the gateposts that marked the entrance to Thibodeaux Farms. They passed down an avenue lined with immaculate white wooden fencing behind which longhorn cattle grazed. In addition to his herd of cattle, Skeeter Thibodeaux had a thousand acres planted in pecans, five hundred planted in soybeans and another five hundred in corn. The pecans would be harvested in October and November. Thibodeaux sold some in his farm market, but most went either to the Pittypat Praline Company in Albany or to Mama Lucy's Home-Cooked Pies in Macon, both of which distributed their products nationwide.

Blanton Trapnell often remarked that Skeeter Thibodeaux was doing all right for himself, considering that he dropped out of school in the tenth grade.

"Tell me again how Trainor ended up in, what was it called?" Aimee said to her brother.

"Collonges-la-Rouge. It's a village in the Dordogne valley. It's like something out of a fairytale. All the buildings are made from red sandstone. It was voted one of the most beautiful villages in France. The whole place has been declared a historical monument. It's got winding cobblestone streets, a twelfth-century church, and marvelous restaurants. Quite a few English-speaking people have second or third homes there. Most of the townspeople speak English. Trainor wouldn't have to learn a word of French. I chose it because it would have been the perfect place for him to lay low and wait to be declared dead, but he managed to screw it up. I should have known he would."

"If he went to France couldn't they trace his passport? If Palmer hires a private detective to look for him, I imagine that's the first thing they'd do. Palmer's no fool. She may suspect there was something fishy about your story of getting separated from Trainor in the swamp and you having amnesia for a month," Aimee said. She wore the sundress and red high-heeled slingbacks that her brother had suggested earlier, although it didn't seem like the best ensemble for meeting a criminal mastermind. Wouldn't black leather be better? But she knew enough to trust her brother's instincts when it came to clothing.

Marsh wore a brown plaid lightweight wool suit by Ermenegildo Zegna. His brown and white pinpoint polka-dot necktie was also by Zegna, as was his light blue cotton poplin shirt. As always, his appearance was impeccable.

"They could go ahead and trace his passport, for all the good it would do them. It hasn't been used since he and Palmer went to Greece last year. It would be a different story if they traced the movements of a speech therapist from Alexandria, Virginia named Travis Montenay. They'd find he flew to Heathrow, then on to Orly, but they wouldn't do that because they're not looking for Travis Montenay," Marsh said.

"Is that Trainor's new identity?"

"It is. Mr. Montenay won't be needing his passport ever again," Marsh said. "He's deceased, although no one's aware of it yet. The individual who caused his demise sold his passport to some people I know. They made a few changes, basically just swapping the photos because Trainor matches the late Mr. Montenay's description as to height, weight, and hair color. The difference in eye color was remedied with brown contact lenses to cover up Trainor's baby blues. Presto change-o, Trainor became Travis."

Marsh braked the Porsche to allow a golf cart driven by a gray-haired woman to cross his path. It was Linh Thibodeaux, Skeeter's wife. She waved at them, and they waved back. Driving on, he continued, "American passports aren't easy to come by. I could have gotten a Canadian one cheaper. I thought of doing it because Americans aren't exactly welcome in some places right now, but no way would anyone believe Trainor was Canadian, not as soon as he opened his mouth and the 'y'alls' and 'them-uns' came rolling out. I went to a lot of trouble to get that passport, even down to finding one with a first name that sounded like his, to make it easier for him to know when someone was addressing him. I shouldn't have bothered."

"What happened in that French village? It doesn't sound like the kind of place where Trainor could run into trouble," Aimee said.

"Trainor could run into trouble anywhere. It comes natural to him, the way some people can add enormous sums in their heads without a calculator," Marsh said bitterly. They'd reached the end of the drive. The Thibodeaux house lay before them. It was a long, low rancher with bottle-green shutters and a façade of tan-colored bricks. A pair of cast-iron jockeys held lanterns beside the steps leading to the front door. The jockeys were black with startling white eyeballs and bright red lips. While it would have been offensive up North, in south Georgia, nobody thought anything of it. Pulling into a parking space, Marsh shut off the ignition. "Skeeter's probably out back, getting the plane ready."

They walked around to the back of the house while Marsh continued his story about how Trainor got into trouble. "There are a lot of rich English-speaking people in Collonges-la-Rouge, or people who pretend to be rich. Trainor fell in with some Irish who welcomed him with open arms and proceeded to rob him at poker. Trainor has no business playing poker. I've seen Jubilee beat him at Go Fish and he wasn't trying to let her win. If a six-year-old child can whip him at a simple game like Go Fish you know what professional card players could do to him."

"Like any card sharks, these let Trainor win the entire pot several nights in a row, insisting that he was a natural card player and marveling that they'd never seen such mastery at poker, buttering him up in their soft Irish brogues. Then when the hook was set, they took him for more than one hundred thousand euros. He telephoned me in a panic, asking for more. I told him I couldn't afford to advance him any more at the moment. He'd have to get a job washing dishes or something. You can imagine how that went over. If I had to guess I'd say he called Peach next and Peach suggested contacting Benjamin to see if he knew of any valuables worth stealing at *Schloss Wilgonhöfferen.* Benjamin told them about the sigul, and the rest is history. Ah, here's Skeeter now."

A tall, lanky old geezer, Skeeter Thibodeaux wore the uniform of the affluent gentleman farmer: madras plaid cotton trousers, pastel polyester golf shirt, and Ray-Bans. On his head was a white sun visor with THIBODEAUX FARMS stitched on it in navy blue. White hair as wispy as cotton candy stuck out from the top of the visor as he came toward them, one hand outstretched.

"Hey, Marsh! Hey Aimee! I was wonderin' when y'all was gonna get here," he said, shaking hands. "The plane's gassed up and ready to go. Linh's been at me to get back before it gets dark. She don't like me flyin' at night. How's your daddy?"

"He's better," Aimee said.

"That's wonderful. You tell him Linh and me are gonna visit him real soon. Right now we got the grandkids stayin' with us, Al Junior's and Stacy-Jo's three, from up in Gilmer County."

Skeeter's given name was Albert. Al Junior was his son.

Just then Lihn Thibodeaux came whizzing up in her golf cart. She was a tiny firecracker of a woman, a war bride from Skeeter's Air Force days in Vietnam. Like her husband, she wore golf attire: plaid madras skirt, white polyester golf shirt, and a THIBODEAUX FARMS sun visor. She brought the cart to a stop and got out holding a brown paper bag.

"I brung you some pecans," she said, handing the bag to Aimee. "How's your daddy, honey?

"Better. He's starting to talk again," Aimee said.

"Praise the Lord! Ain't that fine news! Me and Skeeter been prayin' for him. We got him on the prayer list at Rock of Ages Baptist." She turned to

Marsh. "Hey, Marsh! How you been?"

"Keeping one step away from the law," he said, making her roar with laughter.

Skeeter was shifting from foot to foot, anxious to be off. "Enough jawin', time to get wheels off the ground if we're gonna get to Mobile and back before dark. Can I bring back anything besides crab legs?" he asked his wife.

She compressed her lips, considering. "Shrimp maybe? In case the kids don't want crabs. I wouldn't mind some mudbugs if the season ain't over yet." She was referring to crayfish, the freshwater crustaceans that resemble miniature lobsters.

"Roger-wilco," he said. To Aimee and Marsh he said, "Hop in the golf cart, and we'll ride out to the airstrip. Y'all picked a good day for flyin'. Clear skies and a tailwind from the east. We'll be in Mobile before you can say Jack Robinson. The view over the bay is gonna be pretty. I never get tired of lookin' at it."

"Just don't get so busy lookin' that you go in the bay," Linh said.

Skeeter put his arm around his wife's shoulders and gave her a squeeze. "Darlin', as I told you many times, there are old pilots and bold pilots, but no old, bold pilots. I'm a cautious old pilot. I promise you the bay and my aircraft will remain a safe distance apart."

CHAPTER 16 – THE CRIMINAL MASTERMIND

Skeeter was true to his word. His single-engine plane stayed safely out of Mobile Bay. (He'd traded in his Cessa for something "more up to date," as he put it.) The Cirrus Vision SF50 was white with sporty red pinstripes. A compact thirty feet from its conical nose to its V-shaped tail, it had an instrument panel consisting of flat-panel displays. Skeeter boasted that it could practically fly itself. They landed at Mobile Regional Airport exactly fifty-eight minutes after taking off from the red dirt airstrip at Thibodeaux Farms.

"One time one of the kids left a gate open, and a prize bull we had back then got out. It was on the airstrip when your daddy and me was rollin' along in the first Cessna I had after I traded in the Piper Cherokee," Skeeter reminisced as they flew westward. "We was on our way to the bird dog trials in Texarkana." Below them, the blue water of the bay came into view. It sparkled in the sunlight, dotted with sunfish with colorful sails, catamarans and small yachts.

Continuing his tale, Skeeter said, "I was wonderin' what the heck it was walkin' around down there. I thought at first it was a dog, but it was too big. Then I thought it was a deer, but it was the wrong color. I figured whatever it was would run off when it saw the plane comin'. As we got closer, I saw it was Midnight Oil, the longhorn bull I paid seventy thousand dollars for at a cattle auction in Vidor, Texas. He was black as pitch, and his horns spanned almost eight feet. Well, that ol' bull stood his ground as we bore down on him. I was startin' to think we'd hit him for sure. We was movin' at a good clip. If I braked if would be iffy whether we'd stop in time.

Hittin' twenty-two hundred pounds of Texas longhorn at eighty miles per hour would be like hittin' a brick wall. Seconds before we woulda collided he ambled off into the tall grass, jes' as casual as could be." Skeeter chuckled and ran a tanned hand over his white hair. "That's how I got some of this snow on the roof, from almost hittin' that bull."

"What did Daddy do?" Aimee asked. "Was he scared?"

Skeeter laughed. "Scared? I'll say! He was white as a ghost, but all he said was, 'Damn, Skeet! That was a close one!'"

Aimee and Marsh turned down Skeeter's offer of a ride from the airport. He was meeting a friend, a retired shrimp boat captain, who he said would be glad to take them wherever they wanted to go and wait while they conducted their business. They refused, saying they didn't know how long they'd be.

"It might be ten minutes, or it might take a couple of hours. You never know with these things," Marsh said. "The person we want to see may be in a meeting, and we'd have to wait for them to come out. We'll meet you back here at three o'clock."

They stood outside the airport terminal, Aimee and Marsh waiting for the shuttle that would take them to the car rental lot. A hot wind rustled the fronds of the palm trees that grew in the grassy embankment that separated the pick-up and drop-off area in front of the terminal from the parking lot. It was an even one hundred degrees, and brutally humid.

"I'll meet you in the Chart Room, up on the second floor," Skeeter said, naming a combination bar and coffee shop inside the terminal. "It's before you come to the security checkpoint."

"Sounds good, no need to go through security," Marsh said agreeably. "We'll see you there at three."

Marsh had a reason for wanting to avoid the airport's security checkpoint. He was counting on there being no metal detectors at their next stop, where they hoped to learn Peach's whereabouts, and that of Trainor and Benjamin.

A black Ford F-150, a grinning septuagenarian behind the wheel, honked its horn as it pulled up to the curb. "Here's my ride. See y'all later," Skeeter said, getting in. Aimee and Marsh caught a shuttle and went to pick up their rental car.

"You know the advertising campaign that went 'Porsche, there is no substitute?'" Marsh asked Aimee twenty minutes later as they drove in the rental car along Dauphin Island Parkway.

Aimee said she was familiar with it.

"It was absolutely right. My Porsche is worlds better than this bucket of bolts. The workmanship on this thing is abysmal. Everything inside is made of plastic. The front end shimmies, and it's practically a new car; it's only got a little more than eighteen thousand miles on the odometer."

"You get what you pay for," his sister told him. "There it is, up ahead."

A billboard loomed next to the highway. It read CHECK OUT OUR LOW, LOW PRICES AT FRIENDLY NEIGHBORS SOUTHLAND! WE MOVE IT! WE STORE IT! WE'RE FRIENDLY! WE'RE YOUR NEIGHBORS!

A red arrow pointed toward the entrance. Marsh drove in. The parking lot held a scattering of compact cars and several tractor-trailer trucks bearing the Friendly Neighbors logo of a Cape Cod-style house with a heart around it. Behind a brick building with copper-tinted windows, long rows of blue and white prefab structures fronted with garage doors marched into the distance, the storage part of the moving and storage operation.

Soft chimes went off as they entered the lobby of the brick building, where a young woman sat behind the reception desk. Her shoulder-length hair was crimped and colored the same shade of copper as the coating on the windows. She'd come to Mobile from her native New Orleans and was regretting it. Being stuck behind a desk all day, taking phone calls from irate customers whose belongings had been damaged by movers from Friendly Neighbors was starting to wear on her. "Can I help you folks?" she asked. Her Delta accent made "help" sound like "hep."

"We're here to see the boss," Marsh said.

"Do you have an appointment?" She consulted her computer. "Are you from Begly Boxes? They usually send Tubby Garner to get our box order." It was evident from her puzzled expression that she doubted that Marsh and Aimee were filling in for Tubby Garner, box salesman. They were too well-dressed for one thing, and Tubby always brought coffee and doughnuts for her and the rest of the office staff when he called. These visitors were empty-handed.

"We're not from Begly Boxes. We're friends of Peach Walker. We'd like to have a word with your boss," Marsh told her.

"Mister Walker's not in," she said.

At that moment a door opened behind her, and a pleasant-faced woman in her late sixties came out. Her hair, once carroty red, had faded to a pinkish gray. She wore it short and severely curled, held down by repeated spraying of an aerosol product that gave it a consistency resembling that of cardboard. It was a hairdressing technique favored by Southern ladies of a certain age. Her features bore a distinct resemblance to those of Peach Walker.

"Well, bless my soul, will you look who's here! Marsh Trapnell!" she said delightedly. "And who's this pretty lady with you?"

"This is my sister, Aimee von Helgern. Aimee, this is Peach's mother, Miz Darlene Walker," Marsh said.

"They don't have an appointment," the receptionist said.

"No appointment necessary, not for Marsh Trapnell and his pretty sister." Miz Darlene beamed. "My goodness, Marsh, how long has it been? Too long, that's how long! The last time I saw you must have been four years ago, at the pig roast we had to celebrate Peach finishing his community service over that silly misunderstanding. Come on back and visit for a spell."

She ushered them into an inner office, where she seated herself in a high-backed chair behind a desk. The desk was bare except for a neat stack of invoices and a framed photograph of a gray-haired man with a cigar in his mouth.

"Have a seat," she said, indicating a couch with sagging cushions upholstered in a nubby orange and brown plaid fabric. The walls were pine paneled and decorated with framed watercolor paintings. It could have been a modest den in someone's home. There was an old cathode ray tube television turned to the Weather Channel and a battered credenza where a coffee pot sat on a hotplate next to some ceramic mugs. WORLD'S BEST GRANDMA was printed on one of the mugs. Aimee wondered when they'd meet the criminal mastermind.

"Coffee?" Darlene asked. "Or how 'bout a cold Co'-Cola? I don't know 'bout you, but I'm just about to melt in this heat." She ran a finger under the Peter Pan collar of her white polyester blouse, puffing out her cheeks comically. The temperature in the room was frigid, the ducts in the ceiling blowing arctic air down on them. Nevertheless, it was generally accepted practice in the South to insist it was perpetually blazing hot, unless the outdoor temperature dipped below sixty degrees, then came the complaints of unbearable cold.

Marsh and Aimee declined her offer of refreshment.

"It was nice of you to drop by. Did you happen to be in the neighborhood?" The motherly lady folded her hands on the desk blotter.

Marsh crossed his legs and gave her his most charming smile. "We flew in from Georgia especially to see you."

"Goodness! I'm flattered," she said. She opened a drawer in the desk and produced a box of sandwich cookies. "Would you care for a chocolate mint patty? My granddaughter Danielle is selling them to raise money for her high school marching band to go to the state finals. She plays the clarinet."

Marsh unbuttoned his suit coat. From the inside breast pocket, he withdrew his sterling silver money clip with the white jade cabochon. Aimee was startled to see he wore a large gun in a shoulder holster. Darlene noticed too. Sounding uneasy she asked, "Marsh, what you got there?"

Moving with his usual lithe grace, he got up and placed two crisp hundred-dollar bills on the desk in front of her. "It's a donation for your granddaughter's marching band trip," he said pleasantly.

"I don't mean the money. I mean that gun you're wearing. Why do you have a gun?"

Marsh's face assumed an expression of self-righteous innocence. "I carry it for protection. You never can tell when you might run into somebody who'll give you a hard time. It's a good gun, by the way, a custom-made Les Baer with a textured grip designed to my exact specifications. Want to see it?" He withdrew it from the holster and held it just out of her reach. She scowled at it.

"Now that I've told you about my gun, how about you tell us where Peach is?" Marsh said.

Miz Darlene no longer seemed motherly. Two vertical creases appeared between her eyebrows. "I haven't the faintest idea," she said coldly.

"Now Miz Darlene, think again," Marsh told her, still smiling. "Peach and Trainor are running around with my nephew Benjamin. They're in over their heads in something they shouldn't have gotten involved in. Ben's a troubled boy, and his mama's worried about him. We need to know where they are."

Darlene folded her arms across her chest. "Peach is a grown man. He doesn't report his comings and goings to me. I'm sorry to hear about your nephew, but I can't help you."

"Nice paintings," Marsh said. He strolled over and examined the watercolors on the walls as if he were thinking of buying them. The paintings, in fact, were terrible. One was of a Siamese cat. It looked demented, its turquoise-blue eyes staring crazily in two different directions. The cat's head was too large for its body, as if whoever painted it had painted the head first and then run out of room to paint the right-size body. Another was of a cabin beside a lake in which a freakishly oversized canoe took up almost the entire lake.

"My late husband did them," Darlene said. She sounded uneasy as if she didn't like the sudden change in direction the conversation had taken.

Marsh nodded appreciatively. "A highly talented man. I take it the cat was a beloved pet? And that charming lakeside cabin was where your husband spent many happy hours?"

"Koko lived to be seventeen. She was a sweet kitty. That's my husband's fish camp. He called it his Shangri-La," Darlene told him, frowning. "Why do you care about my paintings?"

"Because it's terribly sad," said Marsh. "These paintings are beautiful memorials to Mr. Walker and dear, sweet Koko. It would be a shame if anything were to happen to them." He stepped back and pointed his gun at the painting of the cat.

"Stop!" Darlene said. "Are you insane?"

"As a matter of fact, I am," Marsh said and released the safety.

CHAPTER 17 – THROW ME SOMETHING, MISTER

"Would you really have shot her paintings?" Aimee asked Marsh as they drove along Mobile's Old Shell Road, having completed their visit to Friendly Neighbors. The tree-shaded street was lined with modest homes and small businesses.

Marsh considered. "I don't know," he said. "Probably. Once you've drawn your weapon and announced an intention to shoot you have to go through with it or risk looking foolish. Miz Darlene has heard about me from Trainor, who no doubt tried to boost his status with the Walkers by making me out to be a ruthless killer. Miz Darlene's no lightweight, by the way. She's running a thriving criminal empire out of that pokey little office: drugs, prostitution, money laundering, fencing stolen goods, the usual tawdry business. I have to admit I was a little apprehensive. She no doubt had a gun stashed in her desk, along with that box of cookies. I'm certain that with a press of a button she could have summoned armed henchmen, but she wouldn't have wanted a shootout, not when all she had to do was tell me where Peach is and we'd be on our way."

"She seemed like such a nice old lady," Aimee said.

"Steel magnolia. It's a Southern archetype. That nice old lady runs just about every racket from here to Galveston. Peach is only her flunky, although he talks big like he's the one in charge. Ah, here we are." Marsh swung the car into a cracked cement-paved parking lot in front of a ramshackle wood-frame building. A sign on the front proclaimed it to be Queen Eustafia's Oyster Shack. Underneath it said WHERE YAT? YAT THE OYSTER SHACK!

"We have time for lunch before we have to return the rental car and meet Skeeter back at the airport," Marsh said, getting out of the car and stretching. The shoulder holster barely made a bulge under his suit coat. If Aimee hadn't been looking for it, she wouldn't have known it was there.

"Are all your suits custom-tailored so you can carry a concealed weapon?" she asked. "What am I saying? Of course, they are."

"*Mais oui, mon sœur,*" Marsh said, taking her by the arm and escorting her to the entrance to the restaurant.

"Why are you talking French and being all gallant?" Aimee asked. They entered a windowless vestibule. As her eyes adjusted to the gloom, she saw the walls were hung with feathered and sequined masks, as well as framed photographs of parade floats. Zydeco music blared from a speaker, rubboard and accordion, bass guitar and fiddle blending to create a toe-tapping, festive atmosphere. Through a doorway, they could see into a dining room where long tables were covered in sheets of newspaper. People were seated family-style, smashing soft-shelled crabs with wooden mallets and hungrily devouring the meat inside. The place was packed and loud with voices raised in happy conversation.

A stately woman with *café au lait* skin, an emerald-green satin tignon wrapped around her head in origami-like folds, greeted them. "Party of two? We got two spots openin' up over dere." She pointed to where an elderly couple was preparing to leave. Her speech identified her as a native of New Orleans, a two-hour drive to the west of Mobile. Sounding similar to a Bronx accent, it was a regional dialect known as 'Yat.' In it, sinks were 'zinks,' and shrimp were 'swimp.' Oil was 'earl.'

"Y'all come back an' see us again real soon, Mister Paul, Miz Rita," the lady said to the departing couple.

"We will. Food was good as always, Queenie," the lady said. "That peanut butter pie is sinful."

"Don't I know it," the proprietress said, patting her abdomen.

"Sit yo'selves down, folks. We runnin' low on fried ersters, but if you wanna wait we got a new batch comin' shortly. We got plenty a crabs, swimp, turnip greens 'n pot likker, okra n' tomato salad, biscuits an' gravy, swee' potato fries, an' be sure to save room for a slice of peanut butter pie, specialty of the house," she told them.

Marsh and Aimee sat. A server appeared and spread sheets of fresh newspaper in front of them. Marsh ordered softshell crabs and a glass of sweet tea. Aimee asked for okra and tomato salad and lemonade. The food was brought out promptly, along with a mallet for Marsh to smash the crab shells with.

The man seated next to him leaned over to give him some friendly advice. "You oughta take off your jacket, so you don't get crab juice on it," he said.

"That's all right, thanks. I'm feeling a bit chilly," Marsh told him.

The man might have insisted that Marsh remove his jacket, thus exposing the gun in his shoulder holster, (not that it would necessarily be a problem, since the state of Alabama permits the open carry of firearms, although it might cause a certain amount of surprise) but his attention was diverted by the appearance of a man who emerged from the kitchen. He wore chef's whites and a hairnet and held strings of brightly colored Mardi Gras beads.

"Over here!" yelled the man seated next to Marsh. He stood up and waved his arms. "Throw me something, mister!"

The man tossed him a string of green beads. There was laughter from the assembled diners and cries to be thrown beads. Somebody turned up the volume of the music. The room took on the feel of a rollicking party.

A woman seated across the table leaned over the table and raised her voice to address Aimee. "You don't have to show them your breasts; they throw them to you anyway," she said.

"Dis is a respectable family place," said Queen Eustafia, coming up behind Aimee and refilling her glass of lemonade. "Nobody has to show they breasts ta get beads, not unless they want to, that is." She laughed at Aimee's startled expression. "I'm joshin' wit' choo, hon. We ain't rowdy here like they is in N'awlins. We don't want the po-lice raidin' us. Did you know the furst Mardi Gras was in Mobile? True fact. Before it started in N'awlins they had the parades, the masked balls, the krewes, kings and queens, the whole enchilada, right here in Mobile, back when it was the capital of colonial French Loo-zanna."

Aimee said she didn't know that. She'd never been to Mardi Gras. She had likewise never been to the Statue of Liberty or to any of the other tourist attractions in Manhattan, despite owning a home there. Aimee tended to shun things that were enjoyed by the hoi polloi, not because she was a snob (although she was) but because her tastes ran in other directions. If there had been a snake festival or a symposium on how to inherit the entirety of a parent's wealth, cutting one's siblings out completely, she would have been the first one there.

Marsh said he avoided Mardi Gras. "It's full of pickpockets. I prefer the French Quarter at around ten o'clock on a weekday morning, when the pickpockets and their victims are still in bed."

They attacked their lunch hungrily. Knowing where Peach was, and by extension, Benjamin, had given Aimee an appetite. The promise of gunplay, even though no shooting had occurred, always made Marsh hungry.

"How can you be sure Miz Darlene won't warn Peach?" Aimee asked when they were finishing their coffee and peanut butter pie. The coffee was mixed with ground chicory root, New Orleans-style. The pie had dollops of real whipped cream on top.

"Because that would irritate me, and she knows better than to irritate me," Marsh said complacently. "If I discovered that she warned Peach we were coming she knows I'd do a lot worse than shoot her late husband's watercolor paintings, or at least she fears I would. In matters like these, it's best to let their imagination take over. The horrible acts of retribution they envision me bringing down on their heads are far more effective in keeping them in line than any threat I could make."

They paid the bill and departed after thanking Queen Eustafia for her hospitality. "Y'all come back and see us again real soon, y'hear?" she said.

"Tu es magnifique et ta cuisine est merveilleuse," Marsh told her, gazing steadily into her eyes while taking her hand and raising it, so it was an inch from his lips.

She gave a delighted shriek. "Go on wit' choo," she said. To Aimee, she said, "This one's a smooth operator."

"You should see him do the tango," Aimee replied, earning another delighted shriek from Queen Eustafia.

CHAPTER 18 – THE BUCKLE ON THE BOOT OF ITALY

Aimee and Marsh had returned from Mobile and were relaxing by the pool at White Oaks when Franz-Albert phoned. "How is the search progressing? Have you found the item?" he asked her.

"We got a lead on it," Aimee said.

"We? Who is 'we'? Who have you spoken to about this?" His tinny voice coming through the speaker sounded angry or panicked, or both.

In one fluid motion, Marsh rose from his lounge chair in his black swim trunks and took the phone from Aimee's hand.

"Hey there, Franz-Albert! How're you doing? This is Marsh Trapnell, Aimee's brother. How're things at the old *schloss*?"

"Things at *Schloss Wilgonhöfferen* are satisfactory, thank you for inquiring. Please put my wife on the phone," Franz-Albert replied stiffly.

Marsh held the phone away from his face. Raising his voice, he said, "What? I can't hear you."

"I said, put Aimee on the phone."

"Sorry, still can't hear you. This phone's all messed up. It fell in the gumbo we had for dinner. You ever have gumbo?" Marsh grinned at Aimee, who was reaching for the phone. He shook his head and put a finger to his lips.

"I do not know what that is. Let me speak to my wife."

"Can't hear a thing you're saying. You're coming through all garbled. *Auf wiedersehen.*" Marsh hung up. It immediately began to ring again. He turned it off and sat down.

"Why did you do that?" Aimee asked.

A pretty brown and gray butterfly, a variety known as Horace's Duskywing, circled the bug zapper on a metal pole set into the paving blocks that bordered the pool. It met its fate with a sizzling crackle.

"You were about to tell him we found out where Peach and Trainor and Benjamin are, along with his precious sigul. We don't want him going there, or sending anybody to get it. We don't want to risk putting them in danger," Marsh explained.

"I wasn't going to say they're in Spiaggia di Tordigliano," Aimee said, although she wasn't sure. It might have slipped out. She hadn't expected Franz-Albert to call. The fact that he had, instead of waiting for her to return the stolen artifact was troubling. Aimee was unsure whether it really did come from outer space, but Franz-Albert had been adamant about it being dangerous and was fixated on getting it back.

"But you might have said they were in Campania, and he could take it from there. Peach and Trainor stick out like sore thumbs. They might as well be carrying signs saying 'Stupid Americans.' In a place like Spiaggia di Tordigliano, a child could locate them in five minutes."

"Have you been there?" she asked. Marsh got around. From the way he talked it seemed as if he'd been everywhere.

"No, but I've heard of it. It's on the Amalfi Coast, along the Sorrentine Peninsula. Think of it as the buckle on the boot of Italy. That area's popular with tourists. There are lemon groves, vineyards, holiday villas and so on, but Spiaggia di Tordigliano's too off the beaten path to appeal to the selfie-taking, limoncello-drinking crowd. There's not enough for them to do there. It's got rugged black granite cliffs covered with conifers and a beautiful beach, very wild and unspoiled. The only way to get there is by boat, or by climbing a narrow rocky trail about two miles long that runs along the cliffs.

He rose from the lounge chair, leaving Aimee's phone on the wrought-iron table beside it. The pool lights came on automatically as darkness drew in, illuminating the turquoise water. "Don't turn your phone back on yet," Marsh instructed. "Let me put a scrambler on it. That way, when Franz-Albert calls back, he won't be able to trace your location. Keep your conversations short. Be vague about where you are. Reassure him that everything's under control and you'll be recovering the sigul shortly."

He climbed the stainless steel ladder to the diving board and gave a couple of experimental bounces before knifing into the water. He surfaced and flicked water from his hair before stroking across the pool.

"How long until we get there?" Aimee asked.

Marsh treaded water, mentally estimating how long it would take. "It's about a twenty-four hour trip from here, give or take. What time is it now?" He consulted his watch. "Six P.M. It's midnight there now. The quickest way would be to fly out of Valdosta Regional Airport to Atlanta. That takes about an hour and twenty minutes. From there you've got several options. Generally, I'd recommend Turkish Airlines. The flight crews are friendly, and they serve strong Turkish coffee that would revive the dead, as well as red lentil soup as good as any you'll find in Ankara. However, the layover in Istanbul waiting to change planes for Naples would take too long. Air France would be another option. They've got an overnight flight to Paris out of Atlanta, but there'd be a six-hour layover in Paris before you could pick up a flight to Rome and from there you'd have to change planes for Naples, so scratch that option. To make a long story short, the fastest way to get to Spiaggia di Tordigliano, once we're at the airport in Atlanta, is to take an Aer Lingus flight to Boston. From Boston, we fly to Dublin. Then from Dublin to Naples. We get down to the coast, get Benjamin and the sigul, and return it to Franz-Albert. Then we put Benjamin back in rehab. Easy-peasy. Piece of cake."

Aimee took that in silently, daunted by the prospect of the long journey ahead of them. It would no doubt be filled with annoyances and delays. She was anxious to get to Benjamin as quickly as possible, fearful that even if they managed to find Peach and Trainor, he wouldn't be with them.

Benjamin liked to think he was street smart, but he wasn't, not beneath his veneer of bored sophistication and the carefully torn clothing he wore to make him look like he belonged with the real street kids, the feral ones with rotten teeth and dirty fingernails. He would be easy pickings for anyone who wanted to take advantage of a teenager who fancied himself tougher than he really was.

Getting him into the Institute for Health and Human Potential had been a struggle, requiring guile and threats on her part and tearful promises to reform on his. She didn't look forward to going through it all over again, but she'd cross that bridge when she came to it.

Despite her anxiety for her son, Aimee was impressed by how it seemed Marsh had every airline route in the world committed to memory.

"What if I said I wanted to go to Antarctica, would you know the fastest way to get there?"

"Yes," he said. He started to swim again. He did the front crawl to the end of the pool, flutter kicking and exhaling face-down in the water between strokes. He turned neatly and backstroked to the other end.

"Cameroon? Osaka? Tierra del Fuego?"

"All of those," he replied. He hoisted himself out of the pool in one fluid motion and retrieved a plush terrycloth towel from the back of his lounge chair. He rubbed his hair with it before wrapping it around his waist.

Aimee got up and adjusted the bottom of her bikini then walked to the edge of the pool. She felt bloated and regretted having that piece of peanut butter pie at Queen Eustafia's. Turning to her brother, she demanded, "Make reservations for us to leave tonight. Get the best seats available. I don't care how much it costs. If I have to spend almost an entire day on planes, I don't want to be sitting in economy jammed up next to some horrible person." She dove in then, so she didn't hear what Marsh had to say in reply, which was just as well.

CHAPTER 19 – MARSH'S SURPRISE

The next twenty-four hours passed in a blur of airport terminals, with their duty-free shops, crying babies, slow-moving senior citizens, and piped-in announcements in a multitude of languages. Aimee rolled her Louis Vuitton tan cowhide suitcase through crowded concourses and across jet bridges. She was on edge, willing the seemingly endless journey to be over.

They were able to get premium seating on each of their flights, mollifying her somewhat. Marsh reclined his seat and slept from Boston to Dublin and most of the way from Dublin to Naples, dropping off almost instantly. Aimee glared at him resentfully as she flipped through the fashion magazines she'd purchased at Logan Airport. The model on the cover of *Elle* was wearing one of Aimee's designs, a pink off-the-shoulder spandex top with PACKAGED FOR THE PATRIARCHY written across the front in block letters, along with the stamped lines of a UPC code.

She picked at the food the flight attendant placed on the plastic tray table in front of her. The scone with its individually wrapped pat of Kerrygold butter failed to please her. She found the Irish stew with its canned peas and carrots and chunks of baked potato equally unsatisfactory.

None of the choices of inflight movies interested her. Bored, she decided to rouse her brother.

"Marsh," she said, taking him by the shoulder and shaking him. They'd crossed the English Channel by then and were over Calais.

"Humf?" He sat up and blinked. "What?"

"Wake up. I'm bored. Talk to me."

A red-haired flight attendant in a smart teal blue uniform appeared and placed a covered plate in front of Marsh. "Thank you, Fiona," he told her.

"You're welcome, Mr. Trapnell," she said, dimpling prettily. "Good to see you again. Will you be having your usual?"

"That would be lovely," he said.

She went into the galley and returned with a bottle of Jameson whiskey. She poured him a shot, neat.

"Let me know if there's anything else," she said and moved on to the next passenger.

Marsh removed the metal salver over his meal, revealing a perfectly cooked salmon steak on a bed of wild rice, served on a Wedgewood bone china plate.

"How did you get that? How come I got stew in a plastic dish, and you got that?" Aimee asked, incredulous.

"I always have the salmon when I fly Aer Lingus. Fiona and Eileen and Declan and the rest of them know that. They're a great bunch."

Aimee poked her fork at the shriveled peas and carrots in their puddle of congealed brown gravy. "You know all the flight attendants?" Aimee frequently flew back and forth to Europe while attending to her fashion business. She couldn't recall ever seeing the same flight attendant twice, and she certainly wouldn't have remembered any of their names.

"Most of them. I know a lot of flight attendants on the international airlines, ANA, Qantas, Cathay Pacific, Qatar, Emirates..."

"I hate these commercial flights, with other people on them. When Daddy dies I'm buying a private jet," Aimee said.

"That's a worthy goal," Marsh said, eating his salmon and rice. "I was going to use some of my inheritance to build a hospital in Burundi and give it a generous endowment so they could treat people for free. Then I thought why should I do that when I could buy myself a Gulfstream with solid gold bathroom fixtures?"

"Exactly," said Aimee, failing to pick up on his sarcasm.

Having finished his meal, Marsh leaned back and closed his eyes.

"Are you going to sleep again? How can you sleep on a plane? I can't," Aimee said.

"I like to nap whenever I can. I want to be fresh for whatever awaits us in Spiaggia di Tordigliano."

A few minutes later the flight attendant who'd brought them their dinner returned to take their plates. "Tea?" she asked Aimee.

Marsh opened his eyes. "My sister would like an Irish coffee, please, Fiona. She's feeling a bit stressed. Family difficulties."

"I'm sorry to hear that. I'll fetch it right away." Fiona O'Shea bustled into the galley. Mr. Trapnell was a nice man, so polite and considerate, not like the passengers who made endless demands on her, running her ragged and treating her like a servant. His sister didn't seem as nice. And what was that dress she had on? Why did it have a picture of a dead monkey on the front of it with DESTROY THE RAINFOREST written in bright red letters that looked like dripping blood? Why would anyone be in favor of destroying the Rainforest? She decided that Mr. Trapnell's sister was odd, but perhaps she wasn't all that bad if she had a nice brother like Mr. Trapnell. She spooned thick cream into the glass of Irish coffee and set it down in front of Aimee. "There you go, love," she said.

Aimee didn't bother to thank her. Instead, she asked Marsh, "How can you sleep when people are talking and walking around? Listen to that. Somebody keeps sneezing back there." She jerked her head, indicating the economy class seating behind them. "It's maddening. I need it to be dark and absolutely quiet when I sleep."

Marsh thought, not for the first time, that his sister would make an excellent vampire. "I trained myself to sleep anywhere," he said. "It's a skill like any other. Once you've acquired it, you can sleep standing up if you have to. It comes in handy in my line of work. One time, one of my associates, Johnny Rolex, and I were in the Atlas Mountains. He's the one who helped out with that librarian Daddy fired, meeting him in Gander with some warm clothes. Johnny's one of the best. Anyway, where was I? Oh yes! Some business rivals had us pinned down behind an outcropping of rock. They had long-range rifles (Browning X-Bolt Hell's Canyons, as we found out later.) They kept shooting at us, but they couldn't get a clear shot. They kept it up all night while Johnny and I took turns, one of us catnapping while the other one shot at them every so often, keeping them well back so they couldn't sneak up and ambush us. The next morning some friendly Berbers whose acquaintance Johnny and I had made came along and helped us out by eliminating our rivals."

"Is that the moral of the story? Make friends everywhere you go, in case you ever need their help killing people?" Aimee asked.

"That's one way of looking at it. I simply find it's good to have friends. And speaking of friends, I have a surprise for you," Marsh said.

"What is it?" Aimee asked. The intercom chimed as the fasten seat belt lights came on over their heads. The pilot announced that they would be encountering turbulence and to stay seated. The plane gave a lurch. Aimee groaned. "I hate this. What's the surprise?"

"You'll see," Marsh said. He closed his eyes and refused to say more.

At the airport in Naples, Aimee and Marsh were the first ones off the plane. "Have a pleasant stay in Naples, or wherever your final destination takes you," Fiona O'Shea told them, having engineered their quick escape from the confines of first class.

"Thank you, Fiona," Marsh said. He placed something in her hand. She looked at it and gasped. "Oh, Mr. Trapnell! Oh, my goodness!"

"Don't tell me you gave her your phone number," Aimee said. They were rolling their suitcases down the carpeted jet bridge, on their way to customs.

He laughed. "Hardly. Fiona has a fifteen-year-old daughter. I gave her two front-row tickets with backstage passes to the Justin Bieber concert in Galway next month. A client gave them to me."

"You're like Santa Claus, aren't you?" Aimee said. Then her waspish attitude softened. "You really are a nice person, Marsh."

"I try," he said.

They passed through the nothing to declare gate at customs easily, having already gone through preclearance at Dublin airport. Aimee moved toward a group of young people who were gathered around an airport map. They were speaking excitedly to each other in Neapolitan. "*Sto pazziann'*" one of them said, laughing. "*Nun sacc' niente.*"

"*Scusi,*" Aimee said, passing between them to study the map. Something called the Alibus Shuttle would take them into the city center. Her phone rang. It was Franz-Albert again. He'd already called twice since they started on their journey.

"Hello," she said.

"Where are you? Do you have the item?" he asked.

"I'm fine, not that you asked," she said crossly.

"Forgive me, *liebchen.* Do you have the item?"

"Not yet. I'll let you know as soon as I do. I'm busy. I've got to go." She hung up.

She and Marsh continued down the escalator toward the exit.

"If he tried to trace that call he'd be out of luck. It would seem like you were in two places at once, Vancouver, British Columbia and Rio de Janeiro, for instance, anywhere but where you actually are. That scrambler I put on your phone blocks GPS signals from satellites. The one in your phone is state of the art. It's tiny and undetectable while passing through airport security unless they took the phone apart and looked inside. Even then if they didn't know what they were looking for they wouldn't realize what it was," Marsh told her. "They're convenient things to have, illegal of course, even the police aren't supposed to use them. It's a federal crime which carries a large fine and the possibility of imprisonment." He didn't seem at all concerned.

Outside, a rank of taxis was lined up at the curb. Idling at the front of the line, the cabs behind it honking their horns angrily, was a white stretch Mercedes-Benz Maybach S650, its windows tinted an impenetrable black. The front passenger window was open just wide enough for the thunderous sound of rap music to come drifting out. The driver of the cab behind it leaped out and began shouting in Neapolitan. Gesturing furiously, he pounded on the limousine's trunk and kicked the rear bumper, once, then again. At that, the driver's door of the Mercedes opened, and a huge man with formidably wide shoulders emerged and glared at him. The cab driver hurriedly got back in his cab.

"Ah, there's our ride," said Marsh.

The man saw them and waved. His thick black hair hung to the middle of his back, and his forehead, cheeks, and chin were tattooed with black swirls and intricate geometric designs. "Hey, Marsh! Get your ass in here before these *paisans* wet their pants," he called.

"Hi, Johnny. Thanks for picking us up. Nice car. Restrained. Understated," Marsh said. He opened the trunk and threw in his carry-on bag. Aimee saw that a mirrored disco ball was revolving from the ceiling of the rear compartment. There was a stripper pole in there, too.

The man took Aimee's luggage in one massive hand. He extended the other to gently clasp hers. "Johnny Rolex. Pleased to meet you," he said, his voice a rumbling, deep bass.

"Surprise!" said Marsh. "Johnny's going to help us get the you-know-what. You couldn't ask for a better man for the job. The thing's as good as ours. Johnny, this is my sister, Aimee von Helgern."

"The fashion designer? Didn't Sienna St. Clair wear one of your designs at Coachella?" he asked, naming a young actress who was famous for going about practically naked.

"Yes," Aimee said, surprised and flattered that he'd know that. She got into the rear compartment, and Marsh got in front next to Johnny. They pulled out into the flow of traffic leaving the airport. Johnny turned the volume of the music down and called over his shoulder to Aimee.

"You comfortable back there?"

There was enough room in the back of the limousine for six or eight people to sprawl out on the supple black leather seating. The floor was covered in ankle-deep zebra-striped carpeting. Burled oak paneling held a multitude of drawers and compartments. The disco ball revolved and neon lights pulsed behind opaque panels on the headliner: red, green, yellow, purple, and blue.

"Very comfortable, thanks," Aimee said. This party wagon wasn't her style, but she appreciated expensive luxury in all of its forms. She stretched out and inhaled the scent of new leather.

"There's a karaoke machine if you want to give it a go," Johnny told her. "There's a bottle of Champagne in the fridge, along with crackers and cheese and wild boar pâté if you're hungry." To Marsh, he said, "I rented this from a place that rents limos for bachelor and bachelorette parties, weddings, pub crawls, things like that. I thought you'd get a kick out of it."

It seemed Marsh and Johnny Rolex had everything under control.

CHAPTER 20 – CASA DI FUGA

It was 1 P.M., but it felt like seven in the morning to Aimee, whose body clock was still on Eastern Standard Time. It was a fine sunny day. The air blowing in through the front windows smelled of diesel fumes and a hint of salt water from the Gulf of Naples.

Johnny said he was staying at the Romeo, a five-star hotel in the ancient city of Naples, opposite the ferry port for Capri and Ischia. He offered to take them there so they could rest before continuing down the coast, but they refused. This close to the end of their journey they wanted to get to Spiaggia di Tordigliano as quickly as possible before Peach and Trainor and Benjamin moved on.

"We can stop in at the hotel on the way back. It's got a two-star Michelin restaurant on the tenth floor with a helluva view of the gulf. I can see Mount Vesuvius from my room," Johnny told them as he expertly piloted the big car through streams of buzzing Vespas and four-wheeled vehicles that darted every which way, seemingly with no regard whatsoever for traffic rules. He swung onto the E45 to SS163, bypassing the crowded city center.

The drive along the southern edge of Italy's Sorrentine Peninsula is among the most scenic in the world. The narrow two-lane road they were on, the SS163, is known as the Amalfi Drive, or the Road of a Thousand Bends. Its serpentine length zigzags as it follows the shoreline, full of tight turns and narrow passes, steep rock on one side and on the other a stomach-clenching sheer drop to the crashing waves of the Mediterranean. Johnny estimated it would take about an hour to reach Turchi, the closest town to their destination.

The limousine swept through the hairpin turns, past Pompeii and Salerno, past medieval pirate watchtowers and picturesque villages with sun-drenched piazzas. Marsh and Johnny discussed how they were going to confront Peach and Trainor. With the element of surprise on their side, they thought it shouldn't be difficult to get the sigul from them. What puzzled them was why they'd chosen Spiaggia di Tordigliano as a place to hole up.

"Who knows why they do anything? They're idiots. Think Beavis and Butt-Head, and you've got them pictured perfectly. Add Benjamin to the mix and you've got the Three Stooges," Marsh said, adding "sorry, Aimee," over his shoulder to his sister for insulting her son. Aimee didn't reply. She was busy opening the burled oak drawers and cupboards in the back compartment and checking out the contents.

"This sigul, you said it's some kind of alien artifact that has the power to destroy the world?" Johnny asked.

"That's the story Aimee's husband told her. Frankly, I'm dubious, but you never know. Let's say I'm reserving judgment. The important thing is the members of a secret society want to get it back. They may be harmless or they may not. My sister and my nephew are mixed up in this so I'm going to do everything I can to make sure they don't get hurt. As for Trainor, I plan on having some sharp words with him. This is all his fault," Marsh said grimly.

Johnny pulled off the road so they could stretch their legs at one of the scenic overlooks where motorists could stop to admire the view. Local farmers were there selling truckloads of lemons, tomatoes, and peppers. A man with a freezer compartment behind his motorcycle was selling gelato. Aimee's phone rang. It was Franz-Albert. She let it go to voicemail.

"He's getting annoying with all these calls asking whether I've got it yet. I'm seriously thinking about divorcing him, I really am," she said. She dug a plastic spoon into the strawberry gelato the man sold her, having greeted her with a "*chiao, bella!*"

The gelato vendor was in his fifties, pot-bellied, with a few strands of black hair combed over his bald head, but he didn't let that stop him from flirting with her. "You have beautiful eyes! So green! Like the sea! And your dress..." He seemed to really look at it for the first time, taking in the dead monkey and the dripping, blood-red letters. His smile faltered, but he kept on valiantly. "Your shoes, they are *molto belle.*"

"*Grazie,*" Aimee said. The ice cream vendor, like most Italians, appreciated a stylish appearance. Her shoes were little more than soles with six-inch heels, held on by a web of thin leather laces. They cost two thousand dollars.

"Frankly, I don't know why you married Franz-Albert in the first place," Marsh told her. They got back into the car and continued on their way.

"He has a castle and a title. I guess I thought he'd be a father figure for Benjamin. I'm beginning to think it's better to be single," she said.

"It works for me," Johnny said.

"Me too," said Marsh. "Although when I'm old, *if* I ever get to be old, I might consider settling down with some sweet young thing who'll push my wheelchair into the sunlight and spoon-feed me gruel while I dictate my memoirs."

At Turchi, tiers of pastel-colored buildings rose vertically along the cliffs. They pulled into a parking spot behind a shop that rented snorkeling gear. A salty sea breeze filled the air and flocks of sunburned tourists sauntered through the streets. A crescent-shaped silvery sand beach was dotted with umbrellas and pop-up tents that gave shelter from the hot Mediterranean sun. Bathers swam in the translucent water and yachts bobbed at anchor at a distance.

It was a scene that could have sprung straight out of a travel brochure.

"We walk from here," Marsh said. "There's a trail that'll take us to Spiaggia di Tordigliano. It's a sheer climb, steep and rocky." He turned to Aimee. "You should change into something appropriate for hiking."

"I brought boots and jeans. I can get dressed back here. There's plenty of room," she said.

Johnny chuckled. "You probably won't be the first person to take your clothes off in the back of this car. While you change Marsh and I can go over there and get espressos." He indicated a restaurant overlooking the water where people were seated outside at umbrella tables.

They left her and Aimee proceeded to change into a black t-shirt and black skinny jeans. She laced up the thick-soled boots, feeling glad she'd had the foresight to pack them. Then she slung her canvas bag over her shoulder and went to join the men

It was a rugged hike to remote, wild Spiaggia di Tordigliano, like climbing stairs, the trail taking them almost straight up along a limestone cliff. They clambered over thick roots of conifers jutting out from the rock, walking single-file, Johnny first, then Marsh, then Aimee. Two miles farther on the trail sloped downward, coming out on a sandy beach. A yacht was moored in the cove. Close to the beach a motorboat was anchored. Seated on a log were three young people, two girls and a boy. The boy was Benjamin.

Aimee felt an overwhelming sense of relief at finding him safe and sound. "Hello, Benjamin," she said.

His mouth dropped open. "Oh, shit, it's my mother," he said.

The girls stared at them. "I thought you lived in New York," one of them said to Benjamin. She spoke with an Australian accent.

"He does," Aimee told her.

"In the South Bronx, where it's really dangerous, yeah? Where you risk your life every time you go out on the street, and where you're in a gang," the other girl said to Benjamin.

Benjamin, it appeared, had been telling tall tales to impress them.

"He lives in a ten-million-dollar apartment on Central Park West, when he's not living in a castle in Germany," Aimee said tartly.

The girls' tanned foreheads furrowed as they took in this new information.

"What about the gang? That part's true, yeah?" the first girl asked.

"Absolutely. Benjamin is the leader of the Spoiled Rich Kids, the SRKs they're called. They're the terror of the Upper West Side. Doormen tremble at their approach," Aimee said.

Johnny snickered.

"Are they in the gang too?" asked the second girl, meaning Johnny and Marsh. The other girl snorted contemptuously. "Catch up, Bree, my God you're a numpty. He's not in any gang. He was havin' us on."

"Oh, so the part about the drive-by shootings and the fights with the other gangs and him getting' shot five times an' being on life-support an' almost dyin', that wasn't true? And these fellas aren't in the gang either?" She seemed disappointed.

"No, it's just my uncle and some other guy," Benjamin muttered.

"Come on, let's go back to the boat. Dad's going to take us to Sorrento. The boys there won't make up stupid stories," said the first girl. She got up from the log and brushed sand from the seat of her bikini. The second girl got up too. They gathered up their sandals and sunglasses and towels and waded into the water. Getting into the motorboat, they started the outboard and roared off toward the yacht without a backwards glance at Benjamin.

"Am I in trouble?" he asked Aimee.

The motorboat reached the yacht. A crewman helped the girls up a ladder while another raised the motorboat with a davit and secured it. The yacht turned slowly and made its way out of the cove. The girls stood at the stern, making insulting gestures in their direction, no doubt intended for Benjamin.

"We'll talk about it later," Aimee told him. "Where's Trainor and Peach?"

"Over there," Benjamin said, indicating a cottage painted a flaking pastel blue. Over the door was a rustic signboard identifying it as Casa di Fuga.

With the yacht gone there were no other boats in the cove. The only sound was the hiss of waves breaking on the shore and the squealing of gulls as they swooped down over the water in search of fish. The four of them were alone on the remote, lonely beach. There were a handful of cottages that had started out as fishermen's shacks and been converted to weekend residences for people wanting a break from the crowds and traffic of Naples and Bari and Reggio Calabria. They were deserted on this weekday afternoon, their doors firmly shut, wooden shutters fastened over the windows.

"Casa di Fuga. Getaway House, how appropriate," Marsh said. "Let's go have a talk with the fugitives."

They went up the beach toward the house, Benjamin padding in his bare feet beside Aimee. He was almost as tall as she was now. He watched her apprehensively, trying to gauge how angry she was at him for having run away from rehab. He wondered if she knew about him stealing the sigul from Franz-Albert's dungeon. He thought it was likely or else she wouldn't be here with his uncle and this big, tough-looking Hawaiian or whatever he was. He slid a glance at Johnny. The guy was definitely a badass. Those tattoos on his face were straight-up gangsta.

Benjamin had a tattoo, Chinese writing on his left wrist inscribed by a man with blond dreadlocks at a scruffy tattoo studio in the Kalkmarkt in

Amsterdam. He forgot what the tattoo guy said it was supposed to mean, something about wisdom, or oneness with nature? (Benjamin had been stoned at the time, having smoked some hashish and taken several panadeine tablets because he'd heard that it hurt to get inked.) He thought that whatever the writing meant, it looked totally chill. He would have been dismayed to learn it was copied from a label on a can of seafood the tattoo artist found in a grocery store in the Nieuwmarkt. The Han characters meant 'pickled squid meat.'

"You're not going to make me go back to the Institute, are you? I mean, I got a lot out of it, don't think I'm not grateful," he told his mother earnestly, running a hand through his curly dark brown hair. "Seriously, I am. They taught me a lot about triggers and addiction and recovery, and I'm completely on board with it. I've been clean for a really long time, like six weeks, so making me go back would be pointless and a waste of money so I was thinking..."

Aimee stopped walking and turned to him.

"Benjamin?"

"What?"

"Shut up."

He shut up.

CHAPTER 21 – BETRAYAL

They found Trainor and Peach in a garden behind the cottage where someone had planted tomatoes and zinnias and basil. They were seated in canvas lounge chairs with wooden frames, hats tipped over their eyes. Trainor's was woven of palm fronds and had a ragged, raw edge, like something a castaway might make from materials he scrounged up on a deserted island. Peach's hat was a Borsalino Panama with a snap brim and a red, white, and green grosgrain hatband.

"Um, Uncle Trainor…" Benjamin began, his bare feet shifting nervously in the dirt.

"Bring me a beer, willya' Ben?" Trainor said sleepily, the hat covering his eyes.

"Bring me one too, make it a Peroni. Make sure you take one from the back of the fridge, so it's good and cold," Peach said. He batted at a fly buzzing around his head. "Shoo, go 'way. He lifted his hat to swipe at it and saw Marsh, Aimee, and Johnny glowering down at him.

"Oh, fuck," he said.

"Hello, Peach. Hello, Trainor. How's it going?" Marsh said cheerfully.

Peach and Trainor exchanged panicked glances.

"What are you guys doing here?" Peach asked. He struggled to rise from the low-slung chair. "Listen, I'm just gonna go inside for a minute and use the facilities. Be right back."

"You're not going anywhere," Johnny said.

"But I gotta pee," Peach protested. "Honest, I gotta go bad."

"Then do it out here. Nobody'll look. I don't want you in the house. My spider senses tell me you've got a gun in there. I'd rather not have you shooting anybody, unless you shoot yourself. It would be fine with me if you did that," Johnny told him.

Peach sank back down. "I guess I don't have to go after all," he said. His face had gone ashen under his sunburn.

Aimee kicked the bottom of Trainor's chair, causing him to yelp and shoot bolt upright. "What were you thinking, taking Benjamin out of rehab so he could rob Franz-Albert? You're a shitty uncle."

"Hey, quit yelling at me. You don't have to yell at me and kick me," Trainor said, looking hurt. "If Marsh had wired me more money like I asked it wouldn't have happened. He's got plenty of money, but he was too stingy to give me some after those Irishmen ripped me off. What was I supposed to do? Starve?"

Aimee gave the chair another kick, glad she was wearing boots so she could deliver a good, solid blow. "You were supposed to get a job and earn money, like other people."

"Ow! stop doing that," he whined. "First off, I faked my death and ran away to France, remember? Second, I have a passport belongin' to a dead speech therapist. Third, I don't know anything about bein' a speech therapist. I don't speak French, and I don't have a work visa to let me work in France and (what number are we at?) fourth or fifth? I don't know how to do anything. I have no skills, okay? I'm not proud of it; that's just the way it is. Blame Daddy for bein' so rich that we never had to work. Blame society or the government or whatever for not makin' me learn how to do something useful, like auto mechanics or farming." He paused, breathing hard, looking like he was about to burst into tears at the injustice of it all. "I don't like it any better than you do, but I there it is: given the choice between goin' hungry and stealin', I stole, like that French guy in the movie."

Marsh snorted with laughter. "If you're comparing yourself to Jean Valjean from *Les Misérables*, who stole bread to feed starving children, you've got a lot of nerve. The plain truth is you're too lazy to work. I work. Aimee works. Karen works. We have a rich daddy, but we make our own way in the world. You're almost forty. You'd better shape up before it's too late and you end up in a bad way."

Aimee nodded self-righteously, although she knew full well that Karen no longer worked (if operating a child sweatshop could be considered working) but instead was lying in pieces in a refrigerated compartment in a morgue back in Georgia.

"That's right. It's not too late for you to learn a skill and get a job. But first, we've got to get the sigul of Jörmungandr back to Franz-Albert. Where is it?" she said.

"Ah," said Trainor.

"Well, you see, it's like this..." Peach began.

Johnny advanced on them, his huge hands bunched into fists, making them flinch. "Quit stalling. You've got it, right?"

"Sure," Peach said quickly. "We got it."

Johnny nodded. "Good." He turned to Marsh and pointed to a spot at the back of the garden, where the tilled soil ended and sand and rocks began. "Go stand over there."

"Huh?" Marsh looked where his friend was pointing. "Why should I go over there?"

A gun appeared in Johnny's hand as if by magic, drawn from a belt clip in the waistband of his trousers where it had been concealed beneath his short-sleeved Guayabera. "This is why," he said.

Marsh's mouth dropped open. He looked back and forth between the gun in Johnny's hand and his stony face as if he was having trouble understanding what was happening. "What's going on?"

"I'm sorry, Marsh. We go back a long way. I wish it didn't have to come to this, but my instructions were clear: no survivors. Go over there and turn around. I promise it'll be quick. It'll be better this way. You'd thank me if you knew what's coming."

"Put the gun down. Let's talk about this," Marsh said. He took a step toward Johnny. If he could get close enough, he intended to rush him and wrestle him for the gun.

Peach and Trainor and Benjamin watched in horror, afraid to move or speak. Aimee edged in front of Benjamin, shielding him with her body as she slowly reached into her shoulder bag. She sent a silent message in Johnny's direction: *Don't look back here. Keep looking at Marsh.*

"Not another step, Marsh. I mean it. Turn around," Johnny said.

"No. Damn it, Johnny if you're going to shoot me, do it when I'm looking you in the eyes. It's easy to shoot somebody in the back, let's see if you have the stones to..."

Marsh didn't get to finish the sentence. There was a loud bang, and the top of Johnny's head exploded, sending up a dark plume of blood and brain matter.

"Holy shit!" Peach yelped. He fell out of his chair and rolled into a ball, his hands covering his head. Trainor, Benjamin, and Marsh gaped at Aimee, frozen in shock. She'd shot Johnny with the Chiappa Rhino revolver chambered for .357 Magnum cartridges that she'd found in one of the compartments in the back of the limousine. It had been left there by some party-goer and had remained undiscovered by the rental company when the car was cleaned.

She fell to her knees in the dirt, her legs suddenly too weak to support her. "Did I get him?" she asked.

"You got him all right," said Trainor, his eyes like saucers. "Who was that guy? How come he was going to shoot Marsh? How come he was going to shoot all of us? No survivors, he said. Man, that would have sucked. Good shot, by the way."

Marsh stood stock still, staring incredulously at Johnny's body lying among the pink and yellow zinnias, arms flung out, blood seeping from his head in a widening pool.

Aimee's phone rang. It was Franz-Albert again. She let it ring.

CHAPTER 22 – A GRAVE IN THE SAND

They buried Johnny Rolex in an isolated spot on the beach, taking turns digging. At first, Peach tried to beg off, claiming he had a bad back, but a searing look from Marsh was all it took for him to take up the shovel they found in the tool shed behind the cottage and dig as if his life depended on it.

Trainor peppered Marsh with questions. "Who was that? How come he was going to shoot us?"

"Johnny Rolex. He saved my life twice. We were like brothers," Marsh said, his voice without emotion as he stared into the deepening hole. They'd wrapped the body in the plastic shower curtain from the bathroom at Casa di Fuga. Marsh first went through the dead man's pockets, removing his keys and cell phone, wallet, and wristwatch.

Trainor asked, "Is that a real Rolex?"

"Yes," Marsh said shortly, pocketing it.

"As long as we're taking it, can I have it? You've already got a nice watch."

Marsh turned an impenetrable gray gaze on him. "I'm going to forget you said that, okay?"

Trainor blinked, realizing he'd gone too far. "Sure, Marsh, whatever."

Marsh took the shovel from Peach. "For your information, I'm not robbing a corpse for my own benefit. Johnny registered all his Rolexes. He was meticulous about it. The watch could be traced back to him through its serial number, leading the *polizia* or the *carabinieri* or whichever law enforcement agency is in charge out here to identify him more easily, in case his body is found." He took off his suit coat, folded it neatly, and handed to Benjamin. Then he started digging.

Once the grave was deep enough, they rolled Johnny's body in and shoveled sand on top. Marsh tamped the sand down with the back of shovel. Aimee had the distinct impression it wasn't the first time he'd dug a grave. "That takes care of that," he said, brushing sand from his hands. He put his jacket back on.

"Are we going to say a prayer or something?" Benjamin asked. He wasn't especially religious, but he thought a prayer would be appropriate. He'd never been to a funeral, not that this was a real funeral, but it seemed like some appropriate words should be spoken. He was still trying to come to grips with the fact that that he'd seen his mother kill someone. Aimee stood with her hand on his shoulder, looking down at the grave that now looked no different from the rest of the lonely beach.

"All right," Marsh said. He drew himself up. His face a frozen mask, he chanted in a loud voice: "Prepare, prepare the iron helm of war,
Bring forth the lots, cast in the spacious orb;
Th' Angel of Fate turns them with mighty hands,
And casts them out upon the darken'd earth!
Prepare, prepare!"

His words were met with uncomfortable silence. "That doesn't sound like a prayer," Peach said.

"It's not; it's from a poem by William Blake." Marsh smiled grimly. "Johnny loved Blake. He could recite all his poems by heart. In this case, it serves as a warning."

"To whom?" Aimee asked. The sky over the water was darkening from clear blue to the color of slate. The wind picked up, ruffling her hair.

"To whomever hired Johnny to kill us," Marsh said. "Johnny was my friend. He was a mercenary but he had a rigid code of honor. For him to agree to kill me meant someone got to him and forced him to abandon his principles. I'm going to find them."

"And I'm sure you're gonna make 'em sorry they were ever born," Trainor said. "Vengeance, that's the ticket! Now that we're done buryin' him, Peach and me should be gettin' back to Rome. That's where we were before we came down here. We'll just pack up our things and be on our way. C'mon, Peach."

He and Peach started toward the house. "Hold on," Marsh said. "Aren't you forgetting something?"

"Oh yeah, sorry about that!" Peach said. He turned to Aimee. "Thanks for saving our lives."

"Yeah, thanks," said Trainor. "For a minute there I was sure we were goners, but you came through like a champ. Good work."

They started toward the house again, moving quickly, as if trying to put the maximum amount of distance between them and Marsh.

"That's not what I meant. I was referring to the item you stole from Aimee's husband, the sigul of Jörmungandr. Let's have it," Marsh said.

Peach and Trainor exchanged glances. "About that," Peach said.

"It's really kind of funny," Trainor said nervously.

"Somehow I doubt it," Marsh said. He took the shovel from Benjamin and swung it experimentally like a bat, stepping closer to the two men.

"They don't have it anymore," Benjamin blurted.

"What? What did you do with it? Where is it?" said Aimee. Without waiting for an answer she kicked furiously at the sand, scattering it. "I flew halfway around the world. It took an entire day. Then I shot a man and helped bury his body. I'm exhausted. I've had enough of you two. I'm fed up, do you hear me? Fed up!"

"Calm down," said Peach.

"You should never tell a hysterical woman to calm down; it just gets them more excited," Trainor advised him.

Aimee rounded on him, kicking sand in his direction. "I'm not hysterical," she seethed. "Call me hysterical one more time, and I'll scream."

Screaming seemed like an attractive option, so worn out and on edge was she. Killing Johnny Rolex had been different than killing her stepsister. When she'd killed Karen, all she'd felt was cold caution and the need to carry it out without getting caught. With Johnny, she'd been afraid she wouldn't be able to get the gun out of her purse without him noticing, or that she'd shoot and miss. She kept playing it over in her head: unzipping her purse, trying to do it quietly so he wouldn't hear the sound of the zipper being pulled, cautiously lifting out the gun, her heart thumping, desperately hoping Johnny wouldn't turn around, then cocking the hammer and looking down the fiber optic front sight, and finally, pulling the trigger. Time seemed to slow to a crawl while all that was taking place, but it had really only taken a few seconds. The only reason she didn't give in and allow herself to scream was she was afraid that once she started, she wouldn't be able to stop.

"Mom, come on in the house. I'll make you a cup of tea and some toast. Or would you rather have orange juice?" Benjamin asked.

Aimee laughed bitterly. "I'd rather have a son who didn't run away from drug rehab and steal a thingamajig that my husband says has the power to destroy the world, that's what I'd rather have, but sure, why not? A cup of tea would be terrific, Benjamin. It's just what I need to top off a super-swell day."

"You're being sarcastic, but tea and toast would make you feel better," Benjamin told her earnestly. "At the Institute they said it's important not to get hungry, angry, lonely or tired. If you had something to eat you wouldn't be hungry, at least. We've got some sweet chestnut preserves. It's good on toast. And you have every right to be mad. I'm sorry I took the sigul. It was totally my fault. Now somebody's dead because of me." He turned a pained expression to her, his chin trembling.

She wrapped her arms around him, noting that he wasn't as painfully thin as he'd been when she dropped him off at rehab. She could feel muscle now beneath his skin instead of bones. "You couldn't have known what would happen," she said gently.

"That's right," Trainor told him. "You stole things before, and nobody got killed. This was a fluke, completely out of left field."

"Your uncle's right, Ben. You should listen to him," Peach added eagerly. "You wouldn't believe how much stuff I stole, entire truckloads sometimes. And did anybody ever get killed? No. Never. Beat up maybe, but not killed. You could go another twenty or thirty years of stealing things, and if you do it right, nobody else is gonna get killed because of it."

"You two are a piece of work," Marsh said. "Don't you know better than to tell a young person to commit crimes? From now on Benjamin's under my protection. If I hear one more word from either of you encouraging him to do anything even the least bit out of line, I don't care if it's something as minor as returning a library book late, I'll make you sorry, understand?"

"Yes," Peach said sullenly.

"How about you, Trainor? Have I made myself clear?"

"Yeah. Got it."

"Good. We understand each other. Let's go inside, and you can tell us who you gave the sigul to."

"Sold," Trainor said timidly, as if afraid of angering his brother further. "We didn't give it away, we sold it."

They reached the cottage and went into the kitchen. Benjamin put the kettle on for tea. Trainor, trying to be helpful, set out cups and plates. He sliced the loaf of bread in the breadbox, putting four slices in the toaster.

Aimee started to sit down in one of the rustic wooden chairs at the kitchen table. Then she remembered something Johnny Rolex had said.

She drew the gun from her purse. "Peach, go get your gun and give it to Marsh. If you've got more than one bring them in here and give them to him. Then we'll talk about how we're going to get the sigul back."

Peach looked as if he was about to argue, but then he thought better of it. He left the room and returned with a silver pistol with a black grip. Handing it to Marsh, he said, "I only had it for protection. Honest. I got it in Rome, in case the people who were gonna pay us for the sigul tried to take it without paying. I wasn't gonna shoot anybody earlier, it's just that Johnny Rolex seemed intimidating, so I thought I'd better go inside and get it, in case he had a gun, which he did."

Marsh was examining the gun, turning it back and forth. Its stainless steel plating shone in the illumination from the overhead light. "A semi-automatic Walther PPK, just like James Bond's."

Peach grinned proudly. "Cool, huh?"

Marsh sighted down the barrel. "I suppose you could say so if it was real, but it's not. You should learn how to tell a real gun from a replica."

Trainor punched Peach in the arm. "You see? I thought that guy was shady, coming up to us like that."

He turned to Marsh. "A guy in a bar on the Via Veneto heard me and Peach talking. An Italian. He comes over and goes to Peach, 'Signore, I couldn't help but overhear that you are planning to travel to the south. What you need is a gun.' I thought he might be a cop, trying to entrap us and get us in trouble, so I asked him if he was. He said no, he was just a concerned citizen who wanted visitors to his country to be safe and not get preyed upon by *banditti,* bandits, he meant. He said there are a lot of bandits where we were going, and we should have a gun for protection. He was gonna sell it to us for five hundred euros, but we talked him down to four-fifty. Damn. You can't trust these foreigners."

Benjamin put the toast on plates and poured the tea. His face wore a thoughtful expression, as if he was beginning to realize how dangerously incompetent Trainor and Peach were.

Aimee drank her tea. The hot liquid revived her. She picked up a piece of toast and spread sweet *crema di marroni* on it. "Let's hear the whole story. Who did you sell the sigul to? We need to get it back."

CHAPTER 23 – A NAME LIKE TEA

It came as no surprise that Peach and Trainor had no idea whom they'd sold the sigul to, other than it was a pair of men who paid them five million dollars. Peach had been too concerned with making sure the money was wired to his bank account in the Cayman Islands to pay attention to what they looked like.

"I remember their names, though. One was called Bob Smith, and the other was called Ed Jones. That oughta help," he said proudly.

Aimee and Marsh stared at him in disbelief.

He paused to reconsider. "Those could have been aliases."

"Gosh, Peach, do you really think so?" Aimee asked.

"What did they look like?" Marsh asked Trainor, not having much hope that he'd do any better than Peach. He was right.

"Average. They looked average," Trainor said, earning groans from Marsh and Aimee.

Benjamin wasn't much help. He'd been on the beach with the two sisters from Melbourne. He'd been making up stories about his life on the mean streets of the South Bronx to impress the girls, and had only seen the men from a distance.

"They were medium height, medium build. They weren't young, but they weren't that old, maybe as old as you and Uncle Trainor," Benjamin told Marsh. "Maybe a little older. They were white guys, I think. They had on sunglasses, and their skin was kind of dark, like they were outdoors a lot, or maybe they were Middle Eastern, or they could have been Latino. Like I said I didn't see them close up. They came down the trail from the town when I was talking to Bree and Shasta," he said.

"Now we're getting somewhere," Marsh said. "They didn't come from a yacht like the girls? You're sure about that?"

Benjamin nodded. "They came over the trail the way you did. They went back the same way."

Marsh turned to Trainor. "What did they sound like? They spoke English, I presume, since you and Peach don't know any other languages. What kind of accent did they have?"

Trainor's face lit up. "They talked American, not like that Englishman you sent to Iceland or those Irish guys who robbed me at poker. They didn't talk regular the way me and Peach do. They talked fancy, like the people who report the news on TV."

Marsh put a slice of bread in the toaster. "That's called a standard American accent, you ninny. Millions of people speak like that. You couldn't possibly be any less help if you tried." The toast popped up and he spread butter on it.

"I wish I could remember the name of the lawyer who came to see me," Peach said, going to the refrigerator and pouring a glass of orange juice. "It was a name like tea."

Peach pursed his lips and drummed his fingers on the scarred pine kitchen table. "Lipton? Bigelow? Red Rose? No, nobody's named Red Rose, unless they're an Indian. Lemme think..."

"Was it Tetley?" Aimee asked. "Beau Tetley?"

Peach nodded eagerly. "Yeah! That's it, Tetley. Beauregard Tetley. He was an old guy. He looked like Colonel Sanders, white goatee, horn-rimmed glasses, white suit and everything."

"That's Daddy's lawyer. I went to see him after Daddy had his stroke," Aimee told Marsh.

"I remember," Marsh said. "You thought Trainor and I were dead, vanished into the swamp. You were all set to get conservatorship of Daddy's money."

Aimee shifted uncomfortably, not liking to remember how pleased she'd been that Karen was dead, thinking Trainor and Marsh were dead, too, leaving her in sole possession of their father's money. It had been a wonderful month, the culmination of a lifelong dream, but then Marsh had returned and ruined everything.

"Daddy got better, so I never had to go to court and apply for guardianship and conservatorship so I could take better care of him. I'm glad he's getting better," she said defensively.

"I'll bet," Marsh said dryly. He turned to Peach. "Getting back to lawyer Tetley, what did he want?"

Peach took a bite of toast, chewed and swallowed. Wiping crumbs from his lips with the back of his hand, he said, "He wanted me to help steal the sigul outta that castle. Duh. I thought that was obvious."

They were digesting that surprising piece of information when a phone rang. For a moment Aimee thought it was Franz-Albert calling again, but the ringing wasn't coming from her phone. It was coming from across the table, where Marsh sat. He reached into the pocket of his suit coat and took out the slim black mobile phone that had belonged to Johnny Rolex. The ringing grew louder.

"No Caller ID," he said, looking at the screen.

He returned the phone to his pocket. Pushing his chair back from the table, he said to Benjamin, "Get dressed and grab your things." To Peach and Trainor he said, "Pack up everything you brought with you. Move it. Hurry. Get your stuff and lock up. We're leaving."

The phone continued to ring. It rang a dozen times, stopped, then started again.

"Aren't you gonna answer it?" Trainor asked.

Benjamin had gone through the doorway leading to a short hallway where there was a bathroom and two small bedrooms. He stuck his head back into the kitchen. "No, he shouldn't answer. It's the person Johnny Rolex was working for. They're checking to see why he hasn't called to say he's got the sigul. For now, they're just going to think he's busy, but they'll keep on calling. Before long they'll figure out something's wrong."

Marsh turned from where he was stacking the plates in the sink. "There's hope for you yet, Benjamin. Now hurry up and get dressed before they come to find out what's taking Johnny so long."

They quickly vacated Casa di Fuga, leaving the key under the doormat. Peach argued that they should return it to the woman they rented the cottage from. She lived in Turchi, where Johnny had parked the stretch limousine, and where Peach and Trainor had left the Fiat they'd rented in Rome.

"We paid for another three days. We should at least try to get a refund," he said.

Marsh refused to consider it. "We don't have time for that. While you're trying to get your money back, somebody could be on their way to find out why Johnny's not answering his phone. Normally I'd enjoy a brisk exchange of gunfire, but not in a place like Turchi, with streets filled with innocent bystanders."

They hurried over the trail, fearing at any moment they'd come face to face with a killer, but they met no one. They went down the hill to the parking lot overlooking the beach, where Trainor and Peach and Benjamin put their bags in the trunk of the Fiat. They'd drive it and the limousine to the airport in Rome and leave both vehicles there. Then they'd decide what to do next. Aimee and Marsh abandoned the idea of returning to Naples, in case someone was watching the airport there.

"Aimee, you ride in the Fiat with Trainor and Peach. Make sure they go straight to Leonardo da Vinci Roma-Fiumicino Airport. Don't let them call Beau Tetley or anyone else," Marsh told her. "I'll be right ahead of you on the Amalfi Drive, in case there're any problems. Benjamin will ride with me." He handed her a plastic grocery store bag. "Throw this in the trash at one of the scenic overlooks."

She looked in the bag. It contained Johnny Rolex's phone and his empty wallet and the fake Walther. Marsh had cut Johnny's ID and credit cards into little pieces and thrown them in the dumpster behind the shop that rented snorkeling gear.

Peach protested, "I wasn't gonna call that lawyer. I don't think we can trust him, although I dunno, maybe we can. Maybe he had nothing to do with that big Hawaiian. It's kinda confusing."

Marsh gave him an incredulous look. "Are you kidding? Of course, you can't trust him. Johnny was Samoan, by the way, but the point is, don't call anyone. Not Beau Tetley, not anyone, all right?"

"Not even my mama?" Peach asked. "Can't I call her and ask her what she thinks we should do?"

Marsh and Aimee spoke in unison: "No!"

Marsh turned to Aimee. "I've got Johnny's gun, and you've got the

Rhino. We'll hold onto those for the time being." He got behind the wheel of the limousine. Benjamin got in next to him. Before closing the door, Marsh said, "See you at the airport. Benjamin and I will meet you at the station for the Leonardo Express. It's in front of Terminal Three. It goes to the Termini, the central train station in Rome. Trains run every half-hour. Good luck."

CHAPTER 24 – SMITH AND JONES AGAIN

Night had fallen by the time they left Turchi, its twinkling lights vanishing in the rearview mirror as the Fiat followed the limousine along the twisting road that hugged the shoreline.

Peach was behind the wheel of the Fiat, with Trainor seated beside him in the front passenger seat. Aimee was in the back. She leaned forward and asked Peach how he happened to meet Beau Tetley.

"He came to the office. Made an appointment with my secretary," Peach said importantly. "He said he'd heard I could get things for people, sometimes, if the price was right. I told him what I always say when somebody I don't know sounds like he's askin' me to do somethin' illegal. I said, 'Mister, Friendly Neighbors Southland Trucking is a moving and storage company. It's a family business that was started by my granddaddy. I'm a little confused. What do you need?' That way it's on him to say it, and I can't get charged with anything in case there's trouble later."

"I don't think that's right," Aimee told him. "But go ahead, what did he do then?"

"He said he understood I was being cautious. He said that was good. He appreciated folks that were cautious. Then he laughed and said he was too old to be a cop but he guessed he wasn't too old to be a police informant, if that's what I was afraid of. He offered to take off his white suit and strip down to his skivvies to prove he wasn't wearing a wire if I was nervous on that account. I told him there was no need. He said in that case, he'd cut to the chase. He said he had a client who'd pay five million dollars to get a ceremonial item out of a castle in Germany that belonged to somebody called Franz-Albert von Helgern. That's what he called it 'a ceremonial item.' I knew who Franz-Albert was from Trainor talkin' about him. I told him I'd look into it and get back to him. We shook hands on it. Before long Trainor called me up from France sayin' he needed money. I called the lawyer and told him we were on. I went and got Trainor. Then we went and got Ben. Then we got the sigul."

"It seemed like a good way to make some money. The hardest part was figurin' out how to divide five million three ways, a third for me, a third for Peach and a third for Benjamin. It don't come out even," Trainor put in, as the car swept around a bend, its headlights piercing the darkness, illuminating the narrow road ahead. A Vespa passed them going in the opposite direction, followed by a tiny pea-green car. Up ahead the limousine vanished around a hairpin turn.

They came to a scenic overlook, a different one from the one where Marsh and Aimee and Johnny had stopped on their way to Spiaggia di Tordigliano. Aimee told Peach to pull in so she could throw away the bag containing the fake gun and Johnny Rolex's phone and wallet. There was no sign of the Mercedes; it had gone on ahead.

The Fiat was a two-door model. Trainor got out and pulled his seat forward to let Aimee out. There was a trash barrel about twenty yards away, next to a low parapet of rugged rocks that overlooked the steep drop to the Gulf of Salerno. Aimee could hear the distant crash of the surf as she walked to the trash barrel. There were no other vehicles in the scenic overlook. If any vegetable sellers and gelato vendors had been there earlier, they'd packed up and gone home.

Aimee threw the bag in the trash, stuffing it beneath other garbage. She leaned over the parapet and looked down, but it was too dark to see anything. She was turning to go back to the car when she heard the roar of engines. Two motorcycles zoomed in, coming from the north. They pulled up to the Fiat where Trainor was standing and stopped. The riders dismounted and removed their helmets.

From where she stood Aimee could hear Trainor say, "How come you're back? Is everything all right?" Aimee had a sinking feeling she knew who the two men were. They were the ones who'd paid Peach and Trainor for the sigul. Now they were on their way to find out why Johnny Rolex wasn't answering his phone.

As if to confirm her suspicions one of them pulled a handgun from the clip he wore on the belt of his black leather racing suit and pointed it at Trainor. The other one opened the driver's side door of the Fiat and roughly hauled Peach out.

Aimee slid behind the trash barrel and squatted down. She'd left her purse with the gun in it in the car. She hoped the men hadn't noticed her standing there in the dark, in her black jeans and black t-shirt. She wrapped her arms around her knees and scrunched down, making herself small. She waited, her heart pounding.

There was a sound of footsteps on the cracked asphalt. Aimee looked up. It was one of the motorcyclists. He held a gun leveled at her and jerked his head in the direction of the Fiat.

"Get up. Put your hands up," he said. "Move."

Trainor was right, she thought, as she got up, her knees trembling. *He sounds like the newscasters on TV.*

Trainor and Peach stood beside the Fiat, hands raised above their heads, being guarded by the other motorcyclist. The one with Aimee pointed his gun in their direction. "Over there."

She went and stood next to them. Glancing into the back seat she could see her purse, so near and yet so far. To get it she'd have to open the door and reach in. She wouldn't be fast enough to do it without being shot unless the gunmen were distracted by something. She hoped another motorist would pull into the overlook, distracting them long enough for her to grab the gun in her purse.

"Where's John Mulinu'u Mata'afa?" asked the man guarding Peach and Trainor.

"I don't know who that is," Peach replied.

"He calls himself Johnny Rolex. Where is he?" There was a snap as he racked the slide on his gun.

"Oh, him! He's in Spiaggia di Tordigliano," Peach said.

"I don't believe you. Where is he?"

He raised the gun.

A pair of headlights swept into the parking lot, followed by the long, low bulk of a stretch limousine. Marsh leaned out the window, a gun in his hand like a cowboy shooting from the back of a galloping horse. The tires screeched as he fired at the motorcyclists. The bullet struck the side of the Fiat with a *whang*.

Benjamin sat beside Marsh in the front seat. Aimee saw her son's face for a split second before the windshield in front of him shattered. One of the motorcyclists had returned fire.

Peach and Trainor scrambled for cover next to where Aimee crouched behind the Fiat, the palms of her hands stinging from where she'd scraped them crawling on the rough asphalt. Shots pinged off the side of the car, shell casings hitting the asphalt, clattering and rolling. One of the side windows blew out. Trainor cowered on his hands and knees. "Oh shit, this sucks," he moaned.

There was a scream as someone was hit, followed by more shots. Finally, there was an ear-ringing silence. A car door opened and shut. Footsteps could be heard coming in their direction. Then Marsh appeared around the back of the Fiat. "Got them," he said. "Are you all right?"

There was no sign of Benjamin.

Aimee ran to the limousine. There was a neat hole punched through the windshield directly in front of where her son had been sitting, the glass around it forming a lacy white web.

"Benjamin!" she shouted.

The two black leather-clad motorcyclists lay motionless in slowly widening pools of blood.

"Benjamin!" Aimee screamed, panicked.

The car door opened and he got out.

"I'm okay, Mom," he said.

She ran to him and hugged him. "I thought you were dead."

He wrapped his arms around her. "Uncle Marsh was awesome, Mom. We came back to see what was taking you so long. When he saw those two guys he whipped out a gun, hung out the window and hit the gas, heading right at them. He was like Batman."

Marsh joined them. Buttoning the jacket of his brown wool-silk herringbone suit, he said, "Benjamin convinced me to turn back. He said he had a feeling something was wrong."

Peach and Trainor were examining the bullet-riddled Fiat, dismay written over their faces. "We're gonna be in trouble with the car rental people," Trainor moaned. "They don't like it if you bring a car back with a dent in it. They're gonna freak out when they see this."

"They've got my credit card number. They'll go after me for the damages," Peach said morosely. One of the windows was blown out, and one side of the car was pocked with bullet holes. Fortunately, the tires were still inflated, and none of the shots had hit the gas tank.

"It's not your fault *banditti* tried to rob you, and then some other *banditti* came along and shot them," Marsh told him.

Peach nodded slowly. "Yeah, there's supposed to be loads of *banditti* around here. Except I'd rather not go to the police. I don't have to, do I?"

"You don't have to. They'll think it's strange that you didn't, but you can always claim to have been too shook up to think clearly. I propose we drive to Sorrento, abandon the Fiat there, and proceed to Rome in the limousine. Someone will either report finding it abandoned, or they'll steal it to sell the parts. You can always tell the car rental people it was stolen and express amazement if they tell you it was discovered abandoned in Sorrento, full of bullet holes. You could say you have no idea how that happened, and that it was in perfect condition the last time you saw it. That way there'd be no obvious connection to two dead motorcyclists in a scenic overlook ten miles away."

"What about them?" Aimee asked, pointing to the motorcyclists.

"Someone will discover them and call the police," Marsh said. He went over and patted the bodies down, going through their pockets. Unfolding his handkerchief, he carefully picked up their guns. Carrying them to the parapet he tossed them over, sending them bouncing and clattering down the side of the cliff. Then he went through the saddlebags on the motorcycles.

"Bad news," he reported. "The sigul's not here. They must have stashed it somewhere, or given it to someone."

They continued up the coast after transferring their luggage to the trunk of the limousine in preparation for abandoning the Fiat. Peach and Trainor discovered a bottle of Champagne in the compact refrigerator in the rear compartment. Before long they were drinking Champagne from crystal flutes and singing along to pop songs on the karaoke machine. The mirrored disco ball spun and the colored lights in the headliner flashed. Peach attempted to hang upside-down from the stripper pole. He tumbled, laughing, to the zebra-skin carpeted floor.

Aimee, seated in front between Marsh and Benjamin, looked over at Marsh and shook her head. He raised his eyebrows and smiled, "I know. They're like cartoon characters the way they pick themselves up after a near-disaster and go bumbling along. Let's hope their luck holds out."

CHAPTER 25 – TELLING PORK PIES

They abandoned the Fiat on a side street in Sorrento, leaving the keys in the ignition and the doors unlocked to make it more inviting to car thieves.

"I give it an hour, two, tops, before someone steals it," Marsh said. He'd parked the limousine in the 24-hour Vallone dei Mulini parking garage. It was situated atop a steep hill overlooking a ravine where ancient, lichen-encrusted steps led down to the remains of an old mill and a dry river bed.

They walked the short distance to Piazza Tasso, the city's palm-tree-lined main square. It was a warm, pleasant evening and the streets were filled with tourists and smartly-dressed Sorrentini. The air smelled of exhaust fumes and salt spray from the nearby Bay of Naples, as well as the occasional whiff of expensive cologne.

As they passed the Hotel Antiche Mura on the Via Fuorimura, who should be coming out but Bree and Shasta, the teenage sisters whom Benjamin had met on the beach in Spiaggia di Tordigliano. Their long, wavy brown hair was wet from swimming in the hotel pool. They wore hip-hugger shorts, bikini tops, and sandals and were drinking a soft drink called Chinotto through straws stuck in paper cups.

"Oi, you! Are you following us?" Shasta said accusingly to Benjamin.

"No."

"Bull dust. We told you we were going to Sorrento and now you're here. You *are* following us," her sister, Bree, said. She shook her cup, so the ice cubes rattled and sucked the fizzy brown drink through a straw. "There are laws against stalking, you know."

"I'm not stalking you," Benjamin said.

"He's not," Trainor said. "My nephew don't stalk girls. Girls stalk him. Ain't that right, buddy?" He punched Benjamin playfully in the arm.

"No. I don't stalk anybody, and nobody stalks me. It's just a coincidence that we're here the same time as you. We're on our way to..."

"Capri," Aimee said hurriedly. "We're on our way to Capri." She didn't want him saying they were going to Rome. It was unlikely anyone would question the girls about them, but she didn't want to take any chances.

Bree bent at the waist and shook her hair, so it hung over her face. Then she gathered it into a bun on top of her head and wrapped an elastic band around it. Straightening up, she said, "We're going to Capri too. Tomorrow. We're going to see the Blue Grotto. Dad has to return the yacht and then we're flying home. Where are you staying?"

"I'm not sure. We haven't decided yet," Benjamin said.

"You should stay here tonight. The honor bar in our suite has these ripper cheese biscuits," Shasta said enthusiastically.

Shasta seemed to be better disposed toward Benjamin than her sister because Bree told her, "Don't encourage him. He's just going to start in again telling pork pies."

"Pork pies?" Peach asked.

"Rhyming slang. It means lies," Marsh told him.

Just then an attendant from the parking garage hurried up to them. "There you are, *signore!* I was hoping to find you," he said to Marsh. "I am afraid there is a problem with your car."

"What's the matter?" Marsh asked.

"The windscreen has a bullet hole in it. My manager said you should report it to the *polizia.* My manager said it did not happen in our *garage per il parcheggio*," he told him pointedly.

Bree stared at Benjamin. "Bullet hole? Somebody shot at your car?"

"It's all right," Marsh told the parking attendant. "It's not a bullet hole. A stone bounced down from the rocks on the Amalfi Drive and struck the windscreen, that's all. We'll sort it out. Thank you for your concern." He removed his silver money clip from the inside breast pocket of his suit coat and gave the man a twenty-euro note. "*Grazie,*" he said.

The man tucked the note in his pocket. He thanked Marsh and wished them all a *buonasera.*

"Best not to alarm the citizens. Sometimes we get shot at. It comes with the job," Marsh confided to the girls after the man had gone. "Of course I'm not saying that Benjamin is a young intern who's learning the ropes of a dangerous profession involving international travel and top-secret documents." He winked.

The girls took in Marsh's beautifully tailored suit, his perfectly trimmed hair and manicured nails, and his hand-sewn Bontoni wingtip shoes. You could almost see the lightbulbs click on over their heads. "Give me your phone," Bree said to Benjamin.

"Why?"

"So we can give you our numbers."

He handed over his phone, and she entered something into it. "Right. Text us sometime, yeah?"

The sisters walked away down the winding cobblestone street.

"You are a major playa, dawg," Peach told Benjamin gleefully. "Two girls wanting you to text them. You da man!"

"It's no big thing," Benjamin replied, blushing.

Aimee decided to turn it into a teaching moment. "You see how good things happen to you when you're not on drugs?" she told him. "When your skin's cleared up, and you've got some color in your face? Then girls want you to text them."

Benjamin stuck his hands in the pockets of his cargo shorts. "You're ignoring the fact that we got shot at. That's not a good thing," he said.

"You could get shot at if you were on drugs. In fact, it would be more likely," Marsh told him as they made their way across the piazza, dodging flocks of pedestrians. At night, motor vehicle access was restricted to emergency vehicles and everyone was on foot. The windows of the shops surrounding the square were lit, showing off the designer goods inside. Ornate art nouveau streetlights with opaque globes lent a quaint old-world atmosphere to the nighttime scene.

Marsh continued, "Look at how fast you dove to the floor of the car when they started shooting. You've got catlike reflexes when you're not stoned. If you were stoned, you would have sat there and been shot."

"Yeah, probably," Benjamin conceded.

The popular Fauno bar and restaurant was crowded, the outdoor tables draped in daffodil-yellow tablecloths. A waiter conducted them to one of the few empty tables and presented them with menus.

"Europe's got some nice things in it. Fountains and old statues and places like this, where you can sit and watch the people go by. Back home it's too hot to sit outside for long," Trainor observed, looking out over the piazza surrounded by ancient pastel-colored buildings. "This place is bigger than that town in France where I was stayin'. There wasn't a whole lot to do there. Rome was better. Why don't we stay in Rome until things cool down?"

Aimee ordered a bottle of San Pellegrino water. "Things aren't going to cool down. Franz-Albert is going to keep pestering me about the sigul. We've got to figure out how to get it back."

"That's why we need to go to Cobbs and confront Beau Tetley, ask him what his part in all this is," Marsh said. He ordered a limoncello. Benjamin said he'd have one, too.

"Nope. No alcohol for you," Marsh told him. "You can have some of your mother's sparkling water."

"That's not fair. I don't have a problem with alcohol," Benjamin said.

Marsh considered him, smiling. "Alcohol is a drug. I'm surprised you didn't know that. Maybe you should go back to the Institute for a refresher course."

Benjamin exhaled angrily. "That's harsh. I almost got shot. Can't I have one glass to settle my nerves?"

"No," said Marsh.

"Do you think you should drink if Benjamin can't?" Aimee asked him.

"I don't see why not. The sooner he gets used to people around him drinking, the better off he'll be, unless you want to keep putting him in rehabs for the rest of his life. It's up to him to decide if he wants a better life or if he'd rather keep doing the same old thing and keep getting the same results," he told her.

Benjamin fixed Marsh with a defiant glare. "Did you read that in a psychology book?"

"No. It's the plain unvarnished truth. Take it or leave it," Marsh said calmly. He unfolded his napkin and placed it on his lap. "Let's move on to something more interesting. What happened to the sigul? Those two motorcyclists had it, but it wasn't on them or in their saddlebags when I searched them. Peach, how long was it from the time you gave it to them to when they turned up at the overlook?"

"About two hours," Peach said.

Marsh nodded, thinking. "Johnny thought you still had it. That means he wasn't working with those two. We'll call them Smith and Jones since that's what they called themselves."

"Those could have been their real names. People *are* called Smith and Jones, you know," Peach said stubbornly. The waiter came to take their orders.

"It's possible but it's not likely," Marsh told him after the waiter had left. "They left with the sigul and were gone for about two hours. Then they came back looking for Johnny. They didn't have it with them then. And don't forget, somebody kept calling Johnny's phone. It could have been Smith and Jones, or it could have been someone else. Whoever it was blocked their number so it wouldn't show where the call was coming from."

Aimee realized something. "Johnny didn't ask about Smith and Jones. He didn't mention them at all. He thought Peach and Trainor still had the sigul," she told Marsh.

"Good point. It sounded like he didn't know about Smith and Jones, but they knew about him. That indicates they were working for different people," he said.

"Let's do a timeline," Benjamin said. "You said Johnny met you at the airport in Naples. What time was that?"

"We landed at 12:30 P.M., Central European Time," Marsh said promptly. "Aimee and I were the first ones off the plane. It couldn't have taken more than ten or fifteen minutes to walk out of the terminal and meet Johnny in front. We'd already gone through customs back in Dublin, so there was no waiting in line for that."

"How long would you say it took you to get to Spiaggia di Tordigliano?" Benjamin asked.

"We got to Turchi around three," Marsh replied. "It was crowded, and it took a while to find a place to park. Johnny and I went to a café while Aimee changed her clothes. I remember looking at my watch when we got to the café and seeing it was three-fifteen. Then we hiked up the trail that leads to Spiaggia di Tordigliano. That puts it at around four when we ran into you talking to those girls on the beach. Smith and Jones were gone by then."

"They left about thirty minutes before you got there. At least it seemed like it was about that long. I wasn't paying attention to the time," Benjamin said.

"Because of those girls. You were paying attention to them; a whole lot of attention," Peach said with a leer.

"You sound like a creeper when you talk like that, just so you know," Benjamin told him.

The waiter brought their food. "Italian food tastes better in Italy than it does back home," Trainor remarked, digging in. "These little round white things are good."

"It's scungilli," Aimee told him.

"What's that?"

"Sea snail."

Trainor paused, his fork halfway to his mouth. He examined the object speared on it. Then he shrugged and popped it in his mouth. "Really? It's good anyway."

Aimee passed around a plate of antipasti consisting of black and green olives, fresh mozzarella, and paper-thin slices of prosciutto. "Smith and Jones left around three-thirty with the sigul. We must have barely missed running into them on the footpath that goes along the cliff. When they came back, they came from the north, down the Amalfi Drive. Where could they have gone in that time? Naples? Sorrento? Someplace else?"

She looked around the table at her companions' puzzled faces.

"They could have gone to a lot of places. There's no way of telling," Peach said. He dipped a piece of bread into a dish of olive oil. "What worries me is what Johnny Rolex said when he was gettin' ready to shoot Marsh."

"You'd thank me if you knew what's coming," Marsh said slowly.

"That's right. Those were his exact words, I think. What did he mean by that? And why would Smith and Jones be looking for Johnny if they already had the sigul?" Aimee asked.

Marsh appeared to be deep in thought. "I propose we ask Beau Tetley those questions," he said.

CHAPTER 26 – BIG MACS IN THE ETERNAL CITY

The Fiat was gone when they went to check on it after leaving the restaurant. A teenager could have gone joyriding in it, or a car thief may have taken it. Either way, it was now someone else's problem.

"When I tell the car rental place it got stolen, aren't they gonna be mad at me for not reporting it to the police?" Peach asked.

"Tell them you're not sure if it was stolen. Say you might have forgotten where you left it. That won't surprise them; they expect Americans to be idiots. Anyway, it's not as if it was a good car. They're insured. If I were you, I wouldn't give it another thought. Don't tell them anything. Just go back home," Aimee advised him. "If they contact you asking where the car is, tell them you returned it to them. Make it seem like they were the ones who lost it."

"You know what Fiat stands for? It stands for fix it again, Tony," Trainor said. "That's because they're always breaking down."

"Hilarious," Marsh said. "Did you think of that all by yourself?"

They were in the limousine, driving on the E45, on their way to Rome. Traffic was heavy. It would be nearly a four-hour trip. Aimee was exhausted. She hadn't slept in over twenty-four hours. Her eyes burned and throbbed with tiredness. She yawned.

"I'm not getting back on an airplane tonight. I'm too tired. I say we stop overnight in Rome. I like to stay at the Hassler. Let's see if they have any rooms available," she said.

"Is it a nice place?" Trainor asked. "Before, when me and Peach were stayin' in Rome, the hotel was full of Norwegians. They roamed the halls at all hours, talkin' loud to one another so you couldn't get to sleep. When you'd go outside, they'd be hangin' around out there, askin' if you had any American cigarettes. They were wild for American cigarettes. If I knew that beforehand I would have brought a couple of cartons and made some money off of them."

"The Hassler is a five-star hotel. Nothing like that happens there," Aimee assured him. She took out her phone and called the front desk, reserving the San Pietro Presidential Suite, along with the double room next door. "I'll take the bedroom in the suite. Two of you can sleep next door. That room's got two queen-size beds. The other two can have the couches in the suite's living room. They should be quite comfortable."

"If they're so comfortable why don't you sleep on a couch and I'll take the bedroom in the Presidential Suite?" Benjamin asked.

"That's very amusing, Benjamin. The answer is no. When you're the one paying you can decide who sleeps where," Aimee told him.

She looked at her phone, frowning.

"What's the matter?" Benjamin asked.

"Franz-Albert hasn't called in a long time. Before, he kept calling all the time, wanting to know if I'd found the sigul yet," she said.

They were driving through Frosinone at that point, surrounded by mountain ranges and following a steady stream of red taillights. Rome was about two hours away.

"Maybe he's busy," Trainor suggested. He and Peach had gotten tired of singing along to the karaoke machine and had eaten all the contents of the refrigerator, except for a jar of capers.

"Maybe he knows you don't have it. That could be why he stopped calling," Benjamin said. "Maybe Smith and Jones were working for him."

"It's like one of those bewildering mysteries, where the one you least expect turns out to be the murderer and he's murdered himself," Peach said, somewhat incoherently. "What do you think, Marsh?"

"I think I'll be glad when I can stop driving. That's what I think." He took one hand off the leather-covered steering wheel and massaged the back of his neck. "I suggest we abandon this car somewhere. If any of you suspect your fingerprints could be on any international law enforcement databases, you should wipe down everything you touched with the wipes I have in my luggage. Be meticulous. That includes the stripper pole, by the way." He looked into the rearview mirror at Peach and Trainor.

"I haven't done anything that cops in Europe would be after me for," Peach said.

"Me neither," said Trainor.

There was silence from Benjamin.

"Benjamin?" Marsh prompted.

"I'd better take some of those wipes and wipe down the door handle where I touched it, and everything up here that I might have touched," he said, not looking at his mother.

"All right then," Marsh said after a moment. "There's parking near the Roma Tiburtina railway station. We'll leave the car there. From the station, we can take a bus or a cab to the hotel. Or we could get on the metro. The A-line goes to the Spanish Steps. From there it's a short walk up the steps to the hotel."

They abandoned the limousine and took the metro to the Piazza della Trinità dei Monti, where the Hassler presided like a grande dame at the top of the Spanish Steps. Within minutes they were in one of the palatial sixth-floor suites. Its elegant furnishings were upholstered in silvery gray fabric. Arranged in a display case was a collection of antique Roman artifacts. From the private terrace, they looked out over one of the finest views in Rome. Down below, illuminated in the darkness they could make out the Pantheon and the dome of St. Peter's Basilica.

"Would you look at that," Trainor marveled, leaning over the balustrade. "There's a McDonald's. Anybody hungry?"

Marsh picked up a leather-covered menu from atop an antique eighteenth-century desk. "The concierge will send out for a couple of Big Macs, if that's what you want. Personally, I'd prefer the ten-course tasting menu. They have foie gras and dried fruit, shabu scallops carpaccio, scampi tartare, and so on. It's a shame it's not porcini season yet. I've heard the chef does wonders with mushrooms. What say the rest of you? There's enough to share if we go for the tasting selection. Or get the sake-glazed black cod or the linguine with blue lobster and wild lemon."

True to form, Trainor and Peach wanted McDonald's, which a room service waiter delivered without a trace of irony. He showed the same graciousness as he placed the white paper bag with the McDonald's logo on the round mirrored table in the suite's dining area as he did when he laid out the vastly more refined and expensive selections from the tasting menu that were chosen by Marsh.

"So what's the plan?" Peach asked as they ate their meal. He dipped a French fry into the ramekin filled with ketchup provided by the hotel kitchen.

"We go back home and confront Beau Tetley, ask him who hired him to get you to steal the sigul," Aimee said.

Trainor took a huge bite of Big Mac and washed it down with Coca-Cola.

Speaking through a mouth full of food, he said, "I'd rather not go back to Georgia, if that's all right with you guys. Palmer's in Georgia. As soon as she finds out I'm not dead, she'll start up tryin' to divorce me again."

"You can't stay here," Marsh told him.

Trainor looked around the room, at the carved oak wainscoting gleaming with a mellow richness in the light of lamps with ecru silk shades. "Why not? It's nice here."

"Because this suite costs sixty-five hundred euros a night, that's why. You don't have that kind of money," Aimee said.

"I could pay for it out of my trust fund."

"Think about it. How can you take money out of your trust fund if you're supposed to be dead?"

He looked downcast. "Shoot, I forgot about that. Guess I'm screwed either way. If I go home, Palmer'll take my money. If I stay here, I'll end up sleeping on the street."

"You could make up with Palmer," Benjamin suggested. He'd found the sweet buffalo mozzarella to his liking and had eaten the lion's share of what Imàgo, the hotel's Michelin star restaurant, sent up as the dessert portion of the ten-course meal. He took a piece of warm bread from the bread basket and mopped up the rest.

"Make up with Palmer," Trainor said slowly as if testing out the idea in his mind.

"Sure, why not? Tell her you love her and whatever it was that made her mad was entirely your fault. Be contrite," Benjamin advised him. At his uncle's puzzled expression he explained, "Act like you're sorry."

Trainor nodded slowly, as if picturing himself acting sorry. "I could do that," he said. "Palmer's not so bad. She's bossy, and she's got a temper, but as wives go, I'd say she's above average." He sat up straighter, a gleam of resolve in his eyes.

"I'll do it. I'll make up with her, for the sake of our marriage vows, and for little Jubilee. She needs her daddy's guidance so she can grow up right."

"And so Palmer don't keep trying to take all your money," Peach said biting into a French fry.

"That too," Trainor said.

"Now that's settled let's get back to the sigul," Aimee said. "It's supposed to have the power to destroy the world. How does it do that? Is there a button on it that you push and the world blows up? That doesn't seem likely. Franz-Albert's ancestor supposedly tried to cut it open with a saw and the world didn't blow up then."

"No, but spacemen came. Isn't that what you said?" Benjamin said.

There was a knock on the door. It was a young chambermaid, inquiring whether they wanted the beds turned down. She turned down the plump duvets, leaving a corner of the starched sheets exposed. As a final touch, she left chocolates wrapped in gold foil on the pillows. On her way out she gave Benjamin an extra one.

"So you have sweet dreams," she told him, placing the candy in his hand. "*Buona notte.*"

As soon as she left, Peach burst out laughing. In a breathy Italian-accented voice he told Benjamin, "*So you have-a the sweet-a dreams, you sexy thing.*"

Benjamin unwrapped the candy. "Bite me," he told Peach cheerfully.

Marsh went to the window and looked out over the view. "I'm not convinced there were any spacemen, but setting that aside for now, you had the sigul. What did it look like?"

Peach rummaged in the paper bag for the last of the French fries. "It was like a hockey puck: flat and round, y'know?"

"Was there anything inscribed on it? Any knobs to turn, or buttons to push or hinges that made it open like a locket?" Marsh asked.

"Nope, just plain old solid metal, gold-colored, maybe half an inch thick with wavy marks on both sides, kinda like the marks there'd be if somebody ran a comb over sand," Peach said.

"How could something like that destroy the world?" Aimee asked. She yawned and rubbed her eyes. "I'm going to bed. Let's talk some more in the morning. We should try and get a flight out of here sometime in the early afternoon. Marsh, call down to the concierge and get him to take care of it. Tell him to arrange a ride to the airport."

She went into the bedroom and shut the door. A moment later she opened it again. "First class seats, don't forget," she said and shut the door again.

Marsh went over to the minibar and considered the selection. He chose a bottle of Rémy Martin cognac and poured some into a tulip glass. "I'm trying to picture her flying economy," he said, swirling the golden liquid in his glass. "Having to get on last after everybody else and squeezing down the aisle to the cheap seats. I can't do it. It's impossible."

He took a drink of cognac. "Oh well, Via Condotti's right around the corner. I can duck into the shoe store as soon as it opens tomorrow and get another pair of loafers to replace the ones that got ruined when we were dumping that carnival worker's body in the swamp.

Benjamin was in the process of unwrapping a Toblerone bar from the selection of snacks provided by the hotel. A smile spread across his face. "Wow, Uncle Marsh. You dumped a body in a swamp? I want to hear about that."

"Maybe I'll tell you later, if you're a good boy," Marsh told him. "Now it's time for bed. It's been a long day."

CHAPTER 27 – ARRIVEDERCI, ROMA

It was shortly after 6 A.M. Benjamin slept tangled in a nest of blankets on one of the couches in the living room. One pillow had been tossed to the floor, and another was bunched up beneath his head. The neighboring couch was empty, although a pillow and a neatly folded blanket showed signs of it having been occupied.

Aimee, wrapped in one of the Hassler's terrycloth robes, pushed aside the floor-length gold drapes and stepped out onto the terrace, where she found Marsh seated in a chaise-lounge. He was fully dressed, wearing a Brunello Cucinelli silk suit, light gray with a chalk stripe. He had on one of his Turnbull & Asser bespoke shirts with a pair of pink gold Dunhill cufflinks. Around his neck was a perfectly knotted blue-and-pink fantasy pattern Christian Lacroix necktie.

"Couldn't sleep?" she asked.

Marsh picked up a tiny white ceramic espresso cup from the marble-topped table at his elbow and downed the contents in a single gulp, Italian-style.

"I was thinking about Johnny," he said.

Aimee sat down on the chaise-lounge next to his. "I'm sorry."

Marsh shook his head. "Don't be. You had to shoot him. If you hadn't, he would have killed us all."

"I meant I'm sorry you're sad. I know you were friends," she said.

Marsh got up and went to the edge of the balcony. He stood looking out, his hands on the balustrade. "Sunrise in Rome," he said. "People have been standing on this very spot watching the sun come up for thousands of years."

Aimee said nothing. It was clear he didn't want to talk about it.

"The city's waking up. You can hear the rumble of traffic on the Via della Conciliazione. Soon the tour buses will be out in force. Earlier, when it was quiet, I could hear the water splashing in the Fontana della Barcaccia at the foot of the Spanish Steps," Marsh said.

"That's the one that looks like a half-sunken boat with water pouring over the sides," Aimee said, going to stand beside him and looking down in the direction of the Piazza di Spagna.

"That's right. A flood in 1598 made the Tiber overflow its banks. A boat was swept all the way into the center of the piazza, causing a sensation. About twenty-five years later Pope Urban VIII commissioned Pietro Bernini to build a fountain in every major piazza in Rome. The boat-shaped one commemorates a real event. The water in the fountain comes from the Acqua Vergine, an aqueduct that dates to 19 BCE," her brother told her.

"Fascinating. You should consider becoming a tour guide," Aimee said.

He smiled. "I'd be good at it. I know a lot of interesting tidbits about all kinds of places, many of which aren't suitable for public dissemination. But getting back to the boat-shaped fountain down there, it reminds me of the poet John Keats. He died at the age of twenty-five in a house at the foot of the steps. It's a museum now. As he lay dying from tuberculosis he could hear the water splashing in the fountain. It became the source of his epitaph: "Here lies one whose name was writ in water.""

"How cheerful," Aimee said. She stretched languidly. "Have you been up long?"

"Since around three. I went for a walk through the narrow side streets where it's all alleyways and overhanging balconies, out toward the Villa Borghese. I took Johnny's gun apart and threw the pieces into several sewer grates along the way, so that's taken care of. Did you know Rome's sewer system is ancient? Parts of it predate the Roman Empire."

Aimee shook her head. She didn't know that, nor did she care.

"When I got back, the night manager said our airline reservations are arranged. We'll be leaving on the twelve forty-five nonstop Delta flight to JFK. From there we'll get a flight to Savannah, and then home again, home again, jiggity-jig."

He stretched his arms above his head and twisted his neck from side to side until he heard it pop. "That'll give us time for a leisurely breakfast, assuming those slugabeds in the next room wake up in time. I can go over to the Via Condotti and buy my shoes as soon as the shop opens. I'm going to get an extra pair this time, in case I have to take another unplanned trek through a swamp."

They'd left the Rhino revolver in the rear compartment in the limousine where Aimee had found it, after wiping it clean of fingerprints. With no firearms in their possession, they should be able to board the flight home with no problems.

"Did you sleep well?" Marsh asked his sister.

"Not really," she said. "I kept my phone charged and turned on, thinking Franz-Albert would call, but he didn't. I'm worried. At first, I was annoyed when he kept calling. Now I wish he would. He was so fired up about getting the sigul back that he flew all the way to New York to see me about it. It doesn't seem right for him to go silent like this."

Marsh went to the espresso maker and poured himself another cup. "Then call him," he suggested.

"And say what? That we don't have the sigul? That we don't know where it is, and oh, by the way, three people are dead? He's not going to like that. No, I'd rather just leave him alone. He'll call eventually." Then she had an awful thought. "What if he's on his way here? He knows I often stay at the Hassler. Maybe he's downstairs right now, furious because I couldn't get the sigul back. What if he's getting ready to kill us?"

Marsh dropped a piece of lemon peel in his espresso. "He would have no way of knowing you're in Rome. Even if he found out somehow, I can't picture him as the type who'd storm into a hotel lobby and start shooting. He *might* be armed. Germany and Italy are both part of the Schengen Agreement, which means there wouldn't be a routine immigration check if he crossed into Italy from anywhere in the Schengen Zone. That includes Switzerland and anywhere along the Austrian and Slovenian borders. However, even if he comes here, the staff won't disclose the names of any guests. If you're worried about him lying in wait outside, that's another issue. I'll keep an eye out for him when I go to buy my shoes. He won't expect to see me. If need be, I can sneak up behind him and disable him." He tossed back the espresso.

Changing the subject, he said, "Benjamin was having bad dreams. I heard him moaning in his sleep."

When he returned from disposing of the gun he'd heard Benjamin get up and go over to the minibar. The boy stood there a long time, apparently surveying what kinds of alcohol were available. Then Marsh heard the pop and sizzle of a can of soda being opened and the sound of Benjamin taking big gulps. Next came rustling as he tore open the wrapper of a chocolate bar and hungrily devoured it. Benjamin, it appeared, had a sweet tooth, like many addicts. Marsh laid there quietly, waiting to see whether he'd get dressed and go out, but Benjamin went back to the couch and rolled up in his blankets. Marsh remained half-awake, listening, but he didn't get up again.

Aimee stood up. "I'm going to take a shower and get dressed. Benjamin will be all right. I'll take him to Cobbs. He can't get in trouble there. It's not like New York or Berlin or Budapest or any of the other places where he's gotten in trouble. Cobbs is quiet. It's safe. He'll be fine there."

Marsh smiled ruefully. "Benjamin is a Trapnell. Believe me, a Trapnell can get into trouble anywhere; it's in our blood."

Franz-Albert wasn't lurking in the hotel lobby or anywhere outside, as far as they could tell. They were able to leave with no trouble, their plane touching down in New York about nine hours after it took off from Rome.

It was then that Aimee's phone rang. It was Palmetto Gardens calling. Blanton was dead.

CHAPTER 28 – AIMEE'S CONFESSION

Blanton hadn't been a favorite of the staff at Palmetto Gardens. He wasn't what you'd call a nice old man, being easily angered and bitingly sarcastic, but still, his death left them feeling unsettled. He'd been so abrasive, so full of demands and harsh, intense opinions. It seemed odd for such a powerful personality to be abruptly snuffed out.

He'd been sitting in a chair in his room, propped up with pillows, talking to Hillman Parks, who visited him every day. He'd been in good spirits when a nurse went in to check his vital signs, according to the director of nursing, a lady named Bonnie Turner. Then Hillman had left, and another friend dropped by. That's when one of the aides heard Blanton shouting.

"This is it. It's all over!" the aide heard him yell. His friend had come rushing out of the room, calling for help. It was another stroke, this one fatal.

Aimee, listening as Ms. Turner told her about her father's demise, wondered who this second visitor could be. Blanton didn't have any friends. He had employees and people he knew from serving on various boards and commissions, but he wasn't the type of man to have pals. Hillman was probably the closest thing to a friend Blanton had, and their relationship, while devoted, was that of employer and old family retainer, so who was this mysterious friend?

"He was an older white gentleman. He was the spitting image of Colonel Sanders, string tie, white suit and all," Ms. Turner said.

Beau Tetley.

Aimee accepted Ms. Turner's condolences and ended the call. "Daddy passed away," she told the others.

Peach patted her shoulder. "I'm sorry, Aimee. That's a shame, losing your daddy without having a chance to say goodbye. I know how bad I felt when my daddy passed, and he used to smack me upside the head and call me an imbecile. But look at it this way: now you're filthy rich. How much do you get? Billions, right? Not millions, billions. With a B. Girl, you got it made!"

Marsh looked at him askance. "Peach, you're unreal. I can't believe you'd say something like that."

"But it's true," Trainor protested. "We're incredibly rich now. This is awesome." His grin faded as he looked around at his disapproving siblings and his shocked nephew. "I'm only being honest. Look, it's sad that Daddy's gone. I'm gonna miss him, but he was ninety. He wasn't gonna live forever. At least he didn't suffer. And yes, it may be in bad taste to bring up money at a time like this, but Sweet Mother Mary lick my leg! We're gonna inherit loads and loads of money!" He beamed as he looked around the bustling concourse at Kennedy Airport. "We could buy this whole place. We could buy all of Manhattan."

"We're in Queens," Aimee told him. "We couldn't even buy all of Queens. We could buy some of it, but who'd want to?" Her pale green eyes took on a covetous expression. "I'm going to use part of my inheritance to buy an island somewhere, where the weather's warm but not too warm and where I get to say who's allowed on it and who's not. I'll also buy more snakes."

"Haven't we forgotten something?" Marsh asked.

"What?" said Trainor.

"The lawyer. Beau Tetley. How come he was with Daddy when he died? What was he doing there?"

Trainor slapped his forehead. "Crap! You don't think Daddy made a new will, do you? That would be awful. Remember Lyman Gwinnette? He was worth twenty billion. He made a new will three weeks before he died. His kids ended up gettin' one dollar each. The rest went to some kinda nature fund for snowy owls. I was friends with his son Frost. He just about went crazy." He looked stricken at the thought of something similar happening to himself.

"Are we going to have a funeral?" Benjamin asked Aimee. "Do I have to see Grandpa's dead body?"

The idea of Blanton on display in a satin-lined coffin disturbed him. It would be the fourth corpse he'd seen lately. It was becoming a trend, one he didn't care for at all.

"We need to see about the arrangements. Daddy prepaid for his funeral at Chapman's," Aimee said, naming a funeral home in Cobbs. It had been in business since before the Civil War. It had a cast iron hitching post out front where Robert E. Lee was said to have once tied his horse. Chapman's was one of two funeral homes in Cobbs. It catered mainly to a white clientele. The other one, Young's, was patronized exclusively by blacks.

"There's going to be a viewing with visiting hours. Daddy would want a lot of people paying their respects. When Mama died, they had a book for visitors to sign. Afterwards Daddy went through it to see who signed," Aimee told Benjamin. "Even though Daddy's dead and he won't be able to do anything like he did to the people who didn't go to Mama's viewing, like blackballing them from the country club or foreclosing on their mortgages, they'll be afraid of offending his heirs. There'll likely be a large turnout. After the funeral, he'll go into a crypt in the family mausoleum. You don't have to see him if you don't want to. Sometimes people prefer to remember the departed the way they were when they were alive."

"The last time I saw Grandpa he said I dressed like a bum and had hair like a wop," Benjamin said.

Peach gave a low whistle. "Damn! That's racist!"

"It's certainly distasteful, but it's not, strictly speaking, racist," Marsh said.

They had some time before their flights boarded. Aimee, Marsh, Trainor, and Benjamin were headed to Savannah. Peach was returning to his home in Mobile, by way of Pensacola, Florida.

Benjamin asked his mother for money to buy a t-shirt. He went off with Trainor and Peach, who wanted to look over the wares in the duty-free shop. Trainor hoped to find a peace offering for Palmer. Peach suggested he get her the largest, most extravagantly packaged bottle of perfume he could find.

"Get her a teddy bear, too. Give a woman perfume and a teddy bear and they'll forgive all the dumb shit you did. Works like a charm," Peach told him.

Aimee and Marsh went to the gate where their flight would be leaving and sat down in vinyl-upholstered seats that were bolted to the floor. Outside the floor-to-ceiling windows they could see airport workers wearing orange day-glow vests busying themselves around a Boeing 757 being maneuvered into position by a vehicle resembling a tow truck.

"We should tell Karen about Daddy," Marsh said. "It's late morning in Nepal. Let's call her."

Aimee had been dreading this moment.

"There's something you should know," she said. "Karen's dead. Nobody else knows besides me. You're the first person I told."

Marsh crossed his legs. He straightened the crease in his trousers and examined his dark brown Berluti leather brogues. There was a smudge of dirt on the toe of one. He removed a Turnbull & Asser silk pocket square from the breast pocket of his suit coat and wiped it away. Then he turned to his sister. "I'm all ears," he said.

Aimee gave the version of the story she'd worked out, one in which Petulia Puddlehopper, the floral print frog-shaped blackjack, did not figure. In this version, it had been Karen who insisted on Aimee accompanying her on a walk in the swamp.

"She must have been planning it all along. Either that or she snapped and went crazy. I guess we'll never know, but it was terrifying," Aimee told her brother. He listened intently, his face betraying no emotion.

"She was saying how pretty the swamp was at night, with the moon shining through the trees. Then without any warning, she pushed me."

"She pushed you," Marsh repeated.

Aimee looked around to make sure she wasn't overheard. Four elegantly coiffed older women seated nearby were complaining about how expensive everything was in Manhattan.

"New York isn't what it used to be. You always used to get bargains on Seventh Avenue, but no more," said one.

"There are no good restaurants anymore. Mama Leone's, Carnegie Deli, Café des Artistes, gone, all gone," mourned another. "Four Seasons has a new location, but it's not what it was, no, not at all."

The other people nearby were a gaggle of teenagers listening to music on earbuds, a soldier in desert camo who was looking at something on a tablet, and a harried young couple who were trying to calm a baby that kept letting out earsplitting shrieks. They all seemed too preoccupied to pay any attention to what Aimee was saying.

Nevertheless she lowered her voice. "She shoved me hard. I almost fell down. Then she came at me again. I put my hands up. I wasn't even thinking. I acted on reflex and pushed her away. She fell and hit her head on a rock and went under the water."

She watched Marsh to see how he was taking it. His handsome face was perfectly still. He raised an eyebrow.

"Did you try to rescue her?"

"No."

"No?"

"No, I was scared. I thought she'd go after me again. You should have seen her, Marsh. It was like she was insane."

He pursed his lips. "Did you consider going for help?"

"No."

"Why not?"

"I told you, I was scared. I pushed her, and her head hit a rock. I didn't mean for it to happen. I just wanted to keep her away from me, but it would look bad. The police would have said I did it on purpose."

"Why would they say that?"

"You know why," Aimee said. "Because of Daddy's money. They'd say I did it on purpose to get a larger share of Daddy's money, which isn't true, but you know how people are; they think money's at the root of everything."

"Most crimes are about money, either money or revenge or wounded pride," Marsh said. "But setting that aside, do you mean to say you let Karen drown and then you went on as if nothing happened?"

Aimee bit her lip. "It sounds bad when you put it that way. I couldn't think what else to do. Like I said, I was afraid I'd get in trouble even though it was self-defense." She met his eyes, her pale green gaze defiant. "Be honest, Marsh, it wasn't as if we liked her. Do you really care that she's dead?"

He grimaced. "That's not the point. I wish you'd said something about this sooner. You understand it leaves us with a problem on our hands. Karen was the executor of Daddy's will. How are we going to settle his estate without her?"

Peach and Trainor emerged from the duty-free shop and were walking in their direction. Trainor carried a shopping bag and had an enormous fluffy brown teddy bear under one arm. They met Benjamin coming out of a souvenir shop and they conferred over their purchases. Trainor showed Benjamin the bottle of perfume he'd bought. It was nearly the size of a bowling pin, wrapped in layers of colored cellophane tied with a gold bow. Benjamin held up a t-shirt. It had FUGGEDABOUTIT DIRTBAG, I'M FROM NEW YORK written on the front.

Aimee hadn't thought about Karen being the executor of their father's will. It was too late to do anything about it now. "I'm sure there's a way to deal with that. And one more thing," she said hurriedly, wanting to get it over with before the others joined them. "An alligator ate her."

Marsh closed his eyes. "So I was right. It was her inside that alligator," he said.

Aimee nodded. "Yes, the one they killed when they were searching for you and Trainor. I'm ninety-nine-percent certain it was her. I mean, who else could it be?"

"Aimee, you never cease to amaze me," Marsh said.

The others were approaching. He lowered his voice. "We'll talk about this later."

CHAPTER 29 – RETIREMENT

It was early afternoon by the time the cab deposited the four Trapnells at White Oaks. To Aimee, her body clock struggling with the change in time zones, it felt as if it was the middle of the night. Letting themselves in they were met not by Hillman but by Louetta, who came out of the kitchen drying her hands on a dish towel.

"I'm sorry 'bout your daddy," she told them. Noticing Benjamin, she added, "And your granddaddy. My, you growed some since the last time you was here! How you like that boarding school over in Switzerland?"

Aimee had told people Benjamin was in boarding school, rather than say he was in rehab.

"It wasn't so good. I'm glad I'm not there anymore," Benjamin said.

Seamus came to greet them, his toenails clicking on the black and white marble floor. He sniffed at their luggage. Trainor placed the teddy bear on the round table by the stairs, out of the dog's reach.

"Where's Hillman? I could use a drink," he asked, looking around.

Louetta twisted the dish towel nervously. "He gone."

"Gone? You mean Hillman's dead, too?" Marsh asked.

It seemed possible, considering how devoted he was to Blanton, that the old butler could have died from grief.

"Not dead. Retired," Louetta said.

"What? He can't do that," Aimee said, causing Louetta to look at her sharply.

"I mean, technically, yes. He can retire if he wants to. We can't force him to keep working here, but we need him to stay on, at least for a little while. There's going to be a lot to do. We've got a luncheon to put on after the funeral. We'll need sandwich platters, a ham, fried chicken, different kinds of salad and deviled eggs, hummingbird cake, some kind of punch in the big crystal punch bowl. Hillman would know what's best. I'll call him and ask him to come back, as a favor to the family. I'm sure he'll understand. There'll be a lot of work for you, too, Louetta," Aimee told the cook.

"Yes, ma'am, I got a good recipe for hummingbird cake, and I've been told my deviled eggs is second to none. The food won't be no problem. I like cooking for big gatherings. The problem is Hillman. He ain't comin' back. He tole me so. The last thing he done was he pressed Mr. Blanton's burial suit and laid it out on Mr. Blanton's bed, up in Mr. Blanton's room. Then he come down the back stairs to the kitchen, where I was wipin' down the counters. He said, 'That's it, Louetta. I'm done. I'm goin' out the front do' an' when it shuts behind me that's the last White Oaks gonna see of me. I'm goin' travelin'. Gonna see some of this country while I'm still able. Gonna see the Golden West.' Then out the do' he went." Louetta seemed pleased to have delivered such dramatic news.

"Well, that's a hell of a thing," Trainor grumbled. "I guess I'll have to go down to the cellar myself and get something to drink. Then we better call an employment agency and get them to send us another butler." Sighing heavily, as if he were forced to undergo a terrible ordeal, he set off toward the swinging door that led to the kitchen and the basement wine cellar.

"I'll do it later. Right now I'm going to bed. I'm dead on my feet," Aimee said. "Benjamin, bring our luggage upstairs."

They headed up the double-reverse spiral staircase. Marsh patted Seamus. The dog looked up at him with sad amber eyes.

"You miss Blanton, don't you?" Marsh asked.

Seamus went to the polished cypress front door. The afternoon sunlight shone through the fanlight above it, falling in pie-shaped wedges onto the marble floor. He barked once, as if he expected his master to come walking through the door.

"He's gone, boy," Marsh said. Tears prickled his eyes. As difficult as his father had been, he was finding it hard to accept that he wouldn't see him again. Marsh stroked the dog's head before carrying his luggage upstairs.

It wasn't even an hour later when a knock came on Aimee's door. She'd gotten into bed, having removed her makeup and moisturized her face and given her hair its routine one hundred stokes with her tortoiseshell-backed brush. She was hoping for eight hours of uninterrupted sleep, but she couldn't relax. Hillman's desertion had put her in a foul mood. *The least he could have done was stay until he could train a new butler, but as soon as Daddy died, he quit on us. That's gratitude for you,* she thought crossly, punching the plump goose down pillows. *Give someone a job for seventy years and how do they thank you? They up and quit with no warning.*

She slid out from between the starched sheets with a muttered oath. Throwing on her white eyelet embroidered cotton robe, she went to open the door. Benjamin and Marsh stood in the hallway. Benjamin was breathless with excitement.

"Holy shit, Mom, you won't believe it! Grandpa was part of that club," he said.

"What club? The Rotary Club? I know. So what?"

"No, the sigul of Jörmungandr club."

"That's ridiculous. He never said anything about it. I would have remembered if he had. Daddy was in Rotary, and Kiwanis, and the Elks, like a lot of businesspeople. Nobody around here's ever heard of the sigul of Jörmungandr club. That's something they do in Germany," Aimee said.

Marsh shook his head. "Not just in Germany, apparently. May we come in?"

Marsh seated himself in the armchair upholstered in turquoise and white Ikat fabric. He wore J. Mueser custom-crafted denim jeans, a blue chambray shirt with mother-of-pearl buttons, and brown suede chukka boots by Foster & Son of Jermyn Street, London. He was freshly shaved, his hair meticulously combed. He'd traveled halfway around the world, but he looked as refreshed as if he'd spent a leisurely day lounging by the pool.

Benjamin sat at the foot of the bed. He looked at Marsh, who gave a slight nod, urging him to go ahead.

"I wasn't being disrespectful of the dead or anything," he began. "And I wasn't going to steal anything, I swear. I was just thinking about that footrest Grandpa had, the one shaped like a rhinoceros. I wondered if it was still in his room, so I went to see."

Aimee knew what he was referring to. The footrest was about two feet high, made of dark brown leather. It had pointed ears like a cat's and a horn on its nose. When he was small Benjamin used to like to sit on it, pretending he was on an African safari and that it was a tame rhinoceros.

"So I went in his room, and there was this black suit on the bed. It creeped me out. I was going to leave, but I noticed something shiny pinned to the lapel. I went to see what it was and it was a gold circle, like a little ring."

"Didn't Franz-Albert say a lapel pin shaped like a gold ring was the symbol of the secret society of the sigul of Jörmungandr?" Marsh asked.

"Yes, but I don't see how Daddy could be a member. I never saw him wear anything like that on his suits," Aimee said. She tightened the belt of her robe and went to her dressing table. Agitated by this unexpected news, she picked up her hairbrush and ran it through her hair.

"Then why is it on the suit he's going to be buried in? Who put it there?" Benjamin asked, shifting restlessly on the thick mattress. He wore the black t-shirt with "FUGGEDABOUTIT DIRTBAG, I'M FROM NEW YORK on the front.

Marsh and Aimee spoke in unison: "Hillman."

Their eyes met, startled that they'd reached the same conclusion.

"Why would Hillman do that?" Aimee wondered.

"Daddy must have told him to. Louetta said Hillman laid out Daddy's suit before he quit. Daddy must have given him instructions about which suit he wanted to be buried in. He must have told him to pin the gold circle on the lapel. People who belong to fraternal orders often want to be buried in their regalia. Daddy must have wanted to be buried with the Jörmungandr symbol, instead of any of his other ones: the Rotary wheel, for instance, or whatever the Elks have," Marsh said.

"They have an elk's head with a clock on top, with the hands pointing to eleven," Aimee said. Her hair crackled with static as she brushed it. She was having difficulty coming to grips with the idea that her father was a member of an ancient secret organization, one based on a Norse myth about a giant sea serpent. Gruff, no-nonsense Blanton seemed like the last person who'd get involved in something like that.

"An elk's head with a clock on top? What's that supposed to mean?" Marsh said. He looked at the rumpled bed linen then consulted his watch. "Why were you in bed? It's mid-afternoon."

"You may not get jet lag, but I do," his sister replied crossly. "The clock on the elk's head is for this thing the Elks do called the eleven o'clock toast. Daddy told me about it. At eleven at night the Elks are supposed to stop whatever they're doing and drink a toast to absent members, living or dead."

"You know who'd know about this, don't you? Beau Tetley. He's the one who asked Peach to steal the sigul. He must have sent those two motorcycle guys to get it. Tetley was Grandpa's lawyer. He was with him when he died. He's the key to this whole thing," Benjamin said.

"Why would a small town lawyer be involved in something like that? The theft of an ancient artifact out of a castle dungeon? An artifact that's supposed to have the power to destroy the world? That's too far-fetched," Marsh said.

"Nevertheless it seems like it's true. Tetley could be the middleman for somebody else, the real person who wants the sigul," Aimee said. "He might know who Johnny Rolex was working for, or Smith and Jones. Let's go see him tomorrow and get him to tell us what he knows. Marsh, you're good at menacing; you can menace him into telling."

At that moment Trainor entered the room. His bearded face wore a broad grin, and he carried an open bottle of Champagne.

"I heard y'all talkin' so I thought I'd join the party," he said. "Guess what? Palmer's agreed to take me back! I called her up and said, 'Baby, I'm a miserable, no-account hound who don't deserve a fine woman like you, however my daddy just died and left me billions. Can you find it in your heart to forgive me?' And she said yes!" At that, he chugged Champagne straight out of the bottle. Wiping foam from his bushy mustache, he held the bottle up by the neck and announced, "Krug Clos d'Ambonnay 1995. It's a pinot noir, which means it's made from extra-fancy grapes. I learned that when I was stayin' in France. Yahoo! My troubles are over! No more divorce! I get to keep my money!"

"If there is any money," Marsh said darkly. "Don't forget, Daddy met with Beau Tetley. What if he made a new will? We need to go see Tetley tomorrow and find out what's going on. By the way, Benjamin stumbled onto something interesting. It seems Daddy belonged to the secret society of the sigul of Jörmungandr."

"No shit?" said Trainor. He didn't seem terribly concerned, the news that his wife was going to cease gouging him for alimony and child support making his spirits soar. "Chill out. Daddy wouldn't change his will, or if he did, it was to make a little bitty bequest of a hundred thousand or so to one of the nurses at Palmetto Gardens. It won't affect our share." He took another swig from the bottle and belched loudly.

"I guess we'll find out in the morning," Aimee said. "We need to stop by the funeral home to see about Daddy's arrangements. He'll be going into the crypt in the mausoleum next to where Mama is."

"Yuck," Benjamin said. "Funeral stuff is creepy."

It was even creepier than he imagined, as they found out the next day. That's when they learned the mausoleum at White Oaks had an extra body in it, one that wasn't supposed to be there.

CHAPTER 30 – THE EXTRA BODY

Chapman's Funeral Home in downtown Cobbs was built in the style of a plantation house, like White Oaks but on a much smaller scale. It had four round white columns in front, reaching up to the second floor where Lycott Chapman and his family lived. On the ground floor were Chapman's office and the casket showroom. The viewing rooms were straight ahead as you came in. These were hushed and somber, reeking of floral air freshener. The basement was where the real work went on, out of sight of the public. Down there were white-tiled rooms with floor drains and metal embalming tables, and racks filled with disturbing-looking implements.

Cicadas shrilled in the trees as the Trapnells pulled up in Blanton's Rolls-Royce shortly before 10 the next morning. Trainor was driving, having insisted it was a good idea to drive the vintage Rolls every now and then in order to, as he put it, "keep the belts and hoses limber, and prevent the oil from gumming up." Trainor knew practically nothing about cars, but he'd heard this advice somewhere, and it stuck in his mind.

Noticing a black and white patrol car parked in the driveway, he joked, "Hey, look! The police are here. You think somebody got murdered?"

"I doubt it. They probably had a report of vandalism at one of the cemeteries or something," Aimee said. She waited for Benjamin to get out and go around to her door and open it for her.

Benjamin was trying to stay in her good graces, and he did so with alacrity, racing around the car and holding the door open. The question of whether he'd be returning to the Institute was still up in the air. He was doing his best to convince his mother that he'd turned over a new leaf, permanently this time.

They went up the Astroturf-carpeted front steps and into the foyer, Marsh carrying Blanton's funeral suit in a zippered suit bag. To the right was Chapman's office. The door was open, and they could see him seated behind his desk, talking with Ewell Haskins, who occupied one of the maroon leather club chairs usually reserved for the bereaved. The deputy turned and gaped at them, consternation written across his broad face.

Chapman, a beefy man with handlebar moustaches who resembled a roadie for a rock band more than an undertaker, looked at the Trapnells in astonishment.

"How'd you hear about it so quick?" he asked.

"Bonnie Turner from Palmetto Gardens called me," Aimee replied.

Chapman looked puzzled. "How'd she know about it?"

"She was there when it happened," Aimee said.

Haskins stood up and took a step toward her. "She was there? She was a witness?"

Aimee didn't understand what he was so excited about. People died in assisted living facilities all the time, unless... She gasped. "Was he murdered?"

Chapman looked at Haskins, mutely imploring him for help.

"We can't say for sure at this point, but it looks that way," Haskins said, adjusting his duty belt with an air of official self-importance. "I'm deeply sorry for your loss."

"Murder? Who's want to murder Daddy? Now, I mean. Back in the day a lot of people would, but they're all dead now. I can't see anybody murderin' him now, unless it was one of those what d'ya call 'ems? Those nurses who kill patients on purpose," Trainor said.

"Angels of death," said Marsh. He hung the suit bag on a hook behind the door.

"I heard of those. That's screwed up," Benjamin said.

"Oh, gosh. Oh, golly," said Haskins. "Hecky darn. Y'all don't know, do you?" The deputy was a deacon in the First United Methodist Church. He never permitted foul language to pass his lips. "Gol-durn" was as close as he got to swearing. His broad-brimmed uniform hat was in his hand at his side. In his excitement, he put it on, thought better of it, and took it off again.

"Y'all think we're talkin' about Mr. Blanton, don't you?" he said.

"Oh, Christ," moaned Chapman. He looked desperately around the room, his eyes lighting on a box of tissues on a shelf. He went over and got it, placing it on the desk in front of an empty chair. Then he went to Aimee and gently took her by the arm. "Have a seat, Miz Aimee," he said solicitously.

Haskins turned his hat awkwardly in his hands. "All y'all better sit down for this," he told Trainor and Marsh and Benjamin. "Oh, golly. This is a heck of a mess."

They sat down, feeling mystified. Had Blanton been murdered? How? Who would have done such a thing? Why hadn't Bonnie Turner said anything when she spoke to Aimee? She'd made it sound as if he'd succumbed to a stroke.

Chapman managed to get control of himself. Forming his features into an expression of professional sympathy he excused himself and went into the foyer. They could hear him hollering up the stairs to his wife. "Joelle, honey, we got some bereaved. Make a pot of tea and put some of them sugar cookies on a tray."

"Be right back," he said, sticking his head into the office. "My wife would normally bring the refreshments in, but she ain't fit to be seen. She's doing something to her face, defoliating it, I think she said. She can't wash it off 'til it's done."

He left to collect the refreshments. The Trapnells turned to Haskins, who was pretending to be engrossed in the books on the bookshelf. They had titles like *Beautiful Verses of Condolence* and *Ten Steps to Delivering the Perfect Eulogy*. There was one intended for children called *Grandpa's Gone Camping with Jesus*.

"Deputy, what's going on? Did someone kill my father?" Marsh asked.

Haskins took a long time to reply. "No," he said finally.

"But you said it looked that way," Marsh said.

"I was gonna go to your place and tell Miz Aimee, her bein' the next of kin. Y'all took me by surprise, comin' here like this," Haskins said sullenly.

"Daddy ain't been murdered? That's good. When somebody's murdered it sort of puts a black mark against their name. Daddy would hate that," Trainor said.

"Hold on! You said I'm the next of kin. Marsh and Trainor would be next of kin too," Aimee said, remembering to add, "and Karen. They're Daddy's children the same as me, so why did you say you were going to tell me? Why not all of us?"

Trainor clapped a hairy hand over his mouth, a terrible idea having crossed his mind. "It's 'cause Daddy wasn't really our daddy, Marsh's and mine. Is that it? 'Cause he was just Aimee's daddy?" he asked the deputy, his eyes wide. "Was he Karen's daddy, too, or just Aimee's? How'd you find out? Did you do DNA, like on Maury Povich?"

He turned to Marsh. "I always suspected you weren't my real brother, 'cause you're so short, but I never thought Daddy wasn't my real daddy. Does this mean I don't inherit nothin'? Holy shit!"

Just then Chapman returned carrying a tray with a teapot, cups, milk, and sugar on it, as well as a plate of cookies decorated with pink sugar sprinkles. He put the tray on the desk and removed a stack of paper napkins from a drawer in his desk. The napkins were imprinted with CHAPMAN'S HOME FOR FUNERALS. WHERE YOUR LOVED ONE ALWAYS COMES FIRST.

"Here we are, nice tea and cookies for everyone," he said cheerfully.

Benjamin took a sugar cookie and ate it in two bites. He took another, his brows drawn together as he tried to figure something out. "If somebody's been murdered and it's not Grandpa, and the deputy was going to tell Mom because she's the next of kin, that means..." He stopped, realizing what it meant.

"I don't get it," said Aimee, accepting a cup of tea from Chapman. "Somebody's been murdered? Cobbs hasn't had a murder in years. It's not like Atlanta. People get murdered there all the time."

"Atlanta's a fine city, perhaps the finest in the South, but it has its disadvantages, murder being one of them," Haskins agreed. "The last murder we had in Cobbs was on Super Bowl Sunday in 1992. Hart McGraw shot Billy Bob Applegate over a two-dollar bet. Hart McGraw was trash; all the McGraws were, but then so was Applegate and all of his kin. Just trashy, trashy people, every last one of them."

"Franz-Albert," Marsh said quietly.

He looked at Haskins. "Am I right?"

"I'm afraid so," the deputy replied. "I'm terribly sorry for your loss, Miz Aimee. So's the sheriff, and deputy Gorman, and Shirlene the dispatcher. We're all just tore up over this."

"Tissue?" asked Chapman, holding the box of tissues out to Aimee.

She shook her head, trying to come to terms with the sudden news that she was a widow. "No, that's all right. Tell me what happened, please. I had no idea Franz-Albert was here. I was in Italy. I got back yesterday. What was he doing here?"

"We still don't have all the answers, but I'll tell you what I can. It's kind of weird," Haskins said, relieved that Aimee was taking the news of her husband's death so well.

"I wouldn't expect anything less, not where Franz-Albert is involved," Aimee said. "Please, go on."

CHAPTER 31 – WHAT PEEWEE PELLETIER FOUND

Earlier that morning a man called Pewee Pelletier drove a pickup truck through a gap in the tall privet hedge in front of White Oaks. A discrete metal sign, white letters on a forest green background, declared it to be the service entrance to the estate.

The truck's tires crunched on the bluestone gravel roadbed as Pewee drove past the kitchen wing, past the greenhouses and the water cascade, water burbling over its stone steps, and down beyond the old slave graveyard. He parked beside the white granite mausoleum. TRAPNELL was carved in lichen-encrusted block letters in the triangular pediment above the door.

It's only seven-fifteen, and already it's hot as a crotch, Peewee thought, squinting at the white disc that was the sun as it blazed mercilessly above the tangle of trees that marked the beginning of the swamp. He wanted to finish the day's work early and go fishing. He'd sweep out the mausoleum and get it looking shipshape for Blanton Trapnell's big send-off. Then he'd swing by Holy Redeemer and White Knoll cemeteries and cut the grass before knocking off for the day. With any luck, he'd be on the lake in his bass boat by noon, along with a cold six-pack and a container of minnows from Buzzy's. Perhaps he'd get Gordon Buzzy to sell him a bottle of Old Rocking Chair. He bit into the egg salad sandwich his wife had made for him.

Chewing egg salad on white bread liberally smeared with mayonnaise he looked at the mausoleum and snorted in contempt. The damn thing probably cost more than his house. *Rich people*, he thought resentfully. At least rich people died, just like everybody else. Blanton Trapnell wouldn't be driving his Rolls-Royce through town anymore, not deigning to wave at Pewee when Peewee drove past going the other way in his truck.

Peewee always waved when he encountered other drivers. It was the neighborly thing to do, but Blanton Trapnell thought he was too good to acknowledge people like Peewee who weren't born with a silver spoon in their mouth. Blanton Trapnell wasn't neighborly. Now he was dead and good riddance. Let's see what Saint Peter would have to say about his lack of neighborliness when he showed up at the Pearly Gates. Peewee bit into the dill pickle his wife had packed along with the sandwich. Pickle juice ran down through the stubble on his chin as he smiled, thinking of Old Man Trapnell being denied admission to Heaven and instead being cast, shrieking, into a lake of fire.

He crumpled the pieces of wax paper the sandwich and the pickle had been wrapped in and stuck them in the hip pocket of his green Carhartt work pants. Then he took the key hanging from a cardboard tag marked 'Trapnell' that Chapman had given him and went to unlock the mausoleum door.

Leaving the bronze door open to let it air out inside, Peewee got a push broom and a pry bar out of the truck. He carried them into the cool interior of the mausoleum and sniffed cautiously. It smelled musty, like closed-up spaces always did. There was also the unmistakable scent of decomposition.

The decomp odor wasn't coming from any of the corpses in the crypts. Those were embalmed and would be as dry as old leather. It was something freshly dead, most likely a possum or a raccoon had crawled through the ventilation shaft on the roof. Pewee figured he'd find whatever it was lying in the shadows, paws-up. He drew on a pair of rubber work gloves and patted the black plastic trash bag tucked in his belt. Ms. Possum or Mr. Raccoon would be going into the bag. He just hoped they weren't too gooshy.

A stained glass window in the rear wall threw splashes of red, blue, and green over the stone floor. The window's subject was utterly inexplicable to Peewee, not Jesus or some saint but three naked men being attacked by huge snakes. He stared at it, trying to recall which Bible story it illustrated. There were several involving animals. There was Daniel in the lions' den, and Jonah and the whale, and the one about a talking donkey that got pissed off when its owner kept hitting it with a stick, but he couldn't think of anything involving snakes, other than the Garden of Eden thing.

"Rich people," he muttered, shaking his head.

He leaned the broom against the wall, intending to sweep the floor before he locked up.

The double crypt where Blanton Trapnell's coffin would go was on the left side, down near the snake window. Trapnell's second wife was in there, and he'd be going in next to her. The late Mrs. Trapnell had been a terror. Peewee wouldn't want to wait for the last trumpet to blow while lying beside a bitch like Deirdre Trapnell. Fortunately, he wouldn't have to. He'd be buried out at Holy Redeemer with his wife and his mama and daddy and the rest of his family. The Trapnells could keep their old mausoleum with its bizarre naked-men-and-snakes window, thank you very much.

Pewee was going to use the pry bar to remove the granite slab that was known in the funeral trade as a shutter from the front of the double crypt. It was inscribed with Blanton's name and date of birth, as well as his wife's name and her dates of birth and death. A stonecutter would add Blanton's final date. It would go back in place and be sealed after his bronze casket went in.

The casket was a model called the Chancellor, made by the Batesville Casket Company. It cost $25,000. It had a variety of high-end features, including a rounded glass seal, bronze swing-bar handles, fully adjustable inner bed, with head and foot velvet pillow, with a matching velvet blanket and a hidden locking mechanism.

Blanton's purchase of the most expensive casket from among those on display in Chapman's showroom had been a red letter day for Lycott and Joelle Chapman and their two children. The family celebrated by taking a trip to Jekyll Island, where they'd gone to a water park.

Peewee walked toward the crypt, pausing to kick at a drift of leaves that must have blown in under the door. As he kicked the leaves, scattering them, his work boot came in contact with something. He looked down to see what it was and found it was a foot clad in a narrow, polished black shoe.

The pry bar hit the stone floor with a clatter as Pewee turned tail and ran.

"Peewee ain't exactly the nervous sort, seein' as how he's a gravedigger as well as helpin' out here at the funeral home, but he didn't expect to find a body. It's one thing when you're expectin' to see a body; it's another when you come upon one unprepared. The medical examiner figured he'd been dead about forty-eight hours," Haskins told the Trapnells.

Aimee sipped tea and reflected on how life was strange. In the past forty-eight hours she'd shot and killed a man, been present when her brother killed two men in a shootout, confessed to killing her stepsister, learned that her father had died, and now here she was, finding out that her husband had been murdered.

"I can't understand what Franz-Albert was doing in the mausoleum. He didn't tell me he was coming to Cobbs. He's only been here once before, shortly after we were married. It doesn't make sense," Aimee told Chapman.

Franz-Albert hadn't liked Cobbs any better than he'd liked New York City. In his opinion, both places were horrible, just in different ways.

"I recall when he was here," Chapman said. "It's not often we get a visit from a prince."

Chapman had met Aimee and Franz-Albert coming out of the Publix supermarket as he was going in. Franz-Albert had struck Chapman as stuck-up. He'd surveyed the funeral director with his lip curled, as if Chapman were something unsavory he'd discovered clinging to the sole of his shoe.

"He's not a prince; he's a margrave," Aimee said. Then she corrected herself. "Was, I mean. He was a margrave."

"And what an honor it is to be one," Haskins said, having no idea what that entailed. Getting down to business, he took a notebook and a pen from his uniform shirt pocket. He flipped the notebook open to a blank page and asked, "You and your husband didn't live together, is that correct, Miz Aimee? I ain't bein' nosy; I need it for the report."

"Sometimes we did," Aimee said, feeling defensive. The citizens of Cobbs had old-fashioned values, one of which was that married couples should reside under the same roof. "Franz-Albert liked to stay home in Germany. I travel a lot for work. He understood."

"Of course he did," Chapman said soothingly. Privately he thought it was damn strange.

"When's the last time you heard from him?" Haskins asked, busily writing.

"I don't know, exactly. I guess it was two days ago. Like I said, I was in Italy, and he called to see how I was," she said.

"Just a casual conversation? He didn't indicate that anything was wrong? Or mention anything about coming to Cobbs?"

"That's right."

"And how come you were in Italy?" Haskins asked, writing.

"I was on vacation, with my brothers and one of their friends, and my son Benjamin."

Then she had a thought. "Is Franz-Albert downstairs?"

"No, the medical examiner took him away. He'll be here later though, don't you worry," Chapman said, adding, "Your daddy's downstairs. He's coming along nicely."

"I took some photos at the mausoleum. Forensic evidence," Haskins said importantly. "Didn't seem like there was a disturbance. Nothin' knocked over or messed up, just the victim lyin' on the floor, stabbed through the heart."

Aimee stared at him in horror, picturing Franz-Albert stabbed through the heart. Overhead a ceiling fan creaked as it slowly turned.

CHAPTER 32 – THE GOLDEN WEST

Their next stop was Beau Tetley's office, several blocks away. The main street in Cobbs was called Trapnell Avenue, named in honor of the town's founder, Ezekiel Trapnell, a fur trapper who signed his name with an X, being unable to read or write. His eldest son was the man who built White Oaks.

As they drove along, they saw Ash Gaynor, owner of the shooting range, coming out of the launderette. Edith Felcher, the town librarian, was watering the flowers in front of the library. Both of them waved at the Rolls. The Trapnells waved back.

"It's going to be all over town about Franz-Albert, if it's not already," Trainor said.

"So what?" Aimee said. "It's not our fault."

"It's my fault," Benjamin said. Ever since they'd gotten in the car, he'd been silent, opening and closing the ashtray in the burled oak panel in the center of the rear compartment, robot-like. Aimee put her hand over his.

"Quit that. It's not your fault," she said.

He turned to her, his face set. "It *is* my fault, Mom. If I hadn't stolen the sigul Franz-Albert wouldn't have been trying to get it back, and he wouldn't have gotten killed. It's all about the sigul. I know it is. Those two guys in Italy, Uncle Marsh's friend, and now Franz-Albert. They're all dead because of something I did."

"Not Daddy, though. He died of natural causes. You didn't kill *him*," Trainor said, trying to be helpful.

"How do you know? Maybe Beau Tetley murdered him with some kind of undetectable poison that made it seem like he had a stroke?" Benjamin said.

Aimee took off her sunglasses and put them in her Judith Lieber clutch bag. She was dressed more conservatively than usual, in a calf-length black dress and opaque black hose, having thought she was going to the funeral home to help make her father's final arrangements. Little did she suspect when she got dressed that morning that she was a widow. She wasn't particularly upset by her husband's death, although given the choice she'd rather he'd died elsewhere. His being murdered in Cobbs looked bad. To the town's way of thinking there was something unseemly about being a murder victim.

"You're letting your imagination run away with you. I don't see how Beau Tetley could get ahold of an undetectable poison," she told her son.

"All adolescents are drama queens. They think everything's about them. That way they can feel sorry for themselves when life isn't one big party, with themselves as the center of attention of an adoring crowd," Marsh said. He twisted around in the front seat and gave his nephew a patronizing smile.

Benjamin scowled. "Cram it, Uncle Marsh. I've had enough of your tough love bullshit."

"Somebody's grumpy," Marsh said, not at all put out. "Here's Tetley's office. Let's go in and see if we can get him to shed some light on things."

The lawyer's office occupied the ground floor of a wood-frame building that had originally been a firehouse before the new firehouse went up on the outskirts of town. Upstairs, where the firemen used to bed down on cots, was now a dentist's office. The sharp scent of antiseptic and the ominous buzzing of a dental drill hit the visitors as soon as they walked in the door.

Alison Fountain, Tetley's paralegal, was putting files into a cardboard box. She straightened up and blinked at them over her half-glasses. Brushing a stray lock of iron-grey hair off of her forehead she said, "I'm so sorry to hear about your daddy's passing. This town won't be the same without him. Mr. Blanton *was* Cobbs. I was saying that earlier to Jimmy Peaks, over at the post office. I said, Jimmy, Mr. Blanton personified this town. He *was* Cobbs, in the exact same way that Winston Churchill was England."

"Thank you, Alison," Marsh said. "Is Beau Tetley around?" He looked toward the inner office. The door was open. It had been cleaned out. The bookshelves were empty of their rows of law books. Tetley's normally cluttered desk was bare.

"Mr. Tetley has retired. The practice is being taken over by a young lawyer." Alison lowered her voice, "It's a female lawyer, not that there's anything wrong with that, but it'll take some getting used to. She asked me to stay on, and I said I would. We'll see how it goes."

This was the second retirement they'd heard of since they'd returned from Italy. First Hillman Parks and now Beau Tetley.

"He retired? Kind of sudden, wasn't it? We were hopin' to talk to him about Daddy's will. He's gonna be at the readin' of the will, ain't he?" Trainor asked.

Alison placed a stack of files in a box and pushed her glasses higher on her nose. She felt a gratifying sense of professional superiority over these laypersons. "That only happens in books and movies. It's a plot device to get all the heirs gathered in one place so they can learn some kind of shocking development."

"Like a fortune goin' to a bunch of owls," Trainor said, thinking of what had happened to his friend, Frost Gwinnette.

"It could be something like that, I suppose," Alison agreed. "Mr. Tetley's taking a trip out West. He's going to visit our national parks."

"He's not going to be at Daddy's funeral? I would have thought he'd want to be there," Aimee asked.

Alison looked embarrassed. "He already left. He closed up his house and hitched his big old Lincoln to one of those cute teardrop-shaped trailers. A turquoise and white one, retro-styled, if you know what I mean. He was in kind of a hurry. It struck me as being unlike him. Mr. Tetley was always what I'd call a deliberate man, but I suppose he didn't want to waste any time getting started on this new chapter in his life."

They thanked her and left, after telling her they hoped to see her at the open house at White Oaks following the funeral. It was scheduled to take place in ten days. It would be almost as big a blowout as the ninetieth birthday party that hadn't happened due to Blanton suffering a stroke as the result of strangling the unfortunate Novak. Garrison Wickwire had been summoned from his Los Angeles base of operations and told to spare no expense with the preparations. He was eagerly anticipating how he'd go about making it a somber, yet splendid occasion, packed with famous faces from the world of business, politics, and the arts.

As they walked to the car, Marsh said, "Something is rotten in the state of Denmark."

Trainor nodded wisely. "If you mean that smell, it's comin' from the fertilizer factory. It always stinks like that this time of day, when they get to a certain point in the fertilizer manufacturin' process. Daddy took me through there once when I was at St. Botolph's to show me where I'd be workin' if I didn't bring my grades up." St. Botolph's was the name of the prep school that Trainor had attended.

Benjamin guffawed. Seeing his mother standing next to the car, impatiently tapping her foot, he ran to open the door for her.

"I was referring to a line in *Hamlet,* a play by William Shakespeare," Marsh told Trainor.

"I know that. Jeez, give me some credit. I ain't a total idiot," Trainor replied.

"What I meant is something strikes me as suspicious about Hillman and Tetley both suddenly retiring. Both of them are going out West, from what Louetta and Alison said. I wish we knew where," Marsh said.

"That's easy. Yellowstone," Trainor replied. "At least Tetley's goin' there. I don't know about Hillman." Pulling the car away from the curb he spoke over his shoulder to Aimee. "We gotta get another butler. It can't be that hard to find somebody to open the front door and who knows what kind of wine goes with whatever we're havin' for dinner."

"There's more to it than that, but go back to what you said about Tetley. You don't know he's going to Yellowstone. Alison said he was going to visit national parks. That could be the Grand Canyon, or Yosemite, or Carlsbad Caverns, or any of the other ones out West," Aimee said. She owned several snakes from that part of the country, including a Western Diamondback that had been captured in Arizona. Western Diamondbacks had the distinction of being responsible for the greatest number of snakebite fatalities in northern Mexico.

Aimee missed her Western Diamondback, as well as the rest of her snakes. She hoped they could get this wrapped up, find the sigul, and get her father entombed so she could go back to New York and rejoin her beloved reptiles. Although now that Franz-Albert was dead, even if they found the sigul what were they supposed to do with it? Should they contact the secret society and ask them? How did one go about contacting a secret society? Aimee sighed, thinking with longing of the tranquility of her Snake House, the only sound the hum of air quietly blowing through the ventilation ducts as the snakes silently moved through the miniature worlds of their habitats.

"There may be lots of national parks out West, but there's only one Yellowstone," Trainor said smugly. He turned the car in the direction of Jackson Avenue, where Hillman lived. "There was a poster on the wall in his office of that geyser, Old Faithful. That's in Yellowstone. I know because the old couple with the RV that Marsh and me met at Walmart went there. They showed us pictures."

"That's possible," Marsh admitted, regarding Trainor with unaccustomed respect. "Let's see what Hillman has to say."

"I was thinking," said Benjamin. "That deputy said Franz-Albert was stabbed, but the killer didn't leave the knife behind. What if it was an ice knife?"

"An ice knife?" Aimee echoed.

"A knife made out of ice. One that melts, leaving no trace. I saw it in a movie once," Benjamin said.

"This is Cobbs, boy. It's hotter than the hinges of Hell. Ain't nobody runnin' around with an ice knife. It would melt in, like, two seconds," Trainor told him. He parked in front of Hillman and Bestie's small cedar-shingled home.

"Hillman's car's here," he said, seeing the Corolla parked in the carport. "That's a good sign. It means he ain't left yet. Maybe we can convince him to come back to work."

But Hillman wasn't there. His granddaughter, Kortney McNamara, said he'd gone on a road trip with Beau Tetley.

"He needed a break from takin' care of Nana Bestie," she told them in a low voice. Her grandmother, tiny and wizened as a dried-out bean, was drowsing in a reclining chair in the living room, facing an eighty-inch flat-screen TV. On the screen a preacher in a light blue leisure suit stalked back and forth, a cordless microphone in his hand, ranting about the End Times.

"I'm sorry to hear about your daddy passing. Paw-Paw Hilly took it hard," Kortney told the Trapnells, meaning her grandfather, Hillman.

"Thank you, Kortney, I don't believe you've met my son Benjamin. Benjamin, this is Ms. McNamara, Hillman and Bestie's granddaughter. She teaches at the high school."

"Algebra, geometry, and calculus," Kortney said, looking Benjamin over. "My oldest grandson's about your age. He's away at football camp. You like football?"

"No," said Benjamin.

"Benjamin lives in Germany most of the time," Aimee said. "They don't have American football there."

"Soccer, then," Kortney said, nodding, her braids swinging. She was used to being around young people and had an easy way with them. "You must be a soccer fan."

"No. I don't like sports," Benjamin said.

"Don't like sports? I never heard of such a thing! A boy who don't like sports!" Kortney said in mock surprise. She laughed to show that she was joking. "That's fine. There's no law sayin' you have to like sports."

"Benjamin has other interests," Marsh said, earning him a caustic look from his nephew.

Bestie woke up and saw she had visitors. "Trapnells!" she crowed delightedly. She fumbled at her mouth, checking to make sure her dentures were in. Then she hoisted herself out of her recliner and tottered toward them, her arms open wide. "Let me hug your neck," she told Aimee, hugging her. She did the same to Marsh and Trainor before turning to Benjamin. "Don't tell me this is little Ben!" she said delightedly. "Look how big you is! Give old Bestie a hug."

Benjamin hugged her, taking care not to squeeze her too hard.

"I'm sorry to hear your daddy passed," Bestie told them. "Now y'all are orphans. No mama and no daddy. That's tragic."

"I'm a widow, too," Aimee said, wanting to get it over with. "My husband recently passed away."

Bestie clung to her. "A widow and an orphan! You poor child! But be comforted! The End Times is approachin'. The righteous is goin' to glory! No more pain and sorrow. Joy everlastin'! We shall be gathered unto the bosom of Abraham, yes, yes." The old lady clasped her hands together and looked up at the ceiling, as if expecting to see Abraham up there, looking down and beckoning her to come on up and join him.

Kortney guided her gently back to the recliner. On the TV, the televangelist was bellowing about how he knew for a fact that certain Democratic politicians were possessed by demons. "That's right Nana. Sit down and watch your show."

Bestie sat down, and Kortney arranged a crocheted afghan over her lap. "Dick Van Dyke came by to see me today," Bestie told her visitors.

"He was on TV, sellin' life insurance," Kortney told them.

Bestie closed her eyes. "Hill and Mr. Beau is doin' the Lord's work. Goin' on a journey through the desert, like Moses and the Israelites."

"That's right, Nana," Kortney murmured, tucking the afghan around her.

"They bringin' the End Times, with the sigul of Jörmungandr. They got a powerful weapon that'll rain fire and ash down upon the wicked earth," she muttered, her voice trailing off into mumbles before becoming snores.

"What?" said Marsh.

"Shush. Come on in the kitchen," Kortney whispered.

They followed her into the kitchen, startled by what the old lady had said. Had they heard correctly? Had she really mentioned the sigul of Jörmungandr?

Kortney went to the refrigerator and took out a pitcher of sweet tea. Dropping ice cubes into glasses, she said, "Nana's got dementia. She gets crazy ideas. She told my sister Kortnessa that all the land around here belongs to her and Paw-Paw Hilly. She said she had to go to town hall right away and register the deed. Kortnessa said she'd take care of it. That satisfied her. She gets agitated if you try and reason with her. It's better if you play along."

"Has she talked about the sigul of Jörmungandr before?" Trainor asked.

"Oh, yeah. She says that a lot. She must have heard it on one of her religious shows. She says Paw-Paw Hilly and Mr. Beau got the sigul of Jörmungandr and they're gonna bring about the End Times. I say, 'That's right, Nana. They got that ol' sigul, and they're gonna put things right and send us all to be with the Lord.' That makes her happy." Kortney said, passing around glasses of sweet tea in which ice cubes tinkled.

The Trapnells stared at each other in amazement.

CHAPTER 33 – GEOLOGY

Back at White Oaks, Marsh, Trainor, Aimee, and Benjamin gathered in the gentlemen's parlor. Wickwire had arrived and been pressed into service as a temporary butler. He wasn't happy about it, thinking it beneath it. Aimee assured him that as soon as he found them a permanent butler, he could go back to planning Blanton's funeral full-time.

"You must meet a lot of butlers in your line of work. Surely you know one who wants to change jobs," she told him. Wickwire said he'd see what he could do. South Georgia didn't have much to recommend it in the way of entertainment. He couldn't imagine anyone wanting to uproot themselves from Malibu or the Hamptons to move there.

"We'll double whatever salary they're currently getting," Aimee said, causing him to brighten. Old Man Trapnell had been worth billions. If he found them a butler they liked, and if he did a good job with the post-funeral gathering, he could expect a generous bonus. The thought made him glow with anticipation as he joined the Trapnell siblings in the gentlemen's parlor for a post-dinner drink.

"I'll make some calls. You'll want them to sign a nondisclosure agreement, of course," he said. That was traditional with his high-profile clients. Everyone who worked for them, from the nanny to the dog walker, had to sign agreements committing them to secrecy about what they'd seen and heard during their employment.

"That won't be necessary. We'll simply have them killed if they talk about anything that goes on around here," Marsh said.

"What?" Wickwire gasped. His hand trembled, causing sherry to spill onto the antique silk Kashan carpet.

"Look what you've done. You've stained the carpet. Now I'm going to have to kill you," Marsh said. He locked eyes with the terrified party planner and unbuttoned his suit jacket, revealing the gun in the shoulder holster strapped to his side.

Wickwire gave a despairing high-pitched shriek, like a mouse caught in a trap.

Marsh laughed and cuffed him lightly on the shoulder, reaching up to do so since Wickwire towered over him. "I'm joking, Garrison, relax. Club soda will take that out. Go get one of the maids and ask her to do it, okay? They're probably in the sunroom, goofing off, or in the kitchen watching TV. We must have half a dozen women who are supposed to be cleaning this house, but I swear they spend most of their time gossiping and watching TV."

Wickwire scurried from the room.

"That was mean, Uncle Marsh," Benjamin told him.

Marsh had the grace to look chagrined. "I suppose it was. I'll make it up to him."

Trainor observed, "That was like somethin' Daddy woulda done."

"Great. Now I feel even worse," Marsh said. "Sometimes I think I inherited Daddy's mean streak, along with his ambidextrousness. Let's go in his office. Wickwire's going to be bringing one of the maids in here to clean the carpet. I've got something to tell you in private."

They followed him down the hall to their father's office, Seamus tagging along. He'd taken a liking to Benjamin and gazed adoringly up at him, hoping for another game of fetch the tennis ball. They went into the office and closed the door. Marsh seated himself behind the desk.

"Okay, here's the deal," he said, leaning back in the desk chair. "As you may have guessed, due to the nature of my business I'm occasionally required to, how should I put it? Do things that could be thought of as somewhat..."

"Illegal," Aimee said impatiently. "We know that. You're an arms dealer. You break the law all the time. What surprises me is that you haven't been locked up yet."

Marsh stirred the Montblanc pens in the pewter mug on the desk, not looking at her. "Then you must be aware that occasionally I'm privy to information that can't be obtained through normal channels. About a year ago I started hearing rumors coming out of the white supremacist community. I brushed them off, thinking it was more of their usual nonsense, but then Franz-Albert came to you demanding the return of an ancient artifact based on Norse mythology that he claimed has the power to destroy the world. Then Johnny got involved. Johnny and I had been through thick and thin together. I trusted him with my life. I know he felt the same about me, and yet somehow somebody got to him and turned him. A man like Johnny doesn't turn, not unless he's got no other options."

He studied them, his jaw set. "The bodies are piling up, Johnny and Smith and Jones and Franz-Albert. It's always bad when the bodies start piling up. Whoever stabbed Franz-Albert had to be somebody he trusted. It was somebody with access to a key to the mausoleum, somebody who could walk up to him without making him suspicious and stab him in the heart. I can only think of one person who fits that description."

"Not me," Aimee said hastily. "I was with you. I didn't even know he was here."

"No, not you," Marsh agreed, adding, "Although you're fully capable of stabbing someone through the heart."

"Hey!" said Benjamin.

Marsh raised a hand, silencing him. "I was thinking of Beau Tetley."

"That little old lawyer? You sure?" asked Trainor.

"Beneath that white linen ice cream suit he wears he's stronger than he looks. I've seen him on the tennis court. He's wiry and fast. He could have gained Franz-Albert's confidence, perhaps by telling him, he had the sigul and inviting him into the mausoleum to claim it. Once there, one quick upward thrust between the ribs would be all it would take."

"How'd he get in? The door to the mausoleum's kept locked, and the only keys are that one, there, and the one Chapman has," Trainor said, pointing to a pegboard on the wall holding a collection of keys to various doors around White Oaks. Among them was an ornate brass key. It had a cardboard tag on which 'Mausoleum' was written in spidery copperplate.

Marsh laced his hands behind his head. "This isn't Fort Knox. Anybody can walk in. There's no security system. That's something I always thought should be remedied, but Daddy insisted it wasn't necessary. I think he secretly hoped someone would attempt to rob the place so he could shoot them." He smiled reminiscently, thinking of the cantankerous old man. "Someone could have taken the key without anyone noticing, stabbed

Franz-Albert, and put it back. Conversely, we don't know for a fact that those were the only two keys. There could be others that we aren't aware of."

"So what did you want to tell us?" Benjamin asked.

"I was getting to that. There's something peculiar about Hillman and Beau Tetley going off on a road trip together. I don't recall them being close, and yet as soon as Daddy died they quit their jobs and left town, driving west in Tetley's land yacht of a Lincoln, towing a trailer. Bestie mentioned the sigul. She talked about Hillman and Tetley going out West to bring about the end of the world. What if that's exactly what they plan on doing?"

Aimee couldn't believe her ears. "How? With the sigul? Trainor and Peach had it. It doesn't do anything."

Marsh regarded her, his eyes grim. "The sigul might not do anything, but a suitcase bomb would."

"What's that?" Trainor asked.

"A thermonuclear bomb small enough to fit inside a casing resembling a suitcase, one that can be detonated by a single operator. There are supposed to be quite a few around. Some one hundred of them allegedly went missing after the dissolution of the former Soviet Union. I suspect Beau Tetley has one in his cute little retro trailer."

"Where would he get something like that?" Benjamin asked.

"You'd be surprised what kinds of things are available for the right price. If someone were determined enough and had enough money, they could get a suitcase nuke. Like I said, there's a rumor going around that someone has one and they're about to set it off," Marsh replied.

"Even if they had one and they set it off it still wouldn't bring about the end of the world. There've been a lot of nuclear explosions since Hiroshima, and the world hasn't blown up," Aimee said.

"The world wouldn't have to blow up. Bringing about an end to life on Earth would take some time, but the process could begin if a nuclear bomb were detonated in just the right place, such as a volcano," Marsh said.

"Like in Hawaii," Trainor said excitedly. "Me and Palmer saw one when we were there on our honeymoon. It had smoke comin' out of it."

"Closer than Hawaii. Yellowstone National Park has a volcano, and not just any volcano, a super volcano, one of about twenty known to exist. If the poster of Old Faithful Tetley's wall means what I think it does, that's where he and Hillman are headed."

"How would dropping a nuclear bomb in a volcano make the world end?" Benjamin asked.

"It involves geology," Marsh replied.

He explained that the last full-scale eruption of the Yellowstone volcano happened about 630,000 years ago. It produced a spectacular explosion that ejected approximately 240 cubic miles of rock, dust, and volcanic ash into the sky, creating the Yellowstone caldera, the massive volcanic depression that lies beneath the national park. The caldera is what causes Yellowstone's geothermal features like its spectacular geysers, among them Old Faithful, and Steamboat, the world's tallest active geyser.

The geothermal activity there is constant and ever-changing. The bubbling geysers, hot springs, and mud pots are evidence of constant churning below the earth's surface. Not long before, in September 2018, Ear Spring, a thermal spring on Yellowstone's Geyser Hill, had suddenly awakened from years of dormancy, blasting a jet of water and steam thirty feet high.

"The last full-scale eruption of the Yellowstone supervolcano is thought to have been powerful enough to have killed every living thing within hundreds of miles. The clouds of ash would have blocked out the sun for months," Marsh said. "Some scientists even believe it was what caused the dinosaurs to become extinct. The last known supervolcano eruption happened in Indonesia about 75,000 years ago. It's known as the Toba Catastrophe. It pumped some eight million tons of hydrogen sulphide gas into the atmosphere, producing a global winter."

"Global winter?" Trainor said. "Winter all over the world?"

"Ten years of it, as far as anyone can tell. There was a massive migration out of Africa around that time. According to the genetic bottleneck theory, a disastrous event took place then, accounting for a steep decline among the hominid population. Some scientists believe the disastrous event to have been the Toba Catastrophe. The Yellowstone volcano is far larger than the one that erupted in Sumatra, all those eons ago. The caldera sits on top of a pool of magma containing about sixty billion cubic miles of molten rock. Unlike common volcanos, which look like tall cones, super volcanos are a collapsed crust of rock covering hundreds of square miles. When they erupt they don't go off with a bang but by slowly sending magma and clouds of noxious fumes creeping across the landscape. If the Yellowstone volcano were to erupt, it would first render Wyoming uninhabitable, and then it would keep on going, eventually blanketing the North American continent under a thick coat of ash and lava. There'd be another global winter, one even longer than the decade-long one caused by the Toba Catastrophe."

Aimee, Trainor, and Benjamin took that in, stunned. Marsh went on, "That's if the volcano erupted on its own. Nuking it would make things worse. The resulting eruption would cause radiation to be dispersed far and wide in volcanic ash. Chances for the human race to survive would be practically nil."

"Ragnarök. Franz-Albert was talking about it when he came to see me in New York," Aimee said.

"That's what the white supremacists are calling it," Marsh said. "White supremacists are fond of Norse mythology, although I suspect they'd shit themselves if they ever came face to face with Odin. Rumor has it that between them and a renegade group of extremist Christian evangelicals who hope to bring about what they call the End Times or the Rapture they managed to raise enough money to buy a suitcase bomb. Rumor also has it that someone is planning to detonate it by dropping it into the Yellowstone caldera, somewhere where fault lines have been causing recent earthquake swarms."

"Earthquake swarms? What are those?" Trainor asked.

"There's significant seismic activity at Yellowstone, producing about twenty-five hundred small earthquakes a year, on average. Those are called swarms," Marsh said. "A geologist who works at the volcano observatory there informed me that the weakest point to punch through to the caldera and release the magma bottled up underneath would be at the northwest end of Yellowstone Lake. I suspect that's where Hillman and Tetley are headed."

"I can't believe our butler would do somethin' like that. I've known Hillman my whole life. I never once heard him say he wanted to destroy every living thing on Earth." Trainor scratched his beard. "Hillman was devoted to Daddy. Maybe Tetley lied to him. Maybe he thinks he's carryin' out Daddy's final wishes by helpin' Tetley with some kinda project, one that won't hurt nobody. Bestie mighta' got it mixed up with somethin' she heard on one of those religious shows where they talk about the End Times. What are we gonna to do about it? Shouldn't we call the cops?"

"The police are unequipped to deal with something like this. I propose we take care of it ourselves," Marsh said. "Who wants to go with me?"

CHAPTER 34 – HOW HARD CAN IT BE TO DEFUSE A NUCLEAR WEAPON?

"If it's okay with you, I'll sit this one out. Palmer's expectin' me back home," Trainor said, rising to his feet.

Marsh studied him expressionlessly. "What do you think your chances would be if an assassin comes after you when you're in Atlanta? You don't think Tetley and Hillman are acting alone, do you? There's the secret society of the sigul to consider. We don't know how many of them there are, or who they have working for them. Do you really want to risk encountering a pair like Smith and Jones when you're with your wife and daughter?"

"No," Trainor said. He sat back down again.

"I didn't think so," Marsh replied. "I phoned Peach and told him to go to ground at that combination trucking company and crime headquarters his mama runs. He'll be safe if he holes up there. You'll be safe if you're with me."

Marsh was the polar opposite of safety. Wherever he went gunplay and mayhem were sure to follow. That his siblings were aware of this was evident by their unhappy expressions.

"Couldn't Benjamin and I stay at the Dakota? They have excellent security there," Aimee said.

"It's not as good as they make it out to be. Beatles fans have managed to sneak into the service elevator, hoping to see where John Lennon lived. One of them even bumped into Yoko Ono. Tourists have gotten inside when the doorman was occupied with hailing a cab. The management tries to keep these things quiet, for obvious reasons. Security aside, I happen to know that the windows of your apartment are not made of bulletproof glass. Just for fun, I took a bead on you one time with a sniper rifle from an apartment in the Langham Building across 73rd Street. You were standing in your living room. I had a good view of you. It was a clear shot. Anyone wishing to kill you would have had no problem at all."

After an astonished silence Aimee said, "You know that's not normal, right? Brothers don't usually take aim at their sisters with sniper rifles."

"It was a theoretical exercise to answer a question that had been puzzling me about bullet trajectory from a certain angle among the canyons of Manhattan. There was nothing personal about it. You wouldn't have known about it if I hadn't told you," Marsh said.

"Most people don't spend their spare time thinking about bullet trajectories," Aimee said. She resolved to have bulletproof glass installed in all the windows in her apartment as soon as possible.

"Really? What do they think about? Boring things, I suppose, like taxes and popular music," Marsh said. "I can't even imagine how dull their lives must be."

"So how are we going to stop them?" asked Benjamin. He sat with one leg slung over his knee. His sneakered foot jiggled with excitement at the thought of the adventure ahead of them.

Marsh beamed at his nephew. "Look at you! You're happy. Never mind that the world will end if we don't succeed. It does my heart good to see you enjoying something that isn't a controlled dangerous substance. To answer your question, we're going to take them by surprise and disarm the bomb."

"Do you know how to do that?" Trainor asked.

"No, but how hard can it be? There's probably a YouTube tutorial on how to do it," Marsh said. He laughed at their startled expressions. "I'm joking! Of course, I know how, although I've never dealt with any of the Soviet-era ones that are small enough to fit in a suitcase. They're rumored to be a little tricky."

A timid tap came on the door. It was Wickwire, wanting them to know that the stain had been removed from the rug. "I put in a call to a butler who might be suitable. He's currently working in Washington D.C., at one of the embassies," he said.

"Tell him to come on down here. You and Louetta can show him where everything's at," Trainor said.

"You'll want to interview him. When would be a convenient time?"

"You can do it, you and Louetta. We're goin' on a trip," Trainor told him, standing up.

Wickwire couldn't believe he'd heard correctly. "You can't leave now. What about your father's funeral? There are arrangements to make. There's the guest list to go over. There are important decisions that must be made."

"That's why we hired you. You'll do fine," Aimee told him. "And just so you know, my husband was murdered in the mausoleum out back, below the formal gardens. If you see yellow police tape strung around out there or police walking around the grounds, that's why."

Wickwire stared at her, his mouth opening and closing soundlessly.

Chapter 35 – Marsh's Romance

The Yellowstone volcano is one of the most closely watched in the world. Among the scientists monitoring it was thirty-four-year-old Hannah Ryczak, Ph.D., a geologist with a degree from Harvard University.

Dr. Ryczak worked for the Volcano Hazards Program of the U.S. Geological Survey. It was one of eight organizations keeping track of volcanic activity in Montana, Wyoming, Colorado, Utah, New Mexico, and Arizona at the Yellowstone Volcano Observatory. Her specialty was volcanology, the study of the processes involved in the formation and eruptive activity of volcanoes.

It was the day after Marsh shared his suspicion of Tetley and Hillman being in possession of a thermonuclear weapon. The Trapnells hurriedly wrapped up their business in Cobbs, letting the sheriff know they had to go out of town for a few days, and asking him to keep them informed about any new leads in the investigation into Franz-Albert's death.

Palmer was irritated when Trainor phoned saying he wouldn't be returning home right away because something he referred to vaguely as "family business" had come up. She was mollified by his suggestion that she buy Jubilee the pony she'd been asking for.

"Get her a nice one, one that don't bite or kick. Get yourself somethin' too," he told her.

"Can I get one of those eternity rings like Chandler Woodbury's got?" she asked. Chandler Woodbury was the mother of one of Jubilee's first-grade classmates. Palmer and Chandler, while ostensibly friends, were engaged in a fierce campaign of one-upmanship.

"They got three diamonds in them, one each for yesterday, today, and tomorrow," Palmer said. "I was thinkin', since you and me are back together, it would make a perfect symbol of our undyin' love."

"Go on and get whatever you want," Trainor said carelessly, thinking of the inheritance money about to come his way.

"I love you, Boo Bear," Palmer told him, using her pet name for him. She smiled, thinking how her ring would be platinum instead of white gold, like Chandler's, and have larger diamonds in it than Chandler's.

"I love you, too, Chicken Legs," he replied, using his pet name for her.

Wickwire was left in charge at White Oaks, with Louetta as his second-in-command. Despite Marsh's attempts to make amends by going out of his way to be friendly, the party planner was jumpy around him. He was relieved when the Trapnells left on their mysterious trip. It seemed odd for them to be going on vacation when they'd just returned from one, and when they had not one but two funerals to arrange, but Wickwire had worked for enough of the ultra-wealthy to know there was no accounting for some of the things they did.

The Trapnells had concluded it would take their quarry almost four full days to reach Yellowstone, a distance of just over two thousand miles from Cobbs. Despite the fact that Tetley and Hillman had a head start of two days, they'd be slowed down by the trailer they were towing behind Tetley's ten-year-old Lincoln Continental. The two old men would encounter steep grades in the mountains, and twisting, narrow passes in the area of the Continental Divide, as well as the long, gradual climb out of the Snake River Plain. The Trapnells would avoid all that by flying. They'd be in place, waiting for them when they arrived. With the element of surprise on their side, it should be easy to catch Tetley and Hillman off guard and get the bomb away from them before the detonation sequence was initiated. Then they'd demand some answers.

Or so they hoped.

Hannah Ryczak picked them up at Jackson Hole Airport in her mud-splattered Range Rover. The airport was located in a valley at the base of the majestic Teton Range of the Rocky Mountains in Teton County, Wyoming. The jagged snow-capped mountains formed a magnificent backdrop behind the airport's rustic wood-beam terminal.

The sky was an intense, cloudless blue as Aimee, Marsh, Trainor, and Benjamin walked outside into the crisp mountain air. There was a clip-clopping of hooves, and they turned, expecting to see a cowboy on horseback. Instead, a bull elk with an enormous rack of antlers strolled casually past.

Aimee had been there before and was disappointed they wouldn't be staying at one of the five-star resorts in the town of Jackson that catered to the rich and famous. Town Square Park beckoned to her, with its four massive arches made of elk antlers gathered from the national elk refuge. The park was surrounded by wooden boardwalks leading to shops and art galleries, all of which she longed to explore. However, the historic Wort Hotel, with more than two thousand uncirculated 1921 Moran silver dollars from the Denver Mint inlaid into the black Formica of its two bars, would not be seeing her this time. The Trapnells would be staying with Dr. Ryczak about an hour's drive to the south, at her A-frame cabin located just outside the western gateway to Yellowstone Park.

"Thank you for your hospitality, Dr. Ryczak," Marsh said to the geologist, who greeted them with a firm handshake.

"It's my pleasure," she replied. She peered through horn-rimmed glasses at their pile of luggage.

"Most of those bags are my sister's. She's what you call a fashionista," Trainor told her.

"I'm sorry to hear about the loss of your husband," Hannah told Aimee, who looked leaner and more elegant than ever in a body-hugging, ankle-length black knit dress and a sheepskin-lined black leather jacket.

"Thank you. It came as quite a shock. We were devoted to each other. You could say we were true soulmates," Aimee replied, her lovely face assuming an expression of stoic grief.

"You're talkin' about Franz-Albert?" Trainor asked, surprised to hear their relationship described in those terms.

Aimee shot him an angry look. Trainor hurriedly began piling their luggage into the back of the Range Rover, assisted by Benjamin.

"Tell me, Dr. Ryczak, how is Pitchstone?" Marsh asked the geologist.

"He's very well, thank you for asking," she replied.

"Who's Pitchstone?" Aimee asked.

"My cat. He's black, with little flecks of white fur. When I got him he reminded me of pitchstone, a type of volcanic glass with white mineral deposits in it."

Aimee was puzzled. How did Marsh know about Dr. Ryczak's cat?

Marsh linked hands with the geologist. "I met Pitchstone shortly after I made Dr. Ryczak's acquaintance. He's a charming cat, attractive and intelligent, like his owner."

Hannah Ryczak blushed and tucked a loose strand of light brown hair into her French braid.

Aimee and Trainor exchanged surprised glances. They'd often speculated about Marsh's love life, concluding that he either didn't have one or he was mixed up with some person he preferred not to talk about, an international jewel thief, perhaps, or a murderer who'd been consigned to a hospital for the criminally insane. That their brother would be romantically involved with someone as prosaic as a geologist had never crossed their minds.

A Conestoga wagon pulled by a pair of long-eared brown mules was waiting for them when they arrived at Hannah's A-frame, having been held up by a herd of bison that took its time crossing the road. The wagon's white canvas top rippled in the wind blowing down from the mountains.

"Cool," breathed Benjamin looking up at it. "I played a video game about pioneers going on the Oregon Trail in wagons like this. I never knew they were so big,"

"There's plenty of room inside, for lots of things," Marsh replied enigmatically.

The driver climbed down from his seat. He carried a clipboard, which he presented to Hannah. "Equipment for the U.S. Geological Survey, sign here," he said, wiping his brow with a red bandana he pulled from the back pocket of his jeans. He pointed to where he wanted her to sign.

"We'll see to it that the mules are stabled and fed. I'll get back to you in a few days and let you know when you can come and get them, and the wagon," she told him.

"No problem. That one's Pat and that one's Mike," he said pointing to the mules tethered to a hitching rail made of galvanized pipe. "They're smarter than most people. They can pretty much take care of themselves. I'll be stayin' at Mammoth Hot Springs. Just give me a call when you're ready for me to get 'em," he said.

Marsh withdrew his silver money clip with the white jade cabochon from the inside pocket of his suit coat. He counted off five hundred-dollar bills, handing them to the driver. "For your trouble, sir. Thank you for entrusting us with your mules."

The man grinned, pocketing the money. "No trouble at all. This delivery gig is all right. It beats driving tourists around. I'll flag down one of the tour buses and hitch a ride with them. You folks have a nice day." He retrieved a duffle bag from the wagon, slung it over his shoulder, and headed off down the road.

"What are we going to do with a Conestoga wagon?" Aimee asked.

"We're going to have fun with it," Marsh replied. "Benjamin and 1 will drive it while 1 entertain him with stories about the Donner party. Then he can help me set up the geological equipment in the cartons in the back."

Benjamin looked dubious. "That doesn't sound like much fun."

Marsh winked. "Trust me. It will be."

CHAPTER 36 – BLOW-UP

Three days passed. They were beginning to wonder if they'd miscalculated and Hillman and Tetley weren't coming after all. Benjamin and Trainor had gone on a hike. Aimee and Marsh were sitting on the deck in front of Hannah's A-frame, the geologist having gone to the seismic station at the Norris Geyser Basin Museum to check on the equipment that recorded earthquake activity.

That was when a black Lincoln Continental towing a turquoise and white teardrop-shaped trailer drove up and Hillman got out.

"Afternoon, Miz Aimee, Mr. Marsh," he said, nodding cordially to them. He limped toward them, wheezing, his gnarled hands rubbing his lower back. "Feels good to be out of that car. Me and Mr. Tetley's been drivin' for days." He climbed the porch steps.

Marsh stood up. "Hillman, what do you think you're..."

That was as far as he got before Hillman pulled a gun from his waistband and shot him in the chest. Marsh was knocked backward by the impact. He fell face-down on the deck.

Hillman sighed regretfully. "Sorry 'bout that," he said to Aimee. "I always liked you and Mr. Marsh and Mr. Trainor. Miz Karen not so much. She was snotty, with her, 'Oooh, I can't eat that I'm a Buddhist.' Far as I'm concerned Buddhists can kiss my ass."

He stepped over Marsh's body and seated himself in one of the Adirondack chairs, holding the gun pointed at her.

"Your daddy and I were cousins. I guess you know that. We had the same granddaddy, Judge George Trapnell. The judge was a well-traveled man. He went over to Europe and met up with some fellows there who inducted him into their club."

"The sigul of Jörmungandr," Aimee said. She looked at Marsh. He lay motionless, his head twisted sharply to one side. Hillman had killed him.

The old man nodded. "That's the one. Old white Granddaddy George and them visited back and forth. He got some fellows from Cobbs to join up with the fellows from Europe. Beau Tetley's granddaddy was among them. They held their ceremonies upstairs in the Masonic Lodge, some of them bein' Masons. The idea was that when the time was right, they'd bring about the end of the world an' let it start over again from scratch."

"How were they going to do that? With the help of the spacemen?" Aimee asked. She wanted to keep Hillman talking. She hoped Hannah would come home, see the car and trailer and go for help.

The old man laughed. "There wasn't no spacemen. Wasn't no meteorite neither. That was a story they told the members that wasn't high enough up to be in on the real deal. The sigul was made by a craftsman your husband's ancestor found. He figured you needed to have a mysterious object that was rumored to have awesome powers if you're gonna start a secret society."

He rubbed his lower back with one hand, keeping the gun trained on her with the other. "Mr. Blanton was one of the higher-ups. He made them let me join too, seein' as how him and me were blood kin. They figured the way things was goin', with worse and worse wars and inventions like machine guns and dynamite, sooner or later there'd be somebody who invented something that could blow up the whole shebang, which is what happened. Scientists in Germany discovered nuclear fission in nineteen hundred and thirty-eight. Fission's how you make an A-bomb. It takes a combination of fission and fusion to make an H-bomb. Did you know that?"

"No." Aimee couldn't believe she was getting a science lecture from her former butler. She looked in the direction of the road. There was no sign of anyone.

"I did," Hillman said smugly. "Before long there were a whole lot of thermonuclear bombs includin' little ones small enough for a man to carry in a suitcase."

"You've got one of those?" Aimee asked. The road stretched out empty, mountains looming in the background.

"We do. We're fixin' to set it off," Hillman said.

"Why? Why would you want to do that?"

"In case you ain't noticed, Miz Aimee, this old world is getting' worse by the day. Wars, pollution, people bein' ugly to one another. Wipe the slate clean and let 'er start over fresh, that's what we're about to do, me and Mr. Beau. Mr. Beau told your daddy that, the last time he saw him."

"It gave him a fatal stroke," Aimee said.

"Guess so, sorry. Once the world ends he woulda died anyway. We all will," Hillman said matter-of-factly.

"Who killed Franz-Albert? Was it you?"

"It was. I didn't want to, but we couldn't let him get the sigul back. Whoever's got the sigul's in charge, see? It's like a king's crown. The fellow with the sigul gets to say whether the world gets destroyed or not. Your husband was in charge of the sigul. He didn't want the world to end. He wanted to keep the sigul locked up safe. Some of the rest of us disagreed. We wanted the End Times, and we wanted them right quick."

He grinned, showing yellow dentures.

"Me and Mr. Beau were competin' to get the sigul. I knew about Johnny Rolex from Mr. Marsh talkin' about him. He sounded like a fellow who could get things done, so I tasked him with gettin' the sigul from Mr. Trainor and Mr. Peach. Johnny Rolex knew I had me a suitcase nuke and was gonna set it off. I told him if he refused we had fellows in the club who'd kill his family, an' they wouldn't be gentle about it. I sent him the contact information for the Russian I bought the bomb from so he'd know I wasn't playin'."

Despite herself, Aimee was intrigued. "Where did you get the money to buy a suitcase nuke? Aren't they awfully expensive?"

"From my little sideline. I'm a day trader. Seems I have a knack for it. I did all right buyin' and sellin' stocks. Mr. Blanton was impressed."

He frowned. "Johnny Rolex quit answerin' my phone calls. Guess that means he's dead."

"Yes," Aimee said.

"*C'est la guerre,*" Hillman said placidly. "Like I said, Mr. Beau and I were havin' sort of a friendly competition. He hired two fellows of his own. They bought the sigul from Mr. Trainor and Mr. Peach. They mailed it to Mr. Beau from a post office in Italy. They wrapped it up and sent it through the mail, the same way that jeweler fellow sent the Hope Diamond from New York to the Museum of Natural History in Washington, D.C. With Mr. Beau havin' possession of the sigul, he won our friendly competition. He was kind enough to invite me to come along while he blew up the volcano." Hillman made it sound as if what he and Tetley had done was of no more consequence than if they'd been competing to see who could do the most push-ups.

Someone was coming down the road. It was an athletic-looking woman. She strode along wearing shorts and hiking boots, binoculars hanging around her neck. She turned up the path in front of the A-frame. Hillman held the gun out of sight. "Get rid of her," he said.

"Excuse me, do you know where the bald eagles are nesting?" the woman called out. She carried what looked like a map and waved it at them. "It should be around here somewhere."

"Sorry, I can't help you," Aimee said. She hoped the woman wouldn't get close enough to see Marsh's body.

"Okay, thanks," the woman said. She turned to go. Walking behind the Lincoln, she called, "Hey! Did you know both these rear tires are flat?"

Hillman went to the edge of the porch. "What? How could they be flat? They were fine when I drove up here."

That's when Aimee body-slammed him. She rammed him as hard as she could. He tumbled over the porch railing, landing with a thud. The gun flew out of his hand. The woman picked it up and trained it on him. "Get up slowly. Let me see your hands," she ordered him.

At that Marsh rolled over and sat up. "I was waiting for the right moment to tackle him," he said. He winced. "Ow. I think one of my ribs is cracked."

"Walk it off, Bad Choices. You ought to be used to getting dinged up by now," the woman said. She pulled Hillman to his feet. Producing a pair of handcuffs from her backpack, she handcuffed him to the porch railing.

"Who are you?" Aimee asked.

The woman flipped open her denim jacket, displaying a gold badge pinned to the inside. "Special Agent Carson Burns, FBI."

"Hold on there. They don't let women in the FBI, not black ones, anyway," Hillman wheezed. "You knocked me clear over that railin'. I think it tore somethin' in my insides," he told Aimee indignantly.

"You'll get medical treatment, don't you fret," Agent Burns told him. "For your information, they do let black women into the FBI. I'm in charge of the Bozeman, Montana resident agency, something that would give J. Edgar Hoover conniption fits if he knew."

"What took you so long, Burns?" Marsh asked. He looked down at his suit coat. A blackened hole was drilled through the Harris Tweed. Wincing, he reached into the inside breast pocket and removed his sterling silver money clip. It was bent, the white jade cabochon shattered, having taken the full impact of the bullet.

"There aren't many people who can say they were shot point-blank in the chest with a Ruger 9mm semi-automatic and lived to tell the tale. I fear I'm going to need a new money clip," Marsh said.

"Bad Choices, you've got more lives than a cat," Agent Burns told him.

"Why do you keep calling him that?" Aimee asked.

"Bad Choices? It's is our code name for him at the bureau," Agent Burns replied. "He's a confidential informant, a fairly useful one. Your brother is a bad man, Ms. von Helgern, but he's our bad man, so we cut him some slack."

"I would have preferred a more flattering moniker," Marsh said.

She ignored him. Addressing Hillman, she asked, "Where's Tetley? Where's the suitcase bomb?"

There was a loud droning as a helicopter passed low overhead, its rotors thumping. Hillman looked up and smiled.

"It's in that helicopter, isn't it? Tetley's up there, and he's going to drop the bomb once he gets over the caldera at its weakest point," Marsh said.

"Any minute now," Hillman replied. "Any minute now he'll be over Yellowstone Lake. He'll activate the bomb and drop it over the side. The volcano's gonna..."

There was a *thwock,* followed by a thunderous explosion. A ball of fire burst above the trees to the east.

"Holy shit! What was that?" gasped Carson Burns.

"That would be my nephew Benjamin, shooting the helicopter with a rocket launcher," Marsh said calmly.

"Is the volcano going to erupt?" Aimee asked.

Marsh waited, considering. "Doesn't seem like it," he said after a moment. "It appears Tetley didn't have time to detonate the bomb. Lucky for us, huh?"

Agent Burns sat down heavily on the porch steps.

Aimee was in shock. "You let Benjamin fire a rocket launcher?"

"Why not? Plenty of people younger than Benjamin have fired them. I saw a picture once of a Russian girl, she couldn't have been more than twelve or thirteen, shooting a rocket launcher at some Germans during World War II. She seemed to be enjoying herself. Why shouldn't Benjamin have the same opportunity?"

Aimee was at a loss for a reply.

Hannah Ryczak pulled up in her Range Rover, her eyes wide. "I just heard on the radio a helicopter crashed near here. The park service is sending fire trucks."

"What about the bomb?" Aimee asked.

"What about my insides? I need a doctor," Hillman said.

Hannah looked at him curiously. She'd failed to notice the old man handcuffed to the porch railing. "Is this your butler? The one who was going to blow up the volcano?"

"The very same. You can't get good help anymore. The minute your back is turned, they try and destroy the world." Marsh pressed a hand to his chest. "I really think one of my ribs is cracked. It hurts when I press on it."

"Suck it up," Carson Burns told him.

"What about the bomb?" Aimee asked again.

"Oh, that." Marsh winced as he removed his jacket and sadly examined the hole drilled through the blue-flecked gray tweed. "Tetley evidently didn't have time to detonate it. It might not have gone off even if he had. Those Soviet-era devices were notoriously unreliable. I told Benjamin, and Trainor, who was acting as his sapper, to fire as soon as the helicopter came within range. The rocket launcher and ammo were in the Conestoga wagon, not geological equipment, in case you're wondering. I ordered it from a friend in Barstow who supplies such things. I thought it would be a nice touch to have it delivered by mule-drawn wagon. It fits in with the frontier theme out here."

"Stop talking," Carson Burns said. She rubbed her temples, as if she had a headache. "Please. I don't want to hear another word. This is so messed up. You let a child shoot down a helicopter with a thermonuclear weapon in it. What the fuck is wrong with you?"

"He's not a child, technically. Benjamin is eighteen. I was pleasantly surprised to see how quickly he caught on to firing that bazooka. He reminds me of myself when I was his age."

"God help us," Agent Burns muttered.

CHAPTER 37 – TWO FUNERALS

Back at White Oaks, Blanton's funeral went off without a hitch. Everyone had heard about Franz-Albert being stabbed to death by the Trapnells' former butler, and Aimee was the object of considerable pity and curiosity, which pleased her.

Wickwire was given a large bonus and sent home to Los Angeles a happy man, proud to have pulled off what became known as the most lavish post-funeral party ever given in the state of Georgia.

A Dixieland band brought from New Orleans followed Blanton's bronze casket to the mausoleum, the musicians strutting and carrying black umbrellas. They amused some of the guests and shocked others by playing a spirited rendition of a song called "I'll be Glad When You're Dead (You Rascal You.)"

Trainor explained it was Blanton's favorite. He used to sing it with great gusto when he was engaged in a dispute with one of his old business rivals. It seemed fitting for it to be played at his send-off.

Franz-Albert was given a more modest funeral and his body was shipped home to Germany, where it was interred in a vault in the foundation of his castle, beside the bodies of his ancestors. An open house was given in his honor in Cobbs the day after Blanton's funeral. Louetta made her famous hummingbird cake and deviled eggs.

Deputy Ewell Haskins was in attendance at both events. The previous week the sheriff had suffered a heart attack, resulting from of years of inactivity combined with a diet high in fat. He had tendered his resignation. Haskins would almost certainly be the new sheriff. There'd be an election, but unless Haskins did something completely off the chain before then, he'd be a shoo-in.

"Benjamin blew up our lawyer. Is that gonna make a difference in us gettin' our inheritance money?" Trainor asked after Blanton's funeral. The guests had gone home, and he and Aimee and Marsh were in the gentlemen's parlor, eating leftover canapés.

Benjamin was outside with Jubilee, throwing a tennis ball to Seamus. Palmer was upstairs, going through a jewelry box that had belonged to her late mother-in-law. The best pieces were in a safety deposit box at a bank, but she found one or two things she liked. A string of carved onyx and carnelian beads went into her pocket. She couldn't wait to show it to her frenemy, Chandler Woodbury.

Marsh picked up his glass of sherry. Their new butler, Boo Sang Lee, was every bit as poised and deferential as a top-notch butler should be. He'd brought the sherry and glasses in on a silver tray which he'd taken the trouble to polish using a silver polish recipe of his own devising. He'd polished all the silver. The heavy old Trapnell silver shone like never before.

"We'll still get our money, despite Tetley having been blown up, as well as the helicopter pilot, who probably deserved it because he was part of the sigul of Jörmungandr club." Marsh took a sip of sherry.

Carson Burns and her fellow FBI agents were in the process of tracking down the people who were in on the plot to blow up the volcano, those who hadn't fled to parts unknown. Hillman had proved to be helpful in supplying their names.

The sigul was one of the few things that were retrieved intact from the wreckage of the helicopter. It and an aluminum suitcase containing an unexploded thermonuclear weapon had been turned over to the government as evidence. Aimee was glad to be rid of it. She didn't want to become the sigul's custodian.

"How much are we gettin'? It's forty billion, right? Divided four ways that's ten billion each," Trainor said.

Marsh looked at Aimee and raised his eyebrows. He cleared his throat. "Make that three ways."

Trainor was confused. "Ain't it supposed to be four? You, me, Aimee, and Karen. Where is Karen, anyway? She wasn't at either funeral."

"Actually, it's only three. Poor Karen met with an accident in the swamp. 1 was waiting for the right time to tell you," Aimee said, reaching for her glass of sherry.

"Really? That's too bad," Trainor said. He didn't seem upset. "That leaves more for us."

They clinked glasses.

The End

ABOUT THE AUTHOR

Jill Hand is a former newspaper reporter from New Jersey. She is a member of the *Horror Writers Association*. Her short stories have appeared in dozens of publications and in many anthologies. Her time-travel novella, *The Blue Horse*, won a Pinnacle Book Award for fantasy and science fiction. *White Oaks* is her first full-length thriller.

Thank you so much for reading one of our **Thrillers**.
If you enjoyed our book, please check out our recommended title for your
next great read!

The Tracker by John Hunt

"A dark thriller that draws the reader in." **—Morning Bulletin**

"I never want to hear mention of bolt-cutters, a live rat and a bucket in the
same sentence again. EVER." **—Ginger Nuts of Horror**

View other Black Rose Writing titles at www.blackrosewriting.com/books

and use promo code **PRINT** to receive a **20% discount** when purchasing.